Star to Deckhand

The Richard Jackson Saga, Volume 5

Ed Nelson

Published by Ed Nelson, 2024.

Table of Contents

Other books by Ed Nelson

The Richard Jackson Saga

Book 1 The Beginning
Book 2 Schooldays
Book 3 Hollywood
Book 4 In the Movies
Book 5 Star to Deckhand
Book 6 Surfing Dude
Book 7 Third Time is a Charm
Book 8 Oxford University
Book 9 Cold War
Book 10 Taking Care of Business
Book 11 Interesting Times
Book 12 Escape from Siberia
Book 13 Regicide
Book 14 What's Under, Down Under?
Book 15 The Lunar Kingdom
Book 16 First Steps

In the Richard Jackson World

Mary, Mary

Stand-Alone Story

Ever and Always

Cast in Time Series

Book 1: Baron
Book 2: Baron of the Middle Counties
Book 3: Count
Book 4: Earl
Book 5: Earl of the Marches

Dedication

This is dedicated to my wife Carol for her support and help as my first reader and editor.

Also, the BHS class of 1962 just because.

Edited by Janet E. Rupert

Quotation

That is exactly how it happened, give or take a lie or two.

James Garner as Wyatt Earp, describing the gunfight at the OK Corral in the movie *Sunset*.

Copyright © 2019

E. E. Nelson
All rights reserved.
Eastern Shore Publishing
2331 Del Webb Blvd. West
Sun City Center, FL 33573

ISBN 979-8-89434-010-4
Library of Congress Control Number: 2022911369

Chapter 1

The week started normally; Dad rousted me out of bed as he had been doing. Now that was strange. When I was on my own, I woke up without an alarm and got right up and at it. With Dad here, I sleep as long as I can. Now that was plain strange. I must be the only teenager in the world like that.

Once up, I got right to it. Exercise and go out to run. Dick was there. He wanted to talk.

"Rick, something weird is going on. I was approached by the FBI, who told me I was going to be considered for a special project. They wanted Janice and me to answer a long questionnaire about our lives and permit them to check our story out. It is like we are being given a top-secret clearance or something. I called the LA FBI office and found the agent is real, so we went ahead.

"One thing Janice and I agree upon is if anything strange is going on in our lives, you are probably involved."

Ouch!

"If it is what I think it is, Dick, you have no worries. You and Janice will like it. In the meantime, I can't talk about it. You should know in a couple of weeks. Nothing will happen if things don't work out as I hope. You can't lose on this deal."

"Is your Mum involved?"

"Yes, she is."

"I have my suspicions about her, so we will see what we see."

Now it was my turn to worry. What were his suspicions? I couldn't ask as I would give away too much. Instead, I just bore down and ran as hard as I could. The high school coach was there and waved as we blasted by him.

As I finished dressing after my shower, the phone was ringing. After a brief conversation, Dad grabbed it and handed me the phone. It was from Mark Downing. The DF flyers were ready to go out to the distributors today. He had one in hand, and it looked really good. In the meantime, the actual hard copy catalog was going to the printers, so we were in business. Mark was as excited as I was.

Dad dropped me off at the studio with a "break a leg."

I think that was for a stage play, but I would take it how it was given. The set was a beehive of activity by the time I was out of makeup and costume. They were doing a scene with Maid Marian and the village children. All the girls were playing with dolls while the boys were shooting small bows.

I had read the script, and it had said nothing about dolls, so I asked more out of curiosity than anything else. A set dresser was standing there, so I asked him where the dolls had come from. "They are not dolls."

I had to look again; they sure looked like dolls to me.

"What are they?"

"Poppets or puppets," he replied.

"Oh," I answered.

I still thought they were dolls.

He laughed, "Poppets is what they called dolls in medieval times. The term dolls didn't come into use until much later."

"Got me," I laughed. "I don't remember any poppets being mentioned in the script."

"There weren't. Sharon Bronson brought them in. She thought the bows and poppets would be appropriate as Maid Marian trying to help the village children."

"It looks like they are a hit."

"So much that there now will be a scene of her making them out of old rags. To add a little drama, she will run out of rags, and rather than not have dolls for all the girls. She will tear up one of her dresses. Of course, it will have sentimental value or good memories. The writers haven't sorted that out yet."

"Well, I'm glad she is buying into the movie."

"Guess who will be making bows?" He asked.

It didn't take a genius to figure that one out. I had better check one out to see what I had to do.

"Yeah, we were surprised; she has a reputation for being a brat. I hope this is the real Miss Bronson."

"Same here," I replied.

Even after the scene was finished, the littles continued to play with their toys. The girls were obviously in love with their dolls and the boys with their bows. The safety man was watching the boys like a hawk.

My scene was a sword fight with Junior. It wasn't to the death or even a severe wound. We had to save him for future movies. I just had to humiliate him by disarming him.

The actor playing Junior seemed like a nice kid. He was almost my size and twenty-three. What he wasn't was a swordsman. How he got past the audition, I will never know. Even though I had to win the fight, there had to be a fight.

They finally put Sammy in costume and had us perform the fight, then had the actor dance around with a sword getting pictures of his face which they could splice into the film.

Sammy and I had fun. We talked briefly about how we wanted the fight to go. We then walked over to the area we would be fighting in. It was the great hall of the castle. We then put on a show for everyone. It went perfectly though we had to go through everything twice for an insurance shot. They then had me standing over Junior with my sword at his throat, saying,

"Yield or die."

He yields. Then, being Junior, he tries to stab me in the back.

Since I am the all-knowing Robin Hood, I know what he is going to try. So, I slap him up the side of his head with the flat of my sword. I had to time and pull that exactly right, or I would have brained him.

I wouldn't have minded doing that to Junior, but the guy playing Junior was okay.

Sharon had watched the scene even though she could have been off set.

I walked over to her and told her, "Nice touch with the poppets."

"You knew what they were called?

"Of course, I do."

So, sue me, she is a pretty girl with a bad reputation, but it is my duty as a red-blooded American boy to impress every female I can.

"Pull the other one. I saw you talking to the set dresser."

"Busted," I replied.

"That's okay, Rick. I had to look it up."

"If you don't mind, where did you get the idea?"

"Anna told me that she used to do little things on the set for people she was working with; I thought of dolls and went to the library where I learned of poppets."

"Keep it up, Sharon. You are heading in the right direction. The smiles on those little girls' faces prove that. Where did the boys get the bows?"

"Junior made them last night."

"Did he know you were doing the dolls?"

"No, we surprised each other."

"That's neat. Well, I have to get to work."

I went onto the set to take my position. I noticed Sharon and Junior leaving together. I had to find out his name again, I had been told, but hadn't paid attention. Anyway, Junior and Sharon seemed friendly. I hope he is a good guy.

Chapter 2

Finally, it was my turn to go to lunch. All the littles were at the commissary along with their parents. Several parents had seen me get my award from the mayor on the late-night news last night, so they congratulated me. One lady wanted me to know I wasn't to shoot that terrible weapon while her little Johnnie was on the set. Her words, not mine.

I assured her that range safety was paramount, and no kids would be on the range. If her little Johnnie were who I thought he was, I would appear to shoot an apple off his head in the finished film. All camera tricks, but she wouldn't know that. Hollywood, you gotta love it.

I looked around at all the strangely dressed characters and laughed at myself. I was the one in tight pants. After lunch, it was back to work. I finished with my scenes at four o'clock, so I got off early. I didn't expect Dad until six, so I went to the stunt area and lifted weights. After that, I went to the prop shop.

There I checked over the curling iron setup and decided it was okay to test. I turned it on, and it didn't spit fire or sparks, so that was a victory. I turned the transformer control up while taking temperature readings with the thermocouple.

The temperature rose smoothly to four hundred and ten degrees, where it then shut off as designed. I had read that human hair would melt at four hundred and fifty-one degrees, so I didn't want to get near that. I then dialed it back to three hundred and held it against a towel. While it warmed the towel up, it didn't set it on fire. At four hundred degrees, the towel started to scorch.

I decided I had enough to start. I would try to get Dad to bring me to the studio early in the morning so that I could talk with the head of makeup about a trial run.

Dad was waiting for me in a panel van!

"What's this?" I asked.

"I need something to haul building materials in, so I traded the T-Bird for it."

"What!"

"You have another one in Ohio; it will be coming out here soon."

"Dad, you didn't! Please tell me you didn't!"

"Okay, I didn't. The company bought this outright. I had you going. It is getting to be a pain to drive you back and forth. Plus, in the future, we will always have a use for the van, even if it is to haul surfboards."

Hallelujah! Who cares if we use it in the future? I get my T-Bird back!

Dad had all sorts of news.

"The Sinatra people contacted John Baxter, who in turn passed the apartment phone number to them. I was there when they called. The record will be released this Saturday, just ahead of the TV special on Sunday. They also told me that you had to spend two weeks on tour with Mr. Sinatra."

"I can't take the time off from the movie!"

"I told them that. They didn't care. They told me that you would regret it if you didn't. I then told them to ask Mr. Sinatra if Mum should call Lucky."

"What happened?"

"They hung up, and I got a call about ten minutes later telling me that it had been reconsidered and that you weren't needed on the tour. When ten more minutes went by, I got a call from a very apologetic Mr. Sinatra. He claims he had no idea what they had been trying to do until I brought up Lucky. I believed him when he said he had no idea. I also believed him when he told me his guy was in the bathroom throwing up."

Mum may be a little heavy-handed, but it is certainly heard when she delivers a message.

Dad then told me, "I have figured out the elevators in Jackson House."

"What elevators?"

Dad looked at me in disbelief, "You didn't notice any of the elevators?"

I shook my head slowly, "No. I didn't."

"When you go in the front door, did you notice doors on either side of the foyer?"

"I looked into the one on the right. It's a coat room. I assumed the one on the left was the same."

"It isn't. It's an elevator that will hold six people and goes from the basement to the fourth floor."

"Oh, what others are there?"

"Well, we didn't go inside the tower, so you get a pass on that one. It also will take six people from the basement to the top floor. There is a staircase from that floor to the roof. You should check it out."

"Okay, but what else did I miss?"

"Only a freight elevator. It's at the back of the building."

"You're kidding!"

"Nope, it is built onto the outside of the residence. It is on the opposite side of the building from the portico."

At least I noticed the portico. You could go from your car to the back door without getting wet.

"Anyway, the freight elevator is used for moving big items around the house. It has a door that opens to the outside and another on the inside. All the upper floors and basement open to the inside only."

"It's a shame it doesn't go to the sub-basement."

"That's what I discovered. You may not have noticed, but in the sub-basement, there is a Chinese screen against one wall. It's hiding the elevator door. I discovered that you could get the elevator to and from the sub-basement with the button down there. None of the upstairs buttons will send it down there. It can be called if it is left down there, but you can't go back."

"Oh." I dumbly waited.

I was still trying to figure out how I had missed the elevators.

"It is a little inconvenient to use it. You would have to load the elevator and then go through one of the secret doors to take the elevator down. It sounds like a two-man job."

I thought we would go out to Jackson House, and he would show me his finds. Instead, we went to Los Angeles to see the buildings he bought for our company.

"I wanted you to see them before we closed."

"I appreciate that, Dad. I don't know what I can add, but it will be good to see them."

We looked at the office buildings from the outside. They looked like buildings to me. The ground floor of each building used to contain small businesses, like shoe stores, barbershops, beauty parlors, newsstands, dentists, coffee shops, and tailors. Small businesses provide the services that make an area livable.

They were all gone now. Dad told me that he would have offices on the first two floors, and the other two floors would be developed as apartments. We drove around the area some more; we got into the section where buildings had already been converted to apartments. As we drove around in the van, Dad kept looking around more and more.

Finally, he said, "I must be missing something, Rick. Where are the stores? People would have to drive for miles to buy basics? Where are the restaurants? People don't want to eat at home every night. Where are the bars? This is what they call a bedroom community. That's fine in the suburbs with good roads; it won't work in the city."

"How do you know it won't work?"

"Since I got into the housing business, I read everything I can get on the property business. There is a magazine which has articles on rental situations. I remember reading about this."

"What can you do about it?"

"I am going to put businesses on the first floor of the buildings. They are configured for it now. It will cost less to do that than to convert them to offices."

"Where will you find the businesses to move in here?"

"I won't. The mayor's office will. They are pouring concrete everywhere for the superhighways. It is displacing entire neighborhoods. They are destroying small businesses and the city tax base. They will beg me to provide space for them in an up-and-coming neighborhood. I have read about cities giving grants for this sort of thing. I have to make some calls tomorrow."

And I was worried about Dad not having enough to do.

We stopped at a drive-in restaurant. The girls were on roller skates, but none had a tiara.

The day caught up with me, and I fell asleep over an economics textbook.

Chapter 3

Tuesday was a beautiful day in southern California. I didn't know about the rest of the country. I was up early, did my exercises, and finished running by the time Dick Wyman showed up.

I wanted to do two things, drive my T-Bird and get to the studio before scheduled so that I could show my curling iron to the makeup department.

When I pushed the curling iron in on a wheeled table, you would think I was going to start up Frankenstein from how they acted. Once the comments settled down, I explained where the project stood. They were more receptive when it was realized that the transformer would not be a part of the finished product.

They decided to try out the device on an extra made-up for a nineteenth-century movie.

As a makeup guy said, "We can always pop a wig on her."

No one thought to ask the young lady if she wanted to participate. I took the time to show her and tell her what was going on.

She was okay with the project after that. Her only question was could she have one when they became commercially available? I took her name and address. For the record, she wasn't my type.

I would check in each morning to see how their experience with the curling iron went.

The filming went well. Sharon took me aside to tell me how good things were going and that she had talked to John Baxter. She compared him to her old agent. It was a night and day difference in how they treated her.

"Mr. Baxter is a gentleman, the other guy a slime bag. I can't believe that I put up with that. What a fool I was."

There was nothing I could say as I agreed with her.

Sharon told me she was a little nervous today because she resolved to call her parents this evening.

"I hope they will take me back. I treated them so badly when they only wanted the best for me."

Now to that, I could reply, "Sharon, your parents will take you back. They have always loved you. They're disappointed, but they love you."

"I owe it all to you, Rick."

"I don't see that. Why do you owe me?"

"Your unabashed fun in that water fight reminded me that life can be fun without drinking and partying. I had gotten so caught up in that lifestyle. The funny part was that it wasn't fun, so I just tried harder. I think I could have tried myself into a grave."

"Now that is what they call overachieving."

"Yes, it would be, wouldn't it? I can see my tombstone now. Sharon Bronson: she was such a success as a party girl that she died young. Rick, what would your tombstone read?"

"Here lies Richard Jackson, an old man!"

Sharon laughed but then asked, "Seriously, what are your goals and ambitions? I see you work hard and well on the set, but you also appear to be passing through. Where are you going?"

I started to give her a flip answer but stopped.

"Sharon, I want to help mankind get into space. I'm not sure how I will do it, but I have several interim goals. One is to complete my education, and the other is to reach financial stability and make enough money to achieve my dream."

Sharon softly replied, "Wow. That is a set of goals. I would laugh at most guys telling me this, but not you. You have an intensity about you that can be felt."

She had such conviction in her voice that I almost believed her but then remembered I was only fifteen.

"I'm glad you believe in me, but I have a long way to go."

"You said you need the education to support you. What will it be?"

"Well, I have to make it through tenth grade before I can go to the moon."

That was such a stupid statement that we both broke out laughing. Before we could continue, we were called back on the set.

On the way to the commissary for lunch, I saw a guy climbing an electric pole with his climbing spikes. He would drive a spike in, rise, then lift his belt, take another step, and do it all over. He went up that pole like a monkey. I looked around for the cameras. There weren't any! The guy was a real lineman. I think Hollywood was getting to me.

At the end of the day, I stopped at makeup to check on how things went. I was told the curling iron worked fine after they rounded the edges off the clamp. The clamp, which was nothing more than a half section of a pipe, had sharp edges where it was cut down the middle.

When they tried it on the first young lady, it was like a paper cutter. It snipped her hair off. They had to shorten it all the way around and put a wig on her. They had a prop man round the edges with a file. As far as curling went, they loved it.

The temperature range was as I thought. Depending on the texture of the hair and its condition, they would vary the heat. There was no question that they could set curls faster with this than any other method they had. We decided to keep the curling iron in place for the rest of the week. The makeup artist wanted a commercial model of the curling iron as soon as possible.

I agreed that if they used them and kept notes for me, they would receive a free curling iron. I even wrote that in front of the hardback notebook I provided.

It was embossed with Jackson Personal Products on the cover. The patent attorney in Columbus had sent me half a dozen of them as a gift. A court would construe any entries in these books as being performed on behalf of Jackson Personal Products. I was learning a little about both science and patents.

I felt bad for the poor girl who had her hair shortened. I asked one of the makeup people what I should do for her. Several of them discussed the issue and asked how much I wanted to spend. I told them that wasn't an issue. What was the right thing to do? They suggested I pay for an appointment at a high-end hairstylist in Beverly Hills.

When they told me the cost, I choked but decided to do it anyway. It was also suggested I give her a hairdryer. Almost every woman who came through the makeup area who saw a hairdryer wanted one. I had one more at the apartment; it was hers.

I made notes in my notebook to buy a gift certificate, bring a hairdryer, and remember to present her with an electric curling iron when they were available. Luckily, Tim, one of the makeup artists, knew Jennifer, whose hair had been cut, so I had her name.

I made it to the set on time to slave away. It wasn't slaving away, really. It was a concentrated effort by everyone; it felt like time was running out, but we were still on schedule. It was a brutal schedule by studio standards, but we were doing it.

That doesn't mean we didn't have fun. There was a scene where the littles were supposed to be running around and playing a game. The game wasn't defined. It turned into a game of tag very quickly. Now a dozen kids ranging in age from eight to twelve running around can make a lot of commotion. The director loved it. He wanted a scene with village kids playing. There was no question that they were playing.

Then I got tagged. Contrary to the story that went around later, I did not tag the producer. I tagged the director, the producer, and a stagehand who tagged...well, you get it. The scene went all to heck quickly.

Once that settled down, there were a lot of smiles and laughter. Fortunately, we were on a series of scenes that were supposed to be cheerful. It was before the tax collector arrived, so we were allowed to be happy.

We went to lunch as a group, and I swear I didn't start a food fight. Honest! This time I had Mr. Monroe as a witness. He saw Sharon Bronson throw the dinner roll at me. Of course, he said I shouldn't have thrown one back at her. The fight was on!

Junior saved the day, though. He poured a glass of iced tea over Sharon's head. That ended the fight in dead silence as she sputtered. Everyone waited for one of her famous tantrums. It didn't happen. She grabbed a towel, dried it off, and then turned to Junior.

She darkly told him, "We will discuss your behavior on the set later."

He was a dead man walking.

I turned to Mr. Monroe, "I would like to hear that discussion."

He got a funny grin, "I think Junior has gotten more than he can handle."

Maybe Bill Bixby should change his stage name to Junior.

Chapter 4

The rest of the day went smoothly. Everyone knew their cues, spots, and lines. The little girls were dressing their rag dolls when they weren't on camera. Barbie would love the outfits. It seems every girl had a seamstress in the family, and they were trying to outdo each other. Somehow, I doubted that the Middle Ages had ever seen a Christian Dior-style dress on a rag doll.

I just hoped they didn't start having tea parties, or if they did, not invite me.

It was a joy to walk out to the parking lot and get into my car. It was too late to go anywhere by the time I got back to the apartment. Dad wasn't there yet, so I fixed a couple of hotdogs and opened a bag of potato chips.

Just as I finished up, Dad came in. He looked like he had been run through the mill.

When I asked him what his day had been like, he groaned. "I hate all of them, no matter what party they are from."

"So, your development proposal didn't go over?"

"Oh, they loved it. It was the conditions they wanted to put on it. Only union labor and, of course, special contributions to the labor bosses. In Ohio, we call those bribes. They requested more money for the mayor's re-election campaign. Also, he has a favorite charity he wants donations for. I imagine if it was investigated, he is using it for kickbacks."

"What are you going to do?"

"Start over. I'm not getting involved with that swamp of corruption. Once you pay them, they will have you forever."

"Will they let you walk away?

"I shared a story with them about how Lucky didn't want Mum upset with him over Paul Grant, who was used to passing the messages. One of their guys knew one of Sinatra's. He placed a call while I was sitting there."

"What happened?"

"I only heard the questions being asked, but when he hung up, it was, I am very sorry that we bothered you, Mr. Jackson. Maybe we can start over."

"I told him that he could be thankful that I was walking away from such a small fry."

"Wasn't that dangerous, Dad?"

"Rick, I was a captain in the MPs. We dealt with some real scum-of-the-earth types. These guys were amateurs."

Sometimes I forgot how cold my father could be. If nothing else, it would take a hard man to impress Mum.

"So now what? We still need offices."

"It doesn't matter if we are in Los Angeles. I was just trying to keep costs down. We will rent space in Beverly Hills, maybe off that Rodeo Drive. It looks like it could use some development."

"Dad, I don't think it is pronounced like the cowboy event, but 'Rodayo.'"

"Whatever, it has potential."

"Are you going to try to develop it?"

"No, that will be too long-term. I have been reading about indoor shopping malls. I think I will scout on the other side of the mountains, in what they call the Valley. It is growing like crazy out there, and they need shopping. There aren't any real established downtowns, so these will fill a need."

"Sounds good; we need some real estate investments to balance out our stock portfolio."

"So, all of a sudden, you are a big-time investor?"

"I'm going to be. I have not firmed up my dream yet, but if I do, it will cost a fortune and make that the largest fortune this world or any other has ever seen."

"That's why I am so proud of you, Rick. You don't think small. Now, what the heck are you talking about?"

As Dad fixed his hot dogs, I told him about my dreams of space.

"So, you want to fly in a rocket ship?"

"Not necessarily. I want to make it possible for others to do so and develop the resources out there."

"How will you do that?"

"I'm not sure yet. I know it will require a heavy technical education, a lot of money, and a lot of influence."

"Well, you understand what you are facing. How long will this take?"

"Probably my lifetime, my children or their children will reap the rewards."

"At least you are not thinking small. Good luck."

At that, we kicked back and watched TV. Later, I read a mystery set in old England. It had Caroline Ross inheriting a fortune if she was married. To avoid turning control of her fortune to a husband, she paid to be married to a convicted murderer. Ex-fencing master Dick Derwent was to be hung the next day. She marries him one hour before the execution. Derwent, with the rope around his neck, at the very last moment, succeeds to the title of Marquis of Derwent and needs to be tried in the House of Lords.

Dick lives but ends up with a wife and mistress under the same roof. He has to prove his innocence to the House of Lords. The story includes a shot fired through the bathroom window at a lady soaking in a tub of hot milk, a riot at the opera, an early-morning duel, and Napoleon Bonaparte. Then for fun, throw in the Coachman, whose coat smells of graveyard mold. What a neat read!

Before I left the house for my morning run on Wednesday, Mum called. She hoped to catch me. The background check on Dick and Janice Wyman came back clean. If they needed it, they could be issued a security clearance. Because of this, Mum asked me to talk to them to see if they would be interested in living at Wall House, as we called it. It had started as the house outside the wall and was quickly shortened to Wall House.

On our morning run, I told Dick that we had bought the old Talmadge estate. There was a house there we would like to offer rent-free for him and Janice to live in.

Since we were running at a rather good clip, Dick panted as he said, "So all this mysterious checking on us was you?"

"Well, Mum triggered it. A bit of a secret is involved, and she is a little paranoid about such things."

"What secret?"

"Why don't Dad and I show you and Janice the house tonight, and if you would like to live there, things will be explained?"

"You are mean. Janice will drive me nuts until she knows this secret."

"It's a mean world, my friend."

My friend then slapped my butt as he took off. I couldn't catch him. My stamina was great, but I would never run fast.

When I got back to the apartment, Dad had our breakfast ready. Having a parent around was pretty handy. I hustled around to get my clothes ready for the dry cleaner. They picked up every Wednesday and returned my pants and shirts on Fridays.

For my underclothes, I had arranged the laundromat. Before starting my run-on Saturdays, I would drop them off with an elderly Mexican lady along with the needed change. She would wash, dry, and fold them. I would pick them up after running, cleaning up, and stopping at the bank before noon. It was a dollar well spent.

Most weeks, I would also work on a trip to the library for three or four books. I certainly didn't have as much time to read for pleasure as I used to. When desperate, I would stop at a grocery store and stock up. Dad did it last week. For some reason, he didn't think a diet of hotdogs and Hostess cupcakes was healthy.

The milkman would drop off four quarts a week, along with butter if needed.

Chapter 5

The movie was proceeding well. We were still on schedule. The director was pleased with how everyone was cooperating. I was still the lead, but the focus of the movie, if I read the scenes correctly, was shifting over to the group as a whole. It was *The Bandits of Sherwood*.

It was funny in a way; John Wayne had told me that working with kids was hard. They would steal the scene. He meant me. Now I was facing the same. I have an ego like everyone else, but this didn't put it on the line for some reason.

The other kids took to calling me Robin all the time. I suspect some of the youngest, five and six-year-olds, would have a hard time remembering my real name later. All the girls revolved around Sharon. She was their role model. She seemed very conscious of it and acted the part. She was calm and patient with all the kids. Since I knew them both, I could see Anna's influence.

Sharon approached me before lunch and asked to speak to me for a minute. We were watching Senior berate Junior for letting me steal the cup for the second time. Somehow Senior was forgetting it was his castle that I was stealing it from. It didn't matter; Junior would get it back when Will Scarlet left it behind when he stopped flirting with a girl.

That poor cup started out looking so good. By now, it had been dropped from the castle wall, run over by a wagon, and dinged by a sword. I think it still had to go for a swim and be launched from a catapult. That last was when Robin was meeting Senior's demand that it be returned to Junior in the castle courtyard or the village would be burned.

It had to be in the courtyard by noon. It was. Senior just hadn't specified how it was to be delivered. It was a dramatic scene, the whole village waiting to see if they would lose their homes, a headsman waiting for Robin. Then suddenly, a clunk, as the cup lands in the open center of the courtyard. There would be wild jubilation from the villagers, pouting and stomping by Junior and Senior, Maid Marian kissing Robin, and fade to black.

Sharon had a question. "I want to meet with my parents and make up. They refuse my calls and return my letters. How can I get them to talk to me?"

Why it occurred to me, I don't know; I certainly hadn't continued going to church since I came to California.

"Do your parents attend church?"

"I've never known them to miss a Sunday unless someone was ill."

"If I remember right, you grew up in Covina, so would it be easy for you to get there on a Sunday?"

"Yes, it would; they would have to acknowledge me if I attended church and sat in the same pew we always sit in."

"It may not be that easy. They may ignore you at first; it may take many trips, but it will wear them down. You just can't afford any more bad publicity."

"I know, and I haven't gone out since I stayed with Anna. It will be this Saturday. Junior has asked me to dinner. We will attend a movie, eat late at the Brown Derby, and then come home. He understands that I have to be careful."

"Maybe I had better talk to him to make sure he behaves and has you home on time."

"Don't you dare Ricky Jackson!"

She came across as so forceful I thought I was about to get smacked. It did turn a few heads on the set, but she broke out into laughter. I was getting tired of people hitting me.

Bill, Sharon, and I went to lunch together. It was apparent they were interested in each other, not in lust, well, maybe a little, but wanted to get to know each other. The commissary menagerie included pilgrims with funny hats, Indians, and a Chinese emperor. Then there was my medieval group. All in all, a normal day.

After lunch, it was back to the set until six o'clock. After that, I stopped by the stunt area and lifted. I was still trying to do that if we finished by seven.

When I got home after a quick stop at In-N-Out, Dad and I went over to pick up Dick and Janice in my car. I was even allowed to drive.

We went to Wall House, where Janice promptly fell in love. Rent-free, she was ready to move tomorrow. Dick wanted to know what the secret was. Dad told him to be patient. It would be revealed in a few minutes. We drove up the hill to Jackson House.

Both the Wyman's thought that was a good name. They wanted a plaque for their residence when we told them how Wall House got its name. Dad had signed a temporary contract with the security guard company to continue until we moved in. After that, he and Mum would decide how they would go. I don't think it will be with a firm that only hired retired policemen.

We gave Dick and Janice a tour of the house. We even used the elevator in the foyer to go to the second floor. I loved the tower. Each of the floors was like a sunroom with many large windows. The fifth floor, which was above the roofline, had windows on all four walls.

There was a staircase leading to the roof. The roof was fantastic. It was grass-covered! It was a miniature garden up there. A little shed still contained a small push mower and gardening tools. The lawn was immaculate, so someone had been maintaining it.

There was a waist-high wall around the roof, so there wasn't a fear of falling. The view was out of this world. All of the Los Angeles basin would be visible on a clear day. It felt like you could reach out and touch the snow cap on Big Bear even though it was almost a hundred miles away.

After oohing and aahing for a while, we took the elevator back down and showed them the rest of the rooms. You could tell Dick was getting antsy; Janice was too involved with seeing all the rooms to think of secrets.

When we came to the library, Dad walked over and turned the knob which moved the panel to reveal the lever that opened the secret door. Now Janice was paying attention. We turned on the lights, closed the door behind us, and descended to the sub-basement.

Dad gave the tour. This time I noticed the door to the freight elevator. It was only twelve or so feet wide. Why wouldn't I have missed it? We showed them the stairs to the bedrooms. While we were walking around, Dad told me how this would be a safe room. Dick wanted to know why we needed a safe room.

Dad hedged a little.

"Money, British nobility, a famous son, all these could lead to trouble."

We started down the steps that led to Wall House. Dick figured it out immediately.

"Does this exit in Wall House?" he asked.

"Yes, in the garage. That is why we had a background check run on you. Rick recommended you and Janice. He feels like he owes you for watching out for him. Peg, and I agree."

"How could you get a real FBI security check run on us?"

"Peg is still on half-pay from the British MI6 for her wartime activities."

"Oh," was all a stunned Dick Wyman said.

We exited into the garage of Wall House. Even though I had now been through the tunnels several times, it was still so cool.

Janice wanted to know when they could move in. Dad told them whenever they wanted as closing was complete. They decided that it would be a perfect time since next week was the first of the month.

Dad had a key with him, so he presented it to them, so they could start cleaning the place up before their move. A formal rental agreement would be signed later, establishing that they could live at Wall House, rent-free, as long as we owned Jackson House.

They agreed that they wouldn't use the hidden tunnel for the time being, but Dick did kid Dad about that old bottle of Scotch.

Dad replied, "I think it belongs in a museum or at least sent back to Glenfarclas."

Dick agreed and promised he wouldn't touch it.

It was starting to get late, so we went back home. I was tired after the long day and fell asleep without knowing how Dick Derwent defeated the Coachman.

Chapter 6

Both Thursday and Friday went by in a blur. My entire focus was on the film. I spent twelve hours on the set. They had the littles rotating through in shifts, so they didn't exceed their hours. Even so, some of them were a little cranky. Sharon worked with the girls while off-camera, and I did the boys.

I found a sure-fire entertainment for the boys was to let them try to draw my bow. It was understood that the littlest ones couldn't, but I allowed them to try. The older boys, including Junior, were a little more frustrated. Even after I showed them how to get their backs into it, they couldn't draw it completely. I think it gained me a new level of respect from the guys.

In the meantime, you could see at lunch several other arrows had found their mark. Cupid's arrow that is. Apparently, some of the teenage girls had selected the guys they wanted. The guys never had a chance. Remember, this is Hollywood. Everyone but me was exceptionally good-looking. I was waiting for them to expel me one day for being ugly. Well, not ugly, but you get the drift.

My favorites were a couple of eight-year-olds. They pretended not to like each other but were together every time you turned around. If anyone noticed, they would promptly say something nasty and part. They would always drift back together. Was I ever that young?

Saturday was all day with Coach and unarmed combat. I felt like I was finally getting it. As usual, we took breaks during the day, so I was able to lift, practice with swords, and shoot my bow. I was getting better at my targeting. I could now hit the bullseye at one hundred yards, eight out of ten shots. Two hundred yards was still a problem. At that distance, if you moved a hair, you were off by two feet at the target. My rate of fire was increasing. I could now get off eight arrows a minute.

Saturday night Dad and I watched TV. It had been a long week for both of us.

Sunday morning, I did my exercises, ran, and then spent half a day on unarmed combat. Sunday afternoon, we went over to Jackson House and started moving furniture out of the sub-basement on the freight elevator.

Dad had picked up six four-wheeled flat dollies to move the stuff. All that was required was to lift the furniture onto the dollies, and wheel it over to the elevator, and take it up to the basement. We were staging it there before making the final disposition. In two hours, we had cleared the sub-basement and swept it.

Dad boxed up all the contents of the bar and set it in a corner. He also boxed up the whips and chains. We both speculated on what you would do with some of that stuff. Why would they have rat traps and clothespins?

He boxed that stuff up and put it in his van to be dropped off in the dumpster at the apartment. I hope no one opened the boxes. He kept a set of handcuffs, which had the key in them as souvenirs. I told him that he would never get them on Mum. He agreed, and when I turned away, he swatted my behind.

We went back to the apartment for the big TV special on that new rising star of Hollywood, Ricky Jackson, and his new movie with John Wayne, *Sir Nicklaus*. I didn't know if I would be able to watch it.

I watched it as though it was someone else. Although it was about me and my life, it didn't seem real the way it was presented. From appearing in the *Mickey Mouse Club*, to *It Never Happened* and then *Hell Fighters*, it was presented as though I was chosen for my talent rather than the dumb luck I knew it was.

They had stills and clips of my involvement in the Colorado bank robbery and my final rodeo ride to win the National Junior Championship. My appearance on Dick Clark, with parts of "Rock and Roll Cowboy" played. There were pictures of my being awarded a Texas Ranger Badge for my part in capturing the rustlers.

Pictures from the Vincennes fire and a film of my subsequent award. They even got in pictures of my shooting arrows at the bank robbers' compound. All the events of the last year were there.

Interspersed were clips to promote John Wayne's *Sir Nicklaus*. The highlight was the stampede and my role. I liked it best when Mr. Wayne appeared on screen and said, "I told you it would be when you were least expecting it, but I would get you."

It then cuts to one of the scenes where he threw me into a horse trough. These were interspersed throughout the show, and each was done at a different time. It looked like I spent the whole movie in the water. At the time, it sure felt like it.

One last scene was the time I took Mr. Wayne in with me, and we were both soaked. The next shot was me standing there, saying, "Oops."

Among the clips, John and I were installing the Detroit Faucet. We called it by name. During the advertisement, DF was the main sponsor. Anna Romanov made her appearance in several ads announcing her new specialty fixtures commissioned with DF. They were high-class ads. She and Viscountess Jackson were looking through Lady Jackson's newly redecorated bathroom featuring the Romanov Collection.

The DF ads were based on over a hundred years of a functional product with a modern flair. Where do they get these words, and what do they mean?

The end of the show had a split-screen of Frank Sinatra and me singing our new release, "Brothers". They didn't miss a marketing trick. I was never in the same room as Mr. Sinatra, with us singing.

I guess it was a good show. It just didn't seem like the real me. When the show was over, the phone started ringing. The first call through was Susan Wallace. She told me to unplug my phone. She would handle all of it. I was glad to do so.

I went to bed and read. It was a collection of short stories set in a bar. The teller would cadge drinks for his stories, which on the surface were unbelievable, but by the time they were finished, you would wonder. I liked "Beasts of Bourbon", "The Better Mousetrap", and "More Than Skin Deep".

Chapter 7

Monday started great. I don't mean that nicely. It was raining outside, really pouring. The news was talking about the possibility of mudslides. There would be no running today. Then the phone rang; it was Paul Samson from Columbus. His news was all bad.

He had called my patent attorney before he spent too much time on the squirt gun. He had a feeling about the technical parts. He wondered if they were patentable. They weren't. Prior art covered everything I wanted to do. The only coverage I could get would be the shape of the gun.

If I presented that to a toy company, they would say they weren't interested, and then if they thought it would sell, they would change the design slightly and go into business. So, I would have no super squirt gun unless I wanted to go into retail sales and manufacturing.

To make matters worse, while Paul was on the phone with the attorney, he mentioned the electric curling iron I had discussed with him. The attorney said hold on. He had seen something about that recently. Less than ten days ago, on April 18, 1959, Lelevie and Lemoine had applied for a patent on an electric curling iron. Win some, lose some. It is said that when it rains, it pours, but this was stupid.

Dad was going to spend the day checking out possible new office sites since he had a truck now. I was free to take my car. I discovered that the front seal on the rag-top leaked. Not a lot, just enough to be aggravating.

When I got to the studio, production was shut down. The state was in; they were going over each kid's working hours. One kid had worked too many hours, and now they were checking all of them. It turned out there was only one violation, and that was me. Everyone else had been monitored by their parents and kept within the rules. It never occurred to me to keep track of my hours.

The guy from the state tried to get me to say I had been forced into it. I told him it was my carelessness causing this problem and that I wouldn't work too much in the future. He kept at me until I pulled out my LA Police Badge and threatened to arrest him. He left the set, telling everyone that I was crazy. No one argued.

I suspected that I would hear more of this shortly. In the meantime, all the kids had been sent to class, which didn't count against their work time. Bored, I went over to the classroom to see how it was going. I got there just in time to hear the teacher try to draw five straight chalk lines at once.

I don't know the name of the chalk holder that holds five pieces. You can draw five parallel lines at once if done properly. It was not done properly. One piece of chalk can make a terrible noise; five at once are hideous. I lost interest in school and went to the stunt area.

I worked off some steam by lifting. Sammy was there and told me to come with him. We went to another set where I was made up as a Waterloo-era British officer and lost a duel to Sammy, who was a stand-in. I guess we were both stand-ins. I would get no credit or pay, but it was better than sitting around.

It was still raining when I started home, and the T-Bird top was still leaking. I would call the dealership in the morning. I was not a happy camper. On the way home, I was thinking about the curling iron and how I had missed the boat by such a slim margin. As I thought about it, I remembered the young lady who lost a portion of her hair over it. I hadn't gotten her the gift certificate from the high-end stylist.

I generally remembered where his shop was, so I drove over there. It was still raining like crazy, and I couldn't find a parking spot close to the beauty parlor. I ran a block to his shop and was soaking wet. The store was closed, and a small sign said, "Not accepting new clients at this time."

It was the day that wouldn't stop giving. I headed home, took a shower, and put on dry clothes. Dad and I made mac and cheese for dinner. His day was a lot better than mine. He had looked at several office buildings. One on Rodeo Drive looked like it would meet our needs, and the price was right. Dad had inquired if the whole building was for sale. The real estate agent was checking.

We went over to Jackson House and cleaned the sub-basement. This time it was wiping and dusting the plaster walls. They had dirt and grime from the years. Spiders and bugs set up housekeeping many generations ago. If we didn't get rid of them, Mum would not be happy.

It took several hours of hard work, but we got it done. We tapped the walls as we went, wondering if we would find any more secrets. We didn't. Dad and I would be laying out the bedrooms on the floor tomorrow evening with tape. It would be easier to do that than make a drawing. He could buy the materials when he could visualize how everything would fit.

We didn't get home until late, so we both went to bed. I didn't even try to read.

Tuesday morning, it was still raining, so there would be no running. I was starting to miss it. I had to move. I did call the Ford dealer and arranged to drop my car off for them to resolve the leak. They would have a driver take me to the studio and pick me up when I called. It had to be before five o'clock.

I didn't think that would be a problem after yesterday. California law said I could only be on the set eight hours a day, five days a week. I think today the law would be enforced. My first stop was at the makeup department, where I collected the prototype curling iron. I told everyone I would keep my word and buy them one when they were available. I explained my problem to the young lady whose hair I caused to be severed.

One of the actresses being worked on shared the same stylist with the young lady. She suggested that I pay for a haircut every two months for the next year. Of course, she knew the prices. It was only a little more than what I would have paid for one visit to the high-end stylist. I wrote one of the checks I carried that Dad had signed for me.

I left the check along with a note on studio stationery in the studio mail drop for her. That took care of that commitment. I returned the prototype to the prop workshop. I told them I would disassemble it later but was told not to worry; it wasn't a big deal. It had cost the studio about five dollars in parts.

I was right about the working hours. The state had a man show up to monitor the hours of all the children even though I had been the only one in violation. I had worked several ten and twelve-hour days which was against the rules. I guess the state figured if the production company turned one kid, me, into a slave, then they might do it to all the others. They were completely wrong, but they didn't care.

The gentleman, and he was a gentleman, was Mr. George Fitzhugh. His job was to make certain that none of us were overworked, put into unsafe conditions, or worked too many hours. There were at least twenty of us on set at any time.

Fortunately, many parents accompanied their children, so they were less likely to be endangered. For some reason, many parents considered me the most dangerous on the set.

Mr. Fitzhugh was in his late fifties and was running around like a chicken with his head cut off, trying to keep track of everyone. He inadvertently kept getting into camera range. Things were getting tense when it hit me.

The director was about to tear into Mr. Fitzhugh when I interrupted.

"I have a suggestion for you, gentlemen."

They both looked at me, then at each other, and shrugged.

"The only place Mr. Fitzhugh can keep track of everything going on is in the center of the set. At least for today, it is the village market square. Put him in costume and set him against the wall over there. He will be able to keep track of everyone and he won't interfere with any shots."

Of course, our ever-helpful union rep reminded us that he would have to be paid scale. The State of California was paying Mr. Fitzhugh, so that wouldn't work. A runner was sent to the front office. An attorney showed up and whisked Mr. Fitzhugh away. We didn't see him again for the rest of the day, so we got work done.

Chapter 8

The dealership was good on its word. They dropped my T-Bird off at the main gate. They replaced the front seal on the top. There was no charge. The rain stopped. Today was better than yesterday.

On the way home, I turned on the car radio and heard "Brothers" for the first time. They hadn't even sent me a copy before release. I bet I wouldn't get a Christmas card from Mr. Sinatra.

When I got home, Dad had dinner ready. He was still planning to tape the outline of the bedrooms on the sub-basement floor. While we were eating, the phone rang, it was Mum. They talked for a while. I couldn't tell what it was about, but it was serious.

When they hung up, Dad filled me in. "The CIA and MI6 have both picked up my name in calls and conversations between the KGB and the East German Stasi. From what they can tell, I was identified in the gallery when you played golf with Ike. I was recognized, apparently. It would be standard practice for them to identify everyone in a picture taken near the president.

"They want me because of my involvement in the Patton investigation. They know I saw the logbook at the hospital. They don't know and wouldn't believe that I don't know the names. They will be after me."

"What are you going to do, Dad?" I asked quietly.

"Keep a low profile; they have to find me out here."

"What about Mum and the kids?"

"They are safe enough. So far, in the entire Cold War, agents have left each other's families alone. It would get really ugly if that started."

"I would feel better if this was finished, and the family was all out here."

"So would I, son, so would I."

We made a trip to pick up masking tape to lay out the bedrooms. It was a very somber trip with us both lost in our thoughts. We picked up the tape we needed and went to the sub, as were we calling it, to lay out the bedrooms.

There was plenty of room; there could be ten bedrooms down there if we wanted them. Instead, Dad made the five of them generous in size. He also laid out the kitchen, living, and dining areas. The small bathroom and shower down there would have to do. I planned to install a different showerhead. This wasn't just a safe room. It was another house.

I asked him why we were doing all this.

"Rick, when you are in a combat situation, every creature comfort counts. To paraphrase Patton, let the other bastard be uncomfortable for his country. We have space, time, and money to make this place comfortable. If there were bad guys laying siege on us, what would it feel like if it were built like a bomb shelter? Anything that can be done to lower the stress levels, the better."

Later that night, I read about Tatiana, Red Grant, Captain Nash, Rosa Klebb, and her shoes. A trip on the Orient Express was a thrill.

It had dried up from the heavy rains, and I could run Wednesday morning. It felt so good. I felt alive and with it for the first time in several days. As I ran, I thought about last night's phone call. Nothing I could do but be aware of what was happening around me.

At the studio, a compromise was made with the State of California. Their man Mr. Fitzhugh was in costume in the center of the set. Whenever the courtyard or village square was used for a scene, he would be sitting at the vantage point where he could keep track of everything.

He would not have a speaking part but, on occasion, be seen in the background telling stories to the little children of the village. Since the state was paying him, he could take no money directly, so it was going to the charity of his choice. He had chosen his church.

The state was happy, the studio was happy, and even the union was happy. Time would tell how I felt; he was there because of me.

After a while, he blended into the background. The funny part was he was a storyteller. When off the set in the times when the littles had nothing to do and weren't in class, he would have a crowd around him. His stories were the old favorites, like the "Pied Piper of Hamelin".

He gave me no grief but did keep track of my hours. I hadn't realized how much time I was putting in. The producers knew, but they were trying to get the movie out, so had let it happen. I was part of the problem as I didn't see it as a big deal to work a few hours over. I can see the concern over the littles, but I was full-grown in size and got all the rest I needed.

Who would have thought I would be complaining about not being allowed to work? The director was clever in his solution. Usually, doubles were used for stunts or revealing scenes in which the actor or actress didn't want to appear or their body shape wasn't appropriate. In *Bandits*, it was a double whenever I was not facing the camera. It was amazing how much this cut my on-set time down.

This extra time was sporadic, so I had to sign in and out of the set formally. When not on camera, they didn't even want me on set. It was extremely erratic, so I couldn't schedule anything, and they had to know where I was going to be, so a runner could be sent if the shooting schedule changed.

I spent a considerable amount of time in the front office. I would find someone who didn't seem too busy and ask them if they would tell me about their job. People were responsive to someone taking an interest in what they were doing. The purchasing department was an eye-opener for me.

First of all, people were milling around, talking, and having a good time. They didn't seem to have urgent duties. I had no problem finding someone to tell me about what went on in the purchasing world.

I had been listening to a lower-level buyer when the Head Purchasing Agent stopped by and inquired what was going on.

When he heard, he said, "Would you come with me?"

I figured I must be in some sort of trouble. It was anything but trouble. He had a presentation he had been working on.

It seems the studio, which means Mr. Monroe, had asked each department head to prepare a presentation of what their departments did and justify their existence. I was a guinea pig for his presentation.

What they had to go through to get the many items needed for both movies and the studio, separate entities, was amazing. It was his first run-through, so he started slowly and roughly. He got better as he went. He asked me to hold questions until the end. I made notes as he went, treating it like a classroom lecture. When he was done, I had my turn. Some of my questions were basics that anyone in business would understand.

Others had him modify his presentation. After that, he went through it again. He was a lot smoother this time. Halfway through, I realized that he wasn't pacing his breathing as my original voice coach had taught me. I stopped him and explained his problem, and we spent some time on that.

He got it. His third run-through was better. I still had several questions, which he answered and modified his presentation once again. The presentation was to be fifteen minutes. We spent three hours on it. The timing was perfect. As we were finishing his fifth and last practice, a studio runner found me as I was needed on set. The purchasing agent shook my hand and thanked me for my time.

That was a little strange, the teacher thanking the student. I didn't know where I was headed in life, but the knowledge I was gaining was valuable. I went back to work on the set. It was strange going from competitive bidding, freight on board, negotiating contracts, issuing releases against a purchase order to a young and tender kiss and then running for your life, at least on stage.

Mr. Monroe must have been concerned about Mr. Handfield's ability to present as he stopped by the purchasing agent's office to ask him how his presentation was coming. He got a dry run of the presentation. Mr. Monroe was happy with it. He was honest and told Mr. Handfield his concerns. I was given credit for my participation and help.

I didn't hear this directly. I was summoned by a runner later in the day to the Human Resources office. It was suggested that they spend time with me on Thursday to sharpen their presentation. They wanted to make certain I was available. I am an expert on presentations now!

Chapter 9

I asked who suggested that I spend time with them. It was Mr. Monroe. He had seen what I had done with Purchasing. He had seen their first efforts and was so impressed with the improvement that he was suggesting it to all department heads. I told them that I would, depending on the shooting schedule. They told me they would have a runner following my schedule and make the time for me when I was free.

From HR, I went immediately to Mr. Monroe's office. I was expected, and his secretary ushered me straight in.

He also handed his secretary a dollar and said, "I thought it would take him at least ten minutes. It was only seven."

"What's going on?" I asked.

"A little payback for the headaches you've caused me."

"What headaches?"

"Fire alarms, food fights, state child labor violations, a few things like that. Not to say anything about my daughter mooning about the house because her boyfriend hasn't called in a week."

"Oh."

"Rick, you aren't in trouble. I have been working with my department heads for two months to get them to put a decent presentation together for our annual meeting. The worst of the lot was the head of purchasing. In a few hours, you helped him bring his presentation together and to be able to present it without fainting."

"It wasn't that big of a deal. I didn't understand anything about how a large purchasing department works, so I asked him to explain it in simple language. As far as him fainting, that wasn't nerves. It was poor speech habits. He was forgetting to take a breath.

"Mr. Monroe, I just shared my first weeks on set with him what the studio voice coach shared with me."

"You mean to tell me that my department heads need to be trained actors?"

"To get the results you are hunting for, yes. This presentation is for your board. Besides simplifying their presentation, I would have your art department build colored charts. Or better yet, have a slide show presentation made of their main talking points. That way, the whole program can be integrated into a Warner Brothers look, whatever that is."

"Fine, you can work with the art department on this."

"Mr. Monroe, I am a fifteen-year-old child actor, for goodness' sake. I can't tell people how to run their business."

"I'm not asking you to do that, Rick; you seem to have a genius for asking the right questions so that what was complicated becomes simple. You also worked with Handfield, who I thought was a hopeless case, and made him into a decent presenter.

"Rick, I know from our conversations that you don't want to be an actor all your life. You are doing this for the initial money and education you are getting. Consider this as part of your education. Do this for me, and you will have special consideration in any projects you are involved in at this studio."

I'm not stupid.

"I will be glad to help in any way I can, sir."

Mr. Monroe continued, "I have been in this job for less than a year. The entire movie industry has yet to recover from being forced to sell our theaters. Now we have to compete to have a movie played. The industry is going through a shakeout. Some things are easy when you have a monopoly on what plays in theaters. That has changed.

"Studios are merging or being bought out. It is that or go under. I need to demonstrate to my board that Warner Brothers is responding to these market changes. I think showing them that we understand our basic business processes will be a good start. The board meets a week from Friday, so that is your target."

This was the beginning of my most educational and satisfying time in Hollywood. I wish I could take more credit for what came out of it. All I did was ask a few simple questions and the professionals made things happen.

For the next two days, I would spend fourteen hours daily at the studio: eight hours on the set, then in on the rest of the meetings with department heads. On Saturday, I worked in more meetings between my sessions with Coach Palmer.

The first thing to occur was three meetings on Thursday with HR, Accounting, and Maintenance. The department heads ran through their presentations for me. The only one with a problem was HR. The person doing the presentation, who shall remain nameless, seemed to have the memory of a gnat. He would forget where they were going and start revising things halfway through.

I suggested he use his notes. This worked well to a point. Unfortunately, he would just stare at his notes, and the sin of all sins, make no eye contact, and then insult to injury, start to mumble. I thought of cue cards at the back of the room. Then it hit me, cue cards in the front of the room so that the audience could follow along.

The cards would only have an outline so the presenter would know where he was at. He would hang the meat of his talk around those bullet points. Blank poster paper and felt pens were summoned. The first half-dozen points were outlined, and suddenly my presenter was a star.

He had his talking points in front of him, so he didn't lose his way. He could glance at them but turn right back to his audience to keep eye contact. By standing straight instead of bent-over reading, he lost the mumble.

The next two sessions were easier. They knew their material and were comfortable with it. They could give their presentations off the top of their head. I suggested that they use the posterboard outline anyway. That way, there would be a more uniform look to the presentations.

They liked this so much that they decided they wanted a meeting Friday morning of all department heads to determine what all the presentations would look like. I did suggest that they invite Mr. Monroe to this discussion.

I was nominated to be the one to invite him. Since I was acting as his liaison, this made some sense. I had to wait five minutes while he completed a phone call, but I seemed to have open access to him.

He thought the idea of a meeting was great. He would be there as soon as I set up the room. His phone rang, and he waved me out as he picked it up.

I bit my lip and said, "Yes, sir."

As I exited the room, his secretary, Donna, a gorgeous redhead, asked me if I needed any help. I looked a little lost. I grabbed that lifeline for all it was worth.

"I'm supposed to set up a meeting for all department heads tomorrow morning."

"What sort of meeting?

"They want to discuss their presentations with Mr. Monroe and come up with a uniform look."

"So, you will need a conference room with a presentation stand. What time of day?"

"Uh, I don't know."

"Make a decision."

"Nine a.m."

"There, that wasn't so hard, was it? How long will the meeting be?"

I didn't have a clue, but being a quick learner, I came up with, "Two hours and maybe an extension to all morning."

"Okay, then, donuts and coffee set up, with a fruit plate for the ladies. If the meeting runs longer, you will need another coffee service. Will there be handouts or working materials for the meeting itself?"

"It wouldn't hurt to have posterboard, several easels, and felt pens available."

Then she asked, "What about meeting minutes? Will they be kept?"

"I don't...yes, they will."

"So, you need to invite a secretary from the pool. Okay, Rick, you need to contact facilities for the room and materials, catering for the food set up, and the office pool for a secretary. Now, how will people know that there is a meeting, much less the time and place?"

"I guess I will have to call them."

"One last question, what budget code will you use to charge all this against? They will want one when you call facilities, catering, and the general office pool."

I had no idea. I was in over my head, and this was setting up a small meeting. What would the real business world do to me? Then I noticed the little smirk on Donna's face.

"Donna, how would Mr. Monroe go about setting up a meeting like this?"

He would call me into his office and say, "Donna, I need a two-hour meeting tomorrow at nine with all department heads to discuss their board meeting presentations. Take care of it." Donna smiled, "After all, that is my job. Do you want me to take care of it for you?"

I felt a little weak as I nodded my head yes.

"And that is your lesson in the value of an executive assistant. Think about how long all that would have taken you."

I thanked her profusely and headed for the set. At least there, I got to escape from the real world. This real-world stuff was hard.

Chapter 10

Back on the set, we were doing the scene, which would be spliced together, where it looked like I shot an apple off the top of a kid's head. Since the sound would be dubbed in later, it didn't matter if there was noise on the set. As I was ready to release the arrow, some clown started playing the Lone Rangers theme song.

I was lucky I didn't kill someone the shot went so wild. There was a large wooden backstop that saved the day. I didn't come close to my target, an apple sitting on a post the same height as the kid. I got it on the third and fifth tries. This was a terrible shooting as I was only ten feet away.

I had a thought, my second one of the day. I asked if we could move out to the archery range and set up. The director didn't want to set cameras up, but since he had what he needed, he didn't care what I did. The construction coordinator was kind enough to have a post set at the same height as inside. Fortunately, they had brought a full bushel of apples.

I promised the apple leftovers to the construction crew for planting the pole. Now instead of ten feet away, I was fifty yards. I demonstrated, at least to myself, that practice at a distance makes you good at that distance, not at all distances. I was an inch low on my first shot; after that, I hit five apples in a row. The construction crew gave me polite applause for my shooting. Pride assuaged. I gave up the rest of the apples and went back to meet with the department heads.

The rest of the day was spent reviewing presentations. Those I looked at were good and presented well, but they were all over the map as far as length and subject matter. I don't know what they were told to present, but it came across like the game we played as kids. Put people in a line and whisper a message in their ear just once, and they would pass it down the line. What came out was always different than what came in.

I asked the art department head where this assignment was given. It was verbal in another meeting with no written follow-up. This was another lesson learned for me.

For dinner, I took Dad to the Mexican restaurant near the apartment. I was now considered a regular, and it gave me a chance to practice my Spanish. The waitress asked me in Spanish about the handsome gringo. I told her he worked in Immigration. Boy, that smile she gave Dad disappeared quickly! Operation Wetback was well remembered in the Hispanic community.

I backed off on my poor attempt at humor and formally introduced my father. That brought her smile back, but she did tell Dad I was a bad boy for scaring her.

He glowered at me and then said, "He gets his sense of humor from his mother."

Wait until I see Mum!

The meal was delicious. Dad surprised me by taking to the hot spicy food immediately. He ate it with gusto. I had hopes of him grabbing for a glass of water. Oh well. Over dinner, he told me about his day. The entire office building on Rodeo Drive was for sale. It wouldn't be as cheap as those in Los Angeles, but it came without any political baggage. We went over his numbers. They sounded okay to me.

Dad had purchased lumber earlier in the day for the rooms in the sub, so after dinner, we went to Jackson House to unload it. After we loaded the elevator, I would go down the staircase in the library to summon it. He would stay on top to make sure no one came near. As we passed Wall House, Dick and Janice's car was in the driveway, and the lights were on, so they must have been cleaning.

It went exactly as planned. We took all the framing two-by-fours down to the sub. While there, we poked around looking for additional secret doors or passages but found nothing.

In bed that night, I read about Operation Retrograde and Ross Murdock's part in it.

After my run, I showered on Friday morning and then put on a suit. It had been so long since I had worn one that I felt more comfortable in my Robin Hood tights, though I did like my hat better than Robin's. Mr. Monroe had arranged for my shooting schedule to be cleared for the morning so that I could attend the department head's meeting.

I was there by eight-thirty and was glad of it. I had coffee and donuts while the others trickled in. I was amazed at how I was treated as one of the group. Their ages ranged from the early thirties to the late fifties, but apparently, age doesn't count as much in a business setting as to how you fit in the pecking order.

Everyone was in place when Mr. Monroe walked in at exactly nine o'clock. Everyone stood when he came into the room, so I knew where we, as a group, fell into the studio pecking order. I was a heartbeat behind the group, but I stood also.

He got right to it, "This meeting is to see where we are on the presentation to the board. The main focus is uniformity. Rick, where are we?"

Now that is something I did not expect!

"Sir, we are all over the place. Everyone has done an excellent job, but no two are alike. I suggest we show you the beginnings of three of them to demonstrate."

I pulled that response out of the air, but it seemed to work.

"Pick three," he replied.

That was easy. Like in class, it was obvious who wanted to be picked and who didn't. I didn't push the issue and selected three who looked eager. I was a little surprised that Mr. Handfield was one of them. He must be proud of his progress.

When he stood up first, a mild rustling went through the crowd. They had suffered through his presentations before. They were pleasantly surprised by his performance. I glanced over at Mr. Monroe, and he winked at me.

When Mr. Handfield was finished, he received mild applause. From the look on his face, we had one happy person.

He was beaming. He looked at me on his way back to his seat and mouthed, "Thank you."

Some days you are glad you got up; this was one of them.

The next two did very credible presentations also but weren't surprising like Mr. Handfield's. It was very apparent that all three were different. As the last gentleman sat down, it started. Everyone had an opinion on what they should look like. This went on for a few minutes. I looked at Mr. Monroe, who was almost glaring at me.

Did he want me to do something? Well, it was obvious that we would be here all day while they made up their minds. Then it dawned on me. This was the art department's specialty. They could come up with the best look. But then I remembered that they always submitted their work for approval. Who would approve of this?

I stood up, "Ladies and Gentlemen, maybe we should leave this to the experts. Your overpaid art department is rather good at this sort of thing."

That got the laugh I was hoping for.

"And if you think they are overpaid, next it should be reviewed by the marketing group."

That one got half a donut tossed in my direction. Not enough of a challenge to start a food fight, but it crossed my mind.

I continued, "And after that, the marketing group should submit their final picks to our poor underpaid president, Mr. Monroe. Hey guys, I'm not stupid."

That finished in laughter.

It gave me the perfect opening to continue.

"Each department head needs to get their presentation to the art department today. If anyone needs help finalizing their message, I'll help if asked."

There, the ball is in their court.

"Now I have a question for the group. I was thinking of this last night. My involvement started with trying to learn how your department worked. You all were kind enough to give me your time, and I was able to give some modest input.

"The problem I see is that you are in the process of creating a tutorial of how Warner Brothers Studio works. Does the board need that or want that? I thought these were the moneymen, the business experts. They should already know this stuff.

"What are your thoughts?"

I was careful not to look toward Mr. Monroe while opening this can of worms. If he frowned, I was dead.

Thoughts were expressed, and I was lucky that this was a sharp group. I had a question. I just didn't have the answer. They did.

It boiled down to how we stacked up department to department against other studios, our competition, and what were we planning to do to get better.

While this was going on, I got the nerve up to look over to Mr. Monroe. He nodded his head. I took this as a sign that I was on the right track.

With my confidence still intact, I asked, "How will we find out how other studios are structured and their staffing?"

It turned out to be easy. People moved around so much that the answers were in the room. As people volunteered to share their knowledge, appointing people to immediate working groups was no big jump.

Chapter 11

Mr. Monroe jumped in. "Take a ten-minute break. After that, each studio group will list the structure and estimated cost of each of our five major competitors."

As the group headed for more coffee or the restrooms, Mr. Monroe came up to me.

"Good work so far, Rick; you are taking them exactly where I wanted this to go. The best part is that they are buying in as a group. I was concerned that I would have to order it."

"Why is that a concern?"

"If I had ordered it, the usual turf wars would start. By them forming teams, they have bonded, at least for this mission. In the Army, orders have to be given. In business, it is different. That is why you seldom hear of a general heading a large firm."

"What about President Eisenhower?"

"He is a politician. That is different."

"So, generals make good politicians?"

"Not all generals, but as a five-star general of the armies from many nations, what do you think Ike was doing? He would have to delegate, approve, convince, cajole, and gather support from the national leaders for the plans his staff developed. Now tell me how that job differs from being a president?"

"I never thought of it like that."

"The opposite of Ike was President Grant. He was used to having all the power of a general, but Lincoln did the political work. When Grant got into office, it was a whole new ball game for him, and it showed in his administration's record."

"I still don't understand completely why you are putting me in front like this."

"Two reasons, Rick. I needed a frontman, so I wouldn't have to command, and I'm curious as to how far you can go with this. Most full-grown adults with years of business experience couldn't get this group to where they are at this minute. I want to see how far you can go."

Now how is that for pressure? When the group filtered in from break, I watched the clock. When the ten minutes expired, I began.

"Find a room or space for each of your groups and flesh out the structure of the other major studios. Choose a presenter and be prepared to give a five-minute report. Report back at eleven o'clock. That will give us time to review things as a group."

Thank you for the Boy Scout leadership training. They spread out to work. Mr. Monroe stayed with me.

"Rick, this is urgent. Keep pushing them."

"Yes, sir."

At exactly eleven, all the groups were in place but one. I made them stop and join the main group. They didn't give me any grief. They were involved with what they were doing. I reminded them they had five minutes to present their findings.

It was amazing the uniformity between all the studios. So, we could prove we were as good as the others.

"I think we have taken this as far as we can this morning."

I turned to Mr. Monroe.

"How urgent is this? Should we schedule a get-together tomorrow morning?"

"Yes, nine o'clock in this room," he replied.

"Okay, we will meet here tomorrow. Each department head is to review this information, incorporate it into their presentation and any thoughts of improvement."

I then nodded at the secretary taking notes. "Miss Knowlton will have copies of the meeting minutes distributed this afternoon. Thank you all. I will see you in the morning."

The meeting broke up with the various working groups making plans.

On the way, I asked Miss Knowlton, "Would you please ask Donna to set up this room for tomorrow with the same arrangements? And thank you for your help today."

She beamed as she said, "Yes, sir."

I didn't expect that response. Mr. Monroe was listening, waiting to have a word with me.

"Rick, you never cease to amaze me."

"Maybe I should become a magician?"

"You made some magic here today. "

"Mr. Monroe, may I ask a question?"

"Certainly, I owe you several of them."

"I noticed in some departments people didn't have a lot to do. They were talking or even playing solitaire in one case."

"That's the bane of our existence. Every movie project in-house has a minimum of staff, but they aren't all needed all the time. We tried working with smaller staffs, but when things got busy, we were too many people short."

"Sir, my dad worked on the railroad, and they have a concept they call the extra board. These are trained people that are on call for when the regular staff is completely scheduled out."

"That must be terrible for the guys on the extra board who are trying to support a family."

"Oh, it is, but you have a special situation here. Another thing I heard time and again was the staff members were trying to get time off for acting classes, rehearsals, auditions, and tryouts. A good number of your employees want to be entertainers and don't want to work full-time. They take any job they can get with a studio hunting for a break."

"So, you think we could reduce staffing by having several people in each department on-call rather than as full-time employees?"

"Yes, sir, and the nice thing is that as a movie finishes when you normally would let staff go, you could ask if any want to be on call.

Then you only call them as needed. From what I understand, there is an average of ten movies in production at any one time, sometimes as few as five and as many as sixteen."

"You have learned about the studio."

"I was thinking that you could have a cross-trained core team. When there are a few movies, the core team works on those. When a new movie goes into production, the core team members spread out to the key positions on the new teams. That way, you have serious experience in-house that can expand to cover many projects."

"Rick, I was wrong. You are more than amazing. You are incredible. Now I have another challenge for you."

"What is that?"

"Lead the groups tomorrow to reach those conclusions without telling them directly. It would be a tremendous boost in morale if they could present it to the board as their way to reduce costs and improve the organization. Since it will be a group conclusion, no one will expect special recognition from it."

The look on my face must have told the story.

"Rick, you, and I as the president of the Studio, will know the truth. You will get special recognition for this."

"Thank you, sir. I guess I am human, after all."

"We all are, Rick."

It was lunchtime, so Mr. Monroe and I went to the commissary, except we used his private dining room.

Once we were settled and placed our orders, he continued, "Rick, you have several things going for you, physical presence and intelligence, but most of all, you are not afraid to work hard. The thing that amazes me most about you is your general lack of teenage arrogance. Most kids your age would be full of themselves if they performed the deeds that you have, hero, movie star, bull rider, and the list goes on."

"Mr. Monroe, I have thought about that. I have concluded it is because I have been working in an adult world, and it has been expected that I act like one. I suspect I would act like them if I spent much time with kids my age."

"So, we will keep you away from anyone your age. That's a shame. Nina was hoping to spend some time with you this weekend."

I had a moment of sheer panic when I heard him say that, but his smile gave him away.

"It's a chance that I will have to take, sir. She may corrupt my solid ways, but so be it."

"Get out of here, Rick," he replied with a chuckle. "They will need you on the set about now, anyway."

He was right. Production was waiting on me, not long enough for the director to be mad, but long enough for him to be a little sarcastic. Not nasty. Just kidding on the square.

"Now that the star has descended from on high, we can do some work. Places everyone!"

I took my place; some battles couldn't be won.

Chapter 12

I hadn't got to the set until one in the afternoon, so my eight hours with an hour dinner break weren't in until ten o'clock. That made it a long day. I still made a point of calling Nina for a date for Saturday night.

The production crew was going to be exhausted, but at least they got the weekend off. I had to be back at the studio by eight in the morning to make certain everything was in place for the meeting at nine. I learned that as a Boy Scout Senior Patrol Leader.

Everything was as it should be, so I poured a coffee and talked with the department heads as they trickled in. Luckily, I had figured out it would be a golf shirt day. Talking to a group of three, I managed to bring up that some departments seemed extremely busy while others had extra people standing around. They straightened me out on how the system worked. I left them at that point; a seed was planted about extra people.

I moved on to another group and hit the mother lode. The purchasing head asked how my father was enjoying California. I had no idea he knew he was here, but it gave me an opening. I told them he loved the real estate business here rather than the railroad and its extra board in Ohio. I forgot to mention anything about rental properties there. They agreed while the extra board was bad for my dad, it was good for the railroad.

Now I had to hope they would put two and two together. I could tell them directly, but where was the fun in that?

It took until the first break before a group brought the excessive number of people up, and another group responded with the extra board, except they called it flex work staffing. Whatever they wanted to call it was okay with me.

Once they had the idea, they ran with it. The group took it much further than I ever could. As the moderator, I had to keep them on track occasionally, but for the most part, they were focused. I glanced over at Mr. Monroe at one point, and he winked at me.

The group decided that they would calculate the possible cost savings and present this as a group at the board meeting. They went so far as to decide that they didn't need individual presentations. They ended up picking the two department heads who were the most comfortable with the presentation. For a horrible minute, I thought they would pick me.

They would work with the art department on the presentations, with marketing input on the appearance. Mr. Monroe would make the final decision; this was to be done by Tuesday, and then they would do practice sessions on Wednesday and Thursday. I was asked to sit in on those.

After the meeting, Mr. Monroe took me aside.

"Rick, you have the makings of a CEO of a large company. I was watching you, and I could see your ideas coming out, but when did you plant them?"

I explained my conversations before the meeting started.

"You know, Rick, those two guys doing the presenting will be viewed as possible successors to me. They will owe you big time and will never know. I know, and I don't know what I will do for you yet, but it will be significant."

"It had better be, or I will want a box of cigars."

"Well, that's easy enough," he replied.

"They will be old-dried-out things, with the Rough Riders on the box."

"Never!" he gasped.

We both laughed at that.

"Would you marry Nina for me?"

"Err...." Now it was my turn to gasp.

"Thought not," he said as we both roared. I hoped he would never tell Nina about this, or I was dead meat. He must have read my mind as he said, "Please don't mention this to Nina, or I am dead meat."

"I promise I won't."

I wasn't that dumb. Come to think of it, both of us might regret her knowing about these remarks.

I spent the afternoon with Coach Palmer practicing my hand-to-hand. It was feeling better and better all the time. I felt like I could hold my own with most people. Of course, give the guy a gun, some distance, and it was all over.

As I drove home, I turned on the radio. The first song I heard was "Brothers". The announcer said it was number four this week, which meant it had a good chance of going to number one. No telling about people's tastes.

When I got back to the apartment, Dad told me I had to call Susan Wallace. She had called three times today. It was about the premiere of *Sir Nicklaus* on Wednesday.

I think I had been told that, but I didn't remember. I wondered if they wanted me to attend. When I called Susan, I found out.

"Rick, you haven't answered the Wednesday premiere invitation. Why not?"

"It was mailed to me?"

"Yes, didn't you receive it?"

"Just a minute," I replied.

I sorted through my unopened mail for the week and found it. So, I am still fifteen in some respects. Sue me.

"I have it here," as I ripped it open. "Yeah, I will go; I have nothing else planned for Wednesday."

She ignored that somewhat stupid statement.

"Who will be accompanying you?"

"I need a date?"

"It's traditional."

"I have a date with Nina Monroe tonight. I will ask her."

"Let me know how that turns out, will you?"

The way she asked that made me wonder what I was getting into.

"Make sure your tux is back from the dry cleaner's in time."

"I don't own a tux."

"You don't need a publicity agent; you need a mother or a wife."

"I will have to rent one for the evening."

"What, a mother or a wife?"

That stopped me cold.

"Err," I started.

Susan interrupted me, "Be prepared to go to a tailor tomorrow. I will let you know in the morning when and where."

"Thanks, Susan. Do I mail the RSVP back to them?"

"It's too late. I will take care of it." I was beginning to see why I was paying her.

When I went over to Nina's, she was dressed for a casual evening in a sporty-looking dress. I don't know how else to describe it. We started at Hamburger Haven. There were plenty of kids our age, so we had many people stop by our table. One thing that was very noticeable since the TV special was the women or girls in this case.

They went out of their way to let me know they liked me and were available. In one case, I could see Nina coming to a slow boil or not so slow.

She told one girl whom, apparently, she had a history with, "Get the hell away. He's mine, and you're not going to steal him like Tommy."

I kept my mouth shut. I did tell her that it was almost becoming a problem at the studio if I ate at the commissary. Women were even approaching me if I sat by the pool at the apartment.

She replied, "That is okay, but not when we are on a date."

I'm going to have to take an acting class on looking unavailable.

To change the subject, I asked her if she would like to accompany me to the premiere on Wednesday.

"Let me make certain I understand, Ricky. This is Saturday, and you are asking me if I will attend a Hollywood premiere with you on Wednesday."

"Yes, that is it."

She started to say something, but all she did was open and close her mouth. All of a sudden, she burst into tears. I remembered Susan Wallace's comment. Several of her girlfriends must have been watching us like hawks because they swooped in and towed her away to the lady's room.

Our Negro waitress was right there and asked me what I had done to that poor girl. I explained to her what I had asked and Nina's reaction.

"Honey, you are so dead. You think giving a girl an invitation to a major event and then only giving her four days to prepare is all right? Your momma is going to have words with you."

Now I was concerned. Nina's crying was bad enough, but words from Mum were over the top. Nina came back to the table, tears gone and face freshly washed. Luckily for me, she was in a calmer frame of mind. She told me it would be my fault if she and two of her girlfriends got in trouble for skipping school on Monday to go shopping. By the way, for not giving enough notice, I would be expected to pay for everything.

I remembered Mum telling me she paid less than ten dollars for a dress at J.C. Penney's. How bad could it be? There would also be the cost of a visit to the beauty parlor on Wednesday, and she would have to skip school. I could see this getting deeper and deeper.

Chapter 13

After dinner, we went to a drive-in movie. To this day, I have no idea what was on the screen. I did learn more about the mysteries of women. Not everything, but a huge advance. I think she learned some things about men also.

I didn't read before going to sleep. I was too busy reliving the evening.

Susan Wallace called right after I got back from my morning run. She wanted to know how it went with Nina. When I told her, she told me I was getting off easy. Talk about a lesson learned. It seems like I have learned more lately than I ever had in school, or at least quite different things.

Susan told me about my tailor appointment. It was within the hour, so I had to hustle over to an area called Chinatown. When inside, I was descended upon by a small army, literally. It was a group of short Chinese men. Well, three of them. They measured parts I didn't even know I had. It took me a minute to understand when he asked me which side I hung.

I was glad to get out of there. I had to go back after lunch on Tuesday for a fitting.

It was a pleasure to go hand-to-hand with Coach. I felt like I controlled this, and he was only trying to physically hurt me!

When I made my weekly call to Mum, I told her about asking Nina to the premier so late.

Her only comment was, "We will have words later."

I am so dead! Maybe I would get lucky and catch my death before then.

That was the end of the excitement for the week. Dad told me how things were going on in the office front. Good. We watched some TV. The part of the shows I remembered was an ad for dancing

Old Gold cigarettes, "Call for Philip Morris", and my favorite, "Hey Mable".

I woke up feeling cheerful on Monday. The rains had stopped, and we had that wonderful southern California glow. It was April, and the rest of the world was rainy and dreary, at least in Ohio, so all was well. I thought this would be a great week. If I had only known.

Exercising and my run are old friends now. I don't know what I would do without them. I did have to spend more time weightlifting. I had missed too many sessions recently. It wouldn't hurt to practice with both sword and bow, then get back in the ring. My hand-to-hand combat training was coming along nicely.

I was keeping up with my Spanish on the set. I was being careful to keep the accent Mrs. Hernandez had taught me. I also worked at my Mayfair British accent. Half the time, I was speaking with my British accent without realizing it, both in English and Spanish. I was wondering if I should start studying French as that was where Nina was heading. I put that decision off for another day.

On the run with Dick Wyman, we saw the track coach warming his team up. We waved but didn't slow down. Dick did ask me if I missed high school and socializing. I told him I missed the socializing a little, but not high school at all. I told him I didn't plan to sit around in a high school classroom again.

It would be too slow and boring. I realized that to teach a group, they had to work at the speed of the group. I just wasn't interested in waiting for the group. Even socializing wasn't as attractive as it had been. Yes, it was fun to be with kids my age, to a point. I enjoyed spending time with my sister Mary, but I wouldn't want to do it constantly. I felt the same way about high school kids. I had moved on and enjoyed working in the adult world.

This conversation made our five miles go quickly. We gave one last wave to the track team, which was starting its rounds. It was almost symbolic of how I was so far ahead of them in my day and life. I also realized that the devil was at my heels, and I couldn't slow down, or life would catch up and pass me by.

After those deep thoughts, a workout, and a run, I needed a shower. Coffee also helped. Dad fixed bacon and eggs for breakfast; if I kept this up, I would be packing on weight. As we finished eating, the phone rang. It was from Mark Downing.

He was excited about the response from the TV special.

"We have so many orders. I started a second shift in production. I've never seen anything like it. The network contacted me, and they are going to rerun the special next week. While the ratings were sky-high, many people missed it, and from the Nielsen ratings, it will be worth rerunning. They wanted to know if we would sponsor it again. What do you think?"

"I think we should, but it should be a corporate expense this time."

"I agree with you, Rick. I appreciate your kicking this off as you did, but the company has to stand on its own. On another subject, Anna Romanov will be calling you. She wants your thoughts on a project."

You could tell from the tone of his voice he was star-struck and could hardly believe that he was in a business relationship with such a star. The fact is, I was still in awe.

Mark and I talked about the business a little more. As its foundations became firmer, it was obvious he didn't need my input. He enjoyed it and certainly was willing to use my connections but was more than able to run the business himself. I could be the silent partner I had envisioned when we started.

We no sooner hung up than Anna called. She wanted to have a lunch meeting tomorrow at the commissary. She arranged a private dining room. Susan Wallace had been invited, and Sally Enright was flying in from Detroit. She didn't want to go into all the details, but she had received an offer that triggered a set of ideas that she wanted to pass by all of us. Of course, I would make it.

I had to hustle to get to makeup and costumes on time. The morning's shoot had me teaching the littles how to stalk game. It was a bit of a hoot. The littles were supposed to be noisy when they went through our little woods. Who had that bright idea? It was a thundering herd. It finally got to the point where the director told them to sneak as quietly as they could through the woods. That worked out to the right sound level.

Mr. Fitzhugh had taken to his part as a village storyteller so well that the director talked to him about another opportunity. I must say I thought he was going to be a real pain, but instead, he was professional as all get out. Once he saw all of us kids were being taken care of safely, receiving our schooling, and weren't overworked, he was fine. For some reason, I had a hard time including myself in that group.

My ninth-grade completion papers were on file at the studio, so he didn't expect me to attend any classes. That was a load off my mind. I thought California Child Services would be causing me all sorts of problems once they started.

The afternoon filming was more of the same. This time I got to lug a dummy deer over my shoulders that supposedly I had shot. It was the king's deer, so it was illegal as all get out. Of course, this lets Junior come on the scene and chase me everywhere. I don't think it is possible to climb up on the roof of a peasant's hut with a deer over your shoulders. You gotta love Hollywood.

After work, I stopped and lifted weights for a while. Nobody was around to sword fight or box with, so I did my sword exercises and shadowboxed for a while, but it was boring, so it didn't last long.

On the way home, my radio was playing. "Brothers" had now reached number one. This was insane! How can someone like me, who can't sing, have a number-one record?

Chapter 14

When I got home, Dad wasn't there yet. I had just barely gotten dinner started when there was heavy knocking at the door. Looking through the peephole, I saw a short fat lady and two policemen, so I opened the door. I quickly regretted that.

"Ricky Jackson?" asked the lady.

"Yes, ma'am," I replied.

"Pack a bag. We are taking you into child protection."

"What?"

"You are a minor, and your parents are abusing you by letting you live in California without supervision."

The two cops were standing there like they wanted nothing to do with this. They must have each been a little under six-feet tall. I might be able to take both in a fight, but there was no reason to think that way.

"Ma'am, I am under the supervision of the studio, and my parents have signed consent forms."

"Well, they aren't through us, luckily for you. We picked up on your being alone on that TV special. Now come along. We will make sure you are safe."

This was getting surreal.

"Young man, you have to come with me. We will put you up tonight and find a family to take care of you."

"Will they make certain I can do my job at the studio?"

"That remains to be seen. You will have to appear before a judge, and we will make recommendations for your safety. Since you have been abandoned, I doubt if we will be able to recommend that you be allowed to work. Besides, you have no way to get around. You are too young to drive."

I realized that this was going nowhere fast. I hoped Dad would show up soon.

"Let me put an overnight kit together."

"Hurry up about it."

I liked this lady less and less.

"I will."

I turned to the policemen, "Does it cut any ice that I am a Detective 4th Class?"

"You are?" Asked the senior of the two, a sergeant, I thought.

"Yes, sir."

My ID was on my desk, so it was easy to retrieve and show it to him.

He asked, "You're the kid with the bow and arrow?"

"Yes, sir."

"I was there. Your parents attended, if I remember right."

"That's right, and I expect my dad home any minute now."

The officer looked at the woman, "Are you sure about this?"

"Yes, I am. We saw it on TV, so it must be true. His parents aren't here."

Sometimes you get lucky.

"What's going on here?" my dad asked.

"She wants to haul me away because you have abandoned me."

"How much is she going to pay for you?" he inquired.

I saw one of the cops nudge the other.

"Nothing. She wants to protect me from whatever wild things are out here in LA."

The policeman who had been at the award ceremony about lost it, but since he was behind the woman, she didn't see it.

"Now wait for a minute young man. I am here for your good. Now, who is this man?"

"My father."

"It can't be. It said on TV that you were living alone."

"Do you believe everything you see on TV or in the movies?" I asked dryly.

Now the woman wasn't totally stupid. She asked Dad to see some I.D., which was a reasonable request from her point of view. Dad showed it rather than get in a hoorah with her. As far as he knew, she didn't have the authority to require it, but the cops did, so he went along with it.

She sniffed after she looked at his license. It is your picture, but how do I still know he is your son? At that point, I retrieved a copy of my birth certificate and passport. She wanted to argue some more, but the police told her that they were satisfied with the situation, and she didn't have to save me.

As they were leaving, the senior cop asked me, "You kill those guys in Colorado and help capture those rustlers in Texas?"

"Yes, sir."

"I think LA needs to be protected from you."

With a smile and a wave, they left. I hoped I had seen the last of that fat little lady, but who could tell.

After Dad and I had completed dinner, I called Nina to see how her day went. Would I have to be sitting in detention for her? I wondered how that would work. Fortunately, she didn't get caught.

She started with, "You owe me for three lunches. Then there are the clothes, having my makeup and hair done, plus the hotel room."

Now all sorts of thoughts went through my head when she said hotel room. I decided to be cool and take it by the numbers. How much for the lunches?

"Four dollars."

I can handle that.

"How much will the clothes cost me?"

"The main outfit was on sale, so I got a real deal."

Now I had heard this from Mum when she started with the words "sale" and "deal." It meant she spent more than she had budgeted. I wasn't worried. A dress should be under ten dollars.

She told me in a hurry, "The dress was forty-five, the clutch handbag fifteen, and the shoes twenty-four dollars."

I about had a heart attack but kept my cool.

"Nina, it is more than I thought, but that is okay."

"I got even a better deal on the outfit for the reception."

What reception?

"Tell me about it."

"As you know, the after-party reception is at the Beverly Hilton, so it's dressier than the premiere itself. The ballgown was ninety-five dollars, the purse and shoes another fifty-five. She proudly told me she saved almost a hundred dollars."

I had heard Mum do this type of math before. Now I understood why Dad had said he couldn't afford to save much more.

"Then the outfit for the after-party was only eighty-five dollars for everything."

My quick math had me at over three hundred dollars.

"What is the hotel room for?"

This might make it all worthwhile. I remembered our last time together. Would the final mystery be solved?

"So, we can change clothes after the parties. You will wear the same tuxedo at the premiere and reception but change for the after-party. A sports coat will do for that. I even saved us money on that. I called Ellen Shelly, and she and her boyfriend will share the cost. Dad suggested it."

I bet he did. I must remember to thank Mr. Monroe for saving me all of that money.

Chapter 15

The next morning as we ran, Dick told me how he and Janice were doing with Wall House. They were getting ready to move in. They would beat us by a month at least. Mum had another trip planned for next week to meet with her decorator. Dad and I had discussed it and decided that even though he was light in the loafers, he was Mum's decorator. In the meantime, a cleaning crew was working on the house, except for the sub-basement.

The decorator was doing a good job for us. Besides coming up with designs and implementing them after Mum's approval, he arranged the cleaning crews. The furniture was being appraised. Some of it was in useable condition, and all of it had been high quality when new, so there was some value. The salvageable good stuff would go to an auction house as-is. The rest would go to the dump.

Mum was coming out to start the long process of choosing the themes and colors of each room. As a room would be decided upon, the painting would be started. As I thought about it, I realized that we might be lucky to be in before school started. That put me off on another line of thought. What was I going to do next school year?

I was still firm in my thinking that there was no way I was going to sit through daily classes again, at least as they were conducted in high school. I had to go through all the material. I was no super genius or anything, but that didn't mean I had to be held to the speed of the slowest pupil in class or the teacher's rate of instruction.

In some of the books I have, real reasons for going to college were explored. They broke down to learning how to study, gathering necessary information, living without adult supervision, and meeting new people and contacts for your future. As far as I could see, the only thing I needed schooling, for now, was the information part.

I knew how to study, as shown by my grades and how fast I did ninth grade. I had been living on my own with limited adult supervision. As I thought that, I did look around for the short fat lady from California Child Services.

In the studio, I was meeting a wide range of people, and many of those might be able to help me in the future. I guess one thing I would have to add to my lack list was peer contact and their future help. Maybe I would always be ahead of my age group.

All these thoughts made the run go fast. On the way to the studio, I turned the radio on. "Brothers" came on, so I changed the station. That didn't help, as it was on that one, also. The third station had "Diana", so I stayed with it. When the next song up was "Brothers", I gave up and turned the dang thing off.

My attention to the radio almost had me in a wreck. The guy in front of me was driving a 1930s Ford that didn't have turn signals. He didn't bother to use hand signals, turning at the last minute and slowing down sharply while doing so. I about rear-ended him. I would be so glad if all cars had turn signals. However, I suppose that guys like that wouldn't use those either.

When I arrived at the set, Mr. Fitzhugh was waiting for me.

"Rick, I heard Child Services was after you."

"Yes, sir, they thought I was living alone. Fortunately, Dad showed up before they hauled me away."

I think Mr. Fitzhugh twinkled when he said, "Most of the people in that department are rather good, and they all are sincere. Some of them go overboard and believe everything they are told. There is one lady who brags she always gets her kids. You will know her if she shows up at your door. She is short and stout."

"I may have met her."

"It would be a disaster to her worldview if she had to go back without the kid because she had her facts wrong. I even know a lot of people who would be happy to see that. Not me, of course."

"I understand," I said with my tongue firmly in my cheek.

"How did you hear about it?"

"The police don't like to accompany her so they may have spread the word of her comeuppance."

"I see," and I did. Sometimes things work out.

I also felt sorry for any child she rescued. The facts wouldn't get in her way.

He continued, "I need to ask you some questions of a more serious nature. I have noticed that you don't go home when you are finished on the set. You are here for many hours. Are you doing any paid work?"

"No, sir. I use weights to keep in shape, the same with sword fighting, archery, and boxing. I am also taking classes in unarmed combat. Then I am extending my business education by asking questions in each department. Is any of that a violation?"

"No, it isn't. Don't be offended, but I will be confirming that, as that is part of my job."

"I have no problem with that. At least you are checking before saving me from those evil capitalists."

I thought he was going to bust a gut. He laughed so hard.

"Rick, I think those evil capitalists need saving from you. My main worry is always some preteen kid being overworked. Here you are way over six feet and two hundred pounds. That is the physical side. On the mental side, you are making a small fortune off them, and I know about your help in those presentations to the board of directors. That is the talk of the commissary. I must ask. Are you getting paid anything for that?"

"No, sir. Mr. Monroe says he owes me in a general sense, but no contract, written or verbal, exists between either of the parties."

"That's what I mean. I fear more for them than you. How many other kids your age would give that answer?"

That brought me up short. Unless their dad were a lawyer, none would give such an answer.

"Anyway, Rick, if you are obeying the letter of the law, I have no concerns. As far as the spirit of the law, you are meeting that. I don't see a child being used."

"Thank you, sir."

From there, it was work, work, and more work. The morning flew by, and it was time for my lunch with Anna and her publicist, Sally Enright, and Susan Wallace. Anna reserved a private dining room for our meeting. I asked her what pull it took to get a room like this. She didn't know. She always asked Donna, Mr. Monroe's assistant, and it happened. I might try it that way someday.

Anna told us why she had called this meeting. She had an offer of ten thousand dollars to personally oversee a bathroom being redone with fixtures from her collection.

"It is obvious they are trying to have me come to their house so that they can brag about it to their friends. What problems do you see with doing this?"

We all looked at each other, wondering who would go first and what they would say. Susan started with a question.

"What do you know about these people?"

"Nothing, this is a cold contact. It came through DF and Sally."

"That would make me leery right away for two reasons, your safety and what bad publicity you might receive from even being close to them. For example, you don't want to be close to anyone with mob connections. I had a first-hand look at the downside of bad publicity."

That last hit close to home as I thought of Mum, Lucky, or even me and Mr. Sinatra. Though I think it was more rumor than reality about Mr. Sinatra and the mob. They knew him and liked his work as an Italian boy from New Jersey, but that didn't mean he had connections.

I thought having connections meant that one could make a phone call and have someone killed. Come to think of it. Mum probably wouldn't make a phone call.

"So, you recommend that I pass?"

"Without your knowing more about these people, pass."

We all shook our heads in agreement.

Sally said, "I have had the most time to think about it. While these people may not be the right people, there is an opportunity here. Anna, do you have a favorite charity?"

"Yes, the Childhood Cancer Fund. They helped my niece's family when they needed it, and they are sponsoring research."

"Why don't you offer personal designs through them? What do you normally receive for a personal appearance?"

"Normally, I receive two thousand dollars."

"Then charge ten and give the other eight to the charity. That would give you a large tax deduction plus your normal fee. That would be a win."

I added, "Why not make a fundraiser out of it, allowing two thousand for the refreshments and whatever, two for you and six from you to the charity? That way, the charity has the potential to make a much larger sum of money.

Anna's lady then added, "We can also invite a large local paper to take pictures and publicize the event, and we can ask a national magazine to follow all of them."

From there, the conversation took fire. The charity would be asked to help recruit the people Anna would work with, and they would check local news sources about their reputation. In the end, Anna decided that she would like events in Boston, New York, Miami, Dallas, Chicago, and Los Angeles. Anna would be the front person, but Sally would do the actual design.

Anna's publicist was picked to write the letter to the Sol Estes family in Pecos, Texas to decline. It was based on the schedule and plans already in place. There would be an offer to have a designer visit and make recommendations.

Every one of us felt that Anna should only be personally involved with preselected people. Of course, there could be an exception if Ike asked her to do the White House. That was doubtful as Harry Truman had just finished rebuilding the place in 1952.

Chapter 16

The afternoon's scenes had me jumping into the moat as I ran for my life. I wondered if I would ever make a movie without looking like a drowned rat. Though, of course, since it was Hollywood, it was a good-looking drowned rat. Well, as good-looking as I could be. They spent more time redoing my makeup after I made the jump than the rest of the scene put together.

It only took five takes, so I did get off lightly. They talked about using a stuntman to jump onto an airbag. They would also have another stuntman jump into the water to get the large splash required. I then would slide into the water and be filmed coming out. They debated this for half an hour. I then made the radical suggestion that I just make the jump. It would save time and money. The producer loved it, the insurance people not so much.

After another half hour, everyone came around, and I was allowed a test jump from the twenty-foot-tall wall. Now let's see a large fifteen-year-old boy jumping into the water. Put that with a crowd of adults, who had been starting to bore him, and then piss him off standing at water's edge. What could go wrong?

It was the best cannonball I ever did. The whole thing can be seen in Technicolor and sound. To this day, I love the shouts and screams from the crowd as they figured out what was about to happen.

While not appearing in the movie, it was seen in every screening room in Hollywood, both studio and private. It became a badge of honor to be in that crowd. The "Splash", as it became known, made the tabloids.

There were letters to the editor about my juvenile behavior and how the younger generation was going to hell. According to teen magazines, I was a hero. I guessed it depended upon where you visualized yourself in that scene.

That was later. Right now, I had a lot of ticked-off people dripping water. There must be a saying about when in doubt, approach boldly. I climbed out of the water and walked up to the director.

I stated, "That went fine. We can do the scene this way. You might want to move the people further back next time."

His sputtering made whatever grief that might be coming down on me worth it. I saw a couple of the makeup people handing out towels, so I helped them pass them out. I don't know where she came from, but Susan Wallace appeared with a cameraman who took pictures of me passing out towels.

When my eight hours on set were up, a runner appeared. I was wanted in Mr. Monroe's office. Now was the time I had to pay the piper. Donna sent me right in. That was a good sign. He wasn't smiling. That was a bad sign. He stared at me for the longest time. I stood there silently.

Finally, I couldn't take it anymore, "Sir, I'm sorry."

That did it. He burst out laughing.

"Rick, you are an inspired genius for publicity. It will come across as good harmless fun and make you more human and likable to the public, especially your public, the teen market."

"You aren't mad?"

"No, Rick, I'm not mad. Now the trick is to never do anything like that again. Find something new and original. Don't do it often. Keep it original. You will be fine. You don't want to bore your public at the same time. You want to keep them on edge with what might happen next."

This was plain weird. I had been trying my hardest to act like an adult. The one time I backslide, I'm praised for it. What does the world want? I expressed those thoughts to Mr. Monroe.

"Good question Rick. You walk a fine line as an entertainer, putting on a show for your audience and being a serious workman behind the scenes. Knowing when to shift behavior can't be taught. If today is an example, you have the knack. Your action costs the production company time and money; then balance that against the increased revenue because of the publicity. Being a clown once increases income. Doing it all the time becomes predictable, costing money and eventually your fans."

"I get your point, sir. I do these things spontaneously. They are not planned."

"You now have done it twice in this movie. Do you think you should do it again?"

"Probably not, unless an opportunity that is different presents itself."

"I think you have it. Are you ready for the premiere tomorrow?"

"I have to go from here for the last fitting on my tuxedo. By the way, thank you for your help in keeping the cost down on our hotel room."

"Rick, I was your age once. I wasn't trying to keep your cost down, and you know it."

This conversation was heading in a direction that I didn't want to go.

'Yes, sir."

Somewhere I read when in doubt, salute and keep your mouth shut. We aren't military, but I could keep my mouth shut.

"I'm a father, Rick, and want the best for my daughter. That depends on her age and where she is in life. At this point, I'm supposed to be protecting her from herself. Like you, her hormones are running wild. All I can do is limit opportunities and pray for the best. Now you had better be on your way. By the way, look like I chewed you out when you leave here."

"How do I do that?"

"Figure it out. You're the actor."

So, I hung my head as I left his office.

Donna took one look and murmured, "Ham."

Well, so much for my acting ability. I drove down to Chinatown. They had my tuxedo ready. It fit like a glove; it seemed perfect to me. It wasn't for them. They stuck a few pins in, fortunately not into me, and did some minor rework.

Besides the tuxedo, they had made me a set of five shirts plus cummerbunds of different colors and matching bow ties along with braces. There were also studs and cuff links, a standard black onyx. They even pulled out shoes for me to try on. I ended up with two pairs of basic-looking but shiny black shoes. A top hat would be provided later. They took longer to make.

They had me try everything on and were even kind enough to show me how to tie the bow tie. I hadn't a clue, and it showed when it was handed to me.

The tuxedo was more of a set of clothes than a suit. There were three jackets: one black, one white, and one black with long split tails. There were two pairs of pants, each with a shiny black silk stripe down the side. Then there were five different waistcoats.

Susan had arranged that I only had to sign the bill. When I saw the bill, I choked. Then again, it was a lot of custom-made items on short notice.

After I signed the bill, I said, "Thank you."

Then on a hunch, I put my two hands together and made a short bow, more of a tipping of the head in the direction of the working team.

It must have been the right thing to do from the smiles I received. My reading taught me a few things.

That night I started a novel that was too dark for me. Mildred, a divorced lady in the middle of the Depression, starts a restaurant. She gets remarried to a bum named Monte; he takes up with her daughter, who is a spoiled brat beyond belief. Then the youngest daughter, the only likable person in the book, dies. She reminded me of Mary, which I found very distressing. I disliked the other characters so much that I set the book aside. Even the thought of anything happening to Mary left me feeling sick.

Chapter 17

Wednesday was a typical beautiful California day. Sunshine, low humidity, and a moderate temperature were great for running. Dick and I bantered back and forth as we went. They were making progress on Wall House and thought they would be ready to move in by the end of next week. He and Janice were both excited about the move. They had put off starting a family until they had a place to raise children. This appeared to be their chance.

From what I knew of life in Bellefontaine, the children came first, sometimes even before the wedding. It sounded like they did things differently in the big city.

Things on the set were calmer than yesterday. We all settled in for a normal workday. The director did ask me how I liked my session in Mr. Monroe's office. I told him that I wouldn't want to go through that again. He walked away with a smirk.

What I didn't tell him was that I wouldn't want to go through a conversation again with my girlfriend's father about hormones. Once was way too many times.

It had been arranged that I would attend the department heads' practice presentations from ten until noon. I had to log out from the set to stop my work clock. Walking into the boardroom where they were set up was really strange. There were all these businessmen in suits and ties and me in a Lancaster green shirt and tights. At least I left my hat on the set.

I sat in the back next to Mr. Monroe. He explained that they were back to the multiple presenters. His team had time to think and realized that those presenting would have a leg up on the others. To keep emotions from running high, he changed the plan.

They started soon after I arrived. Each presenter would stand behind the pulpit and present. There was an aide who had posterboard charts in order. He would change them at need. The artwork was excellent, as one would expect.

Each chart had bullet points. The presenter would expand on each point. They had a wooden pointer to use if they needed to refer to a specific line. Everyone had their talks down pat. I wasn't certain if there was anything to add as they were all slick and professional. It was obvious this wasn't their first run-through.

After the third presenter was finished, I raised my hand.

"Why are you using a lectern?"

"It's for our notes," the next presenter answered.

He was standing empty-handed.

"Where are they?"

"Well, I don't need them. I know my presentation cold."

I asked, "Would you please do yours with the lectern removed."

Believe it or not, I saw this done in Boy Scout leadership training.

He then proceeded to give his presentation flawlessly.

When he was done, I asked, "Did anyone notice anything different about this presentation?"

The answers were as expected: "He was able to move around."

"He appeared more relaxed."

"He didn't appear to be trapped."

"There isn't a barrier between us."

"All true. A pulpit has its place, but it creates every one of the problems you have just noted. Let's see if you all can work without one."

No one needed one. Their presentations took on a new life as the personality of each presenter emerged from behind that barrier.

They could move around using wider gestures. The body language was now part of the presentation. Instead of a dry recital of facts and figures, these confident professionals were able to demonstrate that they had mastered their trade and were running their businesses. These show-businessmen were the showmen of business.

This wasn't my description. It was made by a business reporter much later after he saw a repeat performance at the annual meeting. The Warner Brothers Board of Directors was so impressed with the format they wanted it repeated in public. It didn't include business improvements. Other studios would find out soon enough. Why tell them in advance?

At the end of the practice presentations, Mr. Monroe asked me, "Where did you learn that?"

I explained about Boy Scout leadership training.

"I guess not knowing about that type of training is a disadvantage of not being a Scout or having a daughter and not a son."

"Not too late to be a Scoutmaster, sir."

From the glare I received, I didn't think it was going to happen. As the last presentation finished, I slipped quietly out of the room. I had to get back to work at my real job.

The rest of the afternoon flew by. There were no hiccups in production. Most of the scenes were done in a couple of takes. We were ahead of schedule, especially in my scenes. As typical of movie productions, the scenes were shot in the order of convenience, not in story order.

Because of that, I had no feelings at all about how the actual movie would end up. There was enough different footage that the director could take the story in several different directions or at least emphasize different parts of it.

One example was Mr. Fitzhugh. He was only in the picture because I violated child labor laws. The fine for that was five hundred dollars. To keep track of the safety of all the kids on the set, he had to sit in the center.

He became the village storyteller to account for his presence. Now I was hearing lines where he was the center of communication for Robin. He never had a direct line and was only referred to as the "old man." He was becoming the brains behind the operation. I wouldn't be surprised if he turned out to be King Richard in disguise.

I rushed home, cleaned up, and changed into my Nina and Susan-approved tuxedo combination. A studio limo picked me up on time and drove me over to Nina's. Dad had a ticket but had to drive himself.

I broke down, gave him the keys to the T-Bird, and told him to have a little style. Something about going to a movie premiere in a van didn't seem right. He took the keys.

Nina had to make a grand entrance. She only kept me waiting for a few minutes, so my conversation with Mr. Monroe didn't have time to turn awkward. Only a few comments on how well the presentations were going before it could turn to hotel rooms, Nina made her appearance.

She adopted the Anna Romanov look. It looked good on her. She was breathtaking as she made her entrance. She didn't look like a high school girl but a gorgeous young woman. Even her father gasped a little.

I had to get into the spirit of the event. I walked over to her, gave a half bow, and air-kissed her hand.

Using my most posh British accent, "You look beautiful, My Lady."

Her father applauded, "You remind me of your mother at that age."

Nina beamed as her mission was accomplished. She had wowed the two men in her life.

We took the limo to the staging area. A parking lot near the theater was used for this purpose regularly. There was a strict order of unloading on the red carpet. First would be Mr. Wayne and his wife, then Nina and me, after that Ellen and her boyfriend, the director followed by the producer, and sundry others.

When it was our turn to step out of our limo, the chauffeur held the door while I handed out Nina. The traditional red carpet was in place. Red velvet ropes held back the crowd. Searchlights lighted the sky. The press was represented by all types of reporters from magazines, newspapers, and radio stations. New additions to the group were the mobile TV trucks and cameras.

At the entrance, there were fans. I was surprised to see a lot of Nina's high school friends in the crowd. I found out later that they would allow friends into one small section. The deal was they saw their person in and then vacated the area for the friends of the next person to appear. They all had complimentary tickets. Since I didn't have friends of that nature here, Susan and Nina took care of that detail for me. That was fine with me.

I was asked the usual questions.

"Yes, I am excited by this great night."

"John Wayne is a great person to work with."

"I would love to work with him again."

"Warner Brothers is the best studio in the world," and so on.

My favorite question was, "Was the stampede scene planned all along?"

"No."

The movie itself was fun. I hadn't bothered to watch it before tonight. I had several opportunities but passed. If it hadn't been me in the picture show, I would have been cheering things on like many others were doing. They had made it a Saturday morning feature film that kids would hoot and holler at.

When I kissed Ellen in the show, Nina elbowed me in the ribs.

She whispered, "How many times did you have to shoot that scene?"

No dummy here, I replied, "One take."

That rated another elbow, but that was the end of that questioning line.

Chapter 18

I thought the crowd loved the movie from the talk I heard as it ended, but then it was an extremely biased crowd. I knew half of the audience. The rest were family members of those I knew.

The early-morning papers would have the critics' reviews. Their opinion would be interesting, but this weekend's real test, the first weekend box-office receipts, would tell the tale. Frankly, most of us were in it for the money, not the awards. There were no illusions that this would win any awards. Like a B movie with a relatively small budget, it wasn't even in the running.

Leaving the theater was as orderly as going in. After most of the crowd had dispersed, those of us with prominent roles in the movie gathered in the lobby, where we left in reverse order of arrival. Thus Mr. Wayne and his wife were last.

On the way out, I was asked such brilliant questions by reporters as, "Did you enjoy the movie?"

"How true to life was the movie?"

"Have you met any of Sir Nicklaus's descendants?"

My answers were: "I thought the movie was wonderful; everyone should see it this weekend. The movie was true to life. Give or take a lie or two. No, I have never met any descendants of the fictional Sir Nicklaus."

My absolute favorite was the follow-up on the last question. "Will you be trying to meet any of the descendants?"

"Yes, I will. I just got directions to their house. It is second to the right and straight on to morning."

Hope he tries to go there. I got away before he could ask for a ride.

Once in the limo, it was all hugs and kisses from Nina. She thought the movie was wonderful. Ellen and her boyfriend had beaten us to the hotel. It was a suite with a living room and two bedrooms with their baths. There was a wet bar in the living room, but it wasn't stocked.

One bedroom was for the boys to change and the other for the girls. A makeup artist and hairdresser were waiting for the ladies. We guys were on our own. Any thoughts I may have had about mysteries were put on hold.

I used the restroom and then joined Ellen's boyfriend. I knew his name was Bob Taylor, but I had never met him. We introduced ourselves and went immediately into the time-honored male tradition of whining about how long the women were taking.

We thought we were safe because the women were having their hair touched up in their bedroom. Bob made a particularly snarky comment and from behind closed doors came, "I heard that."

I'm pretty certain it was Ellen, but I quickly changed the topic to be safe.

"Bob, how do you earn your living?"

"I have a small farm, three hundred acres out in the valley. My primary crop is pecans."

We proceeded to make small talk. I very quickly realized that too much rain, not enough rain, too cold, too hot, various molds, rot, and insects, along with high winds, were the bane of pecan farmers. Since I had heard this from every farmer I had ever met, it was no surprise.

The girls came out just before my eyes glazed over. I know that wasn't fair to Bob, but the plight of the farmer didn't interest me. I suspect he would feel the same way if my dad talked about rental housing. Of course, if I talked about myself, it would be fascinating to him. Not!

We went down to the ballroom as a group. I was getting to be an old hand at Hollywood get-togethers. I mingled and shook hands with everyone I knew. I thanked those in the movie or crew for their support and hard work.

When I had a story about the person on set, I shared it with their friend or family member. Only ones that put the person in good light, of course. I did promise grim retribution to the construction crew members who always had a horse trough waiting for me.

As usual, the talk was about the next job or finding the next job. I was getting better at fending these sorts of questions off. What I was still awkward about were the women. Even with Nina standing right there, some of them were very forward. Nina clung to my arm like she was drowning.

It was such a shame that Nina lost control of her drink, a Coke, and spilled it down the front of the gown of one young lady.

Anna Romanov, who was standing there said, "What a mess! I'm certain it was an accident."

"We will have to talk, my dear. I have several tactics I would like to share with you. It is so tiresome having to refresh your drink all night."

Guess who promptly got the job of refreshing the drink.

The first party came to its scheduled conclusion. We retreated to our suite, where we all changed clothes. Bob and I exchanged notes on the attendees while the ladies had their makeup redone. Our clothes were Hollywood casual this time, so it was easy to get ready, at least for the guys.

The next party was exactly that. While the previous one had been self-congratulatory with a job hunt thrown in, this one was for fun. It was the last time this cast and crew would be together, so it was time for "do you remember?"

I took my fair share of ribbing, and I must say it was most pleasant. However, tomorrow will be a school day for Nina and a workday for me, so we left after spending an hour.

As the limo took us to drop off Nina, we necked. I had wistful thoughts of that suite that we had left for Bob and Ellen. At this moment, I didn't like Bob very much. Dad was still up when I got home. He had attended the movie and the first party. He asked me how I could stand it. He had watched me circulate and work the crowd.

I remembered how I had felt about farming when Bob was talking, so I just answered, "I guess each of us is good at something. Circulating like that is part of my job now, so I had better be good at it."

He continued, "As long as you don't go into politics."

Have I mentioned that my dad didn't care for politicians and taxes? I called it a night and went right to sleep.

It was hard to get out of bed Thursday morning, but I was fully awake after my morning run. Dad was spending his day closing on the office building on Rodeo Drive. He was happy with the price which was more than he wanted to pay but less than he thought it would be.

On the set, Sharon was in fine form. She didn't seem like the same person I had met on the first day. She and Junior appeared to be a couple, but a very discrete couple. It was more the way his eyes followed her and her touching his arm when they talked.

The littles were grumpy in the morning, as they were most mornings, but they did their jobs. Today I had to perform a duet with Will Scarlett. This wasn't in the original script but had been added after the success of "Brothers". It didn't take the Director long to decide that he would dub in the singing by someone else for both Will and me. The actor playing Will was even flatter than me!

I gave up worrying about my singing. I knew I wasn't a singer. If the rest of the world chose to think so, it was their problem, not mine.

The morning flew by as we performed. A writer got it into his head the lines we were presenting weren't right, so we had to redo the scene. It did smooth out the flow. My part ended at lunch, so

I went from the commissary to the boardroom, where the practice presentations were starting.

They had their parts down cold. Without the lectern, everything flowed and seemed more natural. I think it would increase the credibility of the presenters. I wished them all good luck at the big show tomorrow and to break a leg. There were offers, in turn, to break one of my legs. I'm not certain if that was the right spirit or not. Everyone laughed at me, so it was good fun.

Mr. Monroe took me aside and said, "Rick, if this goes like I think it will, I will be able to make you an offer later."

Since he didn't seem inclined to take it further, I replied, "Thanks. We will see what happens, and good luck to you, sir."

I spent the rest of the afternoon lifting, sword fighting, and even sparred a little. I was able to make up some lost time on my unarmed combat. It looked like I would get the needed hours in for my brown belt, but not enough time to start the black belt before vacation. There was also the fact that I didn't have another movie lined up. I was like all those people who were job-hunting at the cast party last night.

After work, I called Nina and discussed the premiere and parties. She had seen the reviews. I had heard a little, but she had read them all. They were okay. No one panned the movie, but no one raved either. If there were a grade, we would have gotten a B- or a C+, not bad, but not great. The real test would be this weekend at the box office.

Fortunately, nothing in direct competition with us was opening, so we had a chance. Without competition, anyone looking for our type of movie would select *Sir Nicklaus*. The question was how many people would choose to go to the movie. I heard all sorts of discussions about the influence of good and bad weather. Who knows?

Nina told me she was not comfortable with the attention all the women were giving me. There wasn't much I could do about that. She understood, but it was still a lot for her to handle. We only had a few more weeks together before we parted, her to Europe and school next fall, me to sail the Seven Seas, or at least one of them.

Chapter 19

Friday was just another day. The movie was into a routine that was going well. The cast had settled in. It was fun being around the littles. It made me homesick for Mary. I will be seeing her in a few weeks. I wondered if she still wore her tiara.

Late in the afternoon, a jubilant Mr. Monroe looked me up. He only had a few minutes. The board meeting went extremely well. They had agreed to all his proposals and extended his contract with a pay increase.

I read about a balsa wood raft journey across the Pacific that night. You talk about bravery. One hundred and one days at sea on something that could fall apart at any minute. I wonder how many of the original explorers tried it and died.

Saturday, I spent all day at unarmed combat training. It was coming together for me. I can't say I wanted anyone to jump me, but I felt I was ready for them. Dad and I drove down the coast later that evening and ate at some drive-in when returning home. It was bad, and we made a note never to go back.

Sunday was more of the same: up, exercise, run, then spend half the day with Coach and my training. Dad and I went for a walk after lunch as we had eaten too much but had to cut it short as it started to rain.

Around three in the afternoon, the phone rang. Dad and I had been watching TV as it was still raining. I didn't pay attention until I heard him say, "What!?"

I glanced over. His face had turned to stone. I never knew what that saying meant until now.

He listened some more and then hung up. He didn't say goodbye or anything. This was so out of character, knew it was serious.

The first words out of Dad's mouth were, "You flew on a charter flight with John Wayne once, didn't you?"

"Yes, I did. What's going on, Dad?"

"I will tell you in a minute. Do you know the name of the charter company?"

"Sure, it was Chatham Aviation."

He grabbed the phone book, found the number, and dialed. He asked how soon a charter flight to Dayton, Ohio, could be arranged.

He was as curt as I ever heard him. "No. Not tomorrow, today. I need to be on the ground in Dayton no later than seven o'clock in the morning. I will pay whatever premium you ask."

Dad listened and said, "Two people."

"No, I don't care how big the plane is. We will take it. Be ready to go; wheels up in two hours. If it takes seven hours of flight time, with the time difference, that will get us to Dayton around 5 a.m. That will work."

Dad hung up the phone, "Rick, pack a bag quickly while I arrange a limo in Dayton. I won't want to be driving in the morning. Also, we have to stop at the studio. Peg wants you to bring your big bow and the war arrows."

"Dad, what's going on?"

"Mary's been kidnapped."

"Kidnapped?" I heard Dad's words. They just didn't want to process. What did he mean?

"Mary has been kidnapped."

This time it penetrated. I went from denial to anger in seconds. It went from explosive hot anger to implacable cold hate just as quickly.

"Who are they, and what are they asking?"

"Your mum thinks the East German Stassi is working for the Soviet KGB. As to what they want, they want me. We will talk about it on the plane. Now move."

I moved. I packed a suit, shirt, and gear in five minutes. There were also several sets of jeans and a pair of steel-tipped boots from my roughneck days. With my shaving kit, I was good to go.

I was fast, but Dad was waiting for me. I still took the time to call Mr. Monroe at home. Nina answered the phone. I asked her for her dad. The tone of my voice must have told her something. She put him on without any questions.

"Mr. Monroe, this is Rick Jackson. Would you please let the production company know that I have a personal emergency and have to make a quick trip home?"

He asked, "Is there anything I can do?"

"No, sir," I replied. "I will call as soon as I know what is going on. Tell Nina I will call her when I can."

"Godspeed, Rick."

"Thank you. We will need it."

I hung up, and we went to the studio. Luckily, it was a twenty-four-hour seven-day operation. I packed my bow and arrows away every day in their lockable travel case. They weren't kept in the studio armory, but I didn't want the littles to get their hands on the arrows. They were wicked sharp and would cut like a surgeon's scalpel.

I drove at the speed limit. It wouldn't be good to get stopped for speeding now. I wasn't worried about the ticket; it was the time. They didn't hassle Dad with taking a company check at the Chatham desk.

When asked how long he would need the plane and reconfirmed Dayton as a first stop, he told them as long as next Wednesday. The first stop would be Dayton, Ohio, and there might be a continuation on to Washington, D.C., before returning to Burbank.

He wrote a check for ten thousand dollars as a down payment. If more was needed, it wasn't an issue. I wondered what sort of aircraft we were getting for that much money.

I found out shortly. Dad chartered the only aircraft available, a Boeing 707. They had the stairs in place, so it only took us a few minutes to board. After stowing our gear in the front closet, we barely settled into the first-class seats as the door closed, and we were taxiing.

I looked at my watch. It had been one hour and forty-five minutes since the phone rang at the apartment. There was a stewardess, but she didn't give us a safety talk. After the seatbelt light was turned off and we were offered a drink, which was coffee for both of us, Dad brought me up to speed.

"Rick, apparently, the Russians want me because they think I know the names in the visitor's logbook from Patton's hospital. They will want to know if I told them to anyone. They have taken Mary and want to make an exchange, me for her."

"I gather I am not bringing my bow to send love messages."

"Your Mum had an idea based on what she knows about these exchanges. There is no question that we have to get Mary back. I just hope we can do it and not leave me in Russian hands."

"What does Mum see happening?"

"At this time, we don't have a plan. It depends on what we find when we get there. Mum thought your bow may give us an advantage if you can kill silently from a distance."

"I thought that agents weren't going after each other's families."

"They haven't until now. I don't know what has changed. They want me badly enough to up the ante for everyone. One of the names on that log must be someone now high enough in the hierarchy to order this to protect themselves."

Dad continued, "I know Army Intelligence always thought rogue Soviets did the Patton operation. They may still be trying to cover their tracks."

We talked in circles for another hour but came to no conclusions. For the first time in a long time, I said a prayer. It was for Mary's safety.

We both tried to sleep, but it was to no avail. The pilot came back and talked to us for a while. I even took him up on his offer to see the flight deck. The co-pilot, navigator, and radioman all explained their jobs to me. Normally, I would have been excited and asked dozens of questions.

I spent about ten minutes up front; normally, I could have been there for hours. I even walked back and forth to the tail of the plane. When empty, they looked enormous. It was configured for one hundred and sixty passengers.

Chapter 20

Daylight was breaking when we landed in Dayton. A limo was waiting as arranged. It took one hour to make the drive to Bellefontaine. Dad and I tried to doze during the ride, but like on the flight, it didn't work.

When we arrived at our house, the lights were on. Mum was waiting. This wasn't the loving mother I had known all my life. This was a face that had seen and dealt with death. There was no doubt in my mind that she would do it again.

Mum and Dad hugged for a moment, and then she gave me the same treatment. I heard activity in the bedrooms. The boys were up and doing something. I learned quickly as they started hauling suitcases to the limo. I was really surprised when Mrs. Hernandez came into the house, suitcase in hand.

I didn't ask anything, just raised an eyebrow. This brought a grin to Mum's face that disappeared as quickly as it came.

"No matter what, Rick, this house and town are no longer safe for us. We are moving to California and Jackson House now! Mrs. Hernandez is moving with us."

The boys, who had barely acknowledged me, continued hauling suitcases and boxes to the limo. They would go in the limo with Mrs. Hernandez and wait at the plane for us. If we didn't make it, Mrs. Hernandez was to take the boys to my apartment and contact Mr. Monroe. Dad had prepared a letter for him.

Mum told me to change to outdoor clothes, so I went to my old room and put on the rough clothes I had brought. It was actually what I would wear rabbit hunting. The tough cotton fabric wouldn't get caught up in a thicket.

As I came into the kitchen, the phone was ringing. It was the kidnappers. Mum did the talking. After a few questions, she hung up.

"Fortunately, they are not very imaginative. They are using the same method they have always used."

How did Mum know this?

"Out at the field by the Guest Yards, Jack will walk towards a man who will be holding Mary. They will have a sniper team doing overwatch. The spotter and sniper will be there to shoot me, Jack, and Mary if anything goes wrong."

She went on, "Rick, your task will be to take out the sniper, then the spotter if you can. I will have a rifle to take out the guy holding Mary. If you can take out the sniper while I take out the exchange man, one of us can then take out the spotter."

"That is counting on the team being as you see it and me being able to hit the sniper."

"It should be a clap shot for you. They won't want to be far away. What I am counting on is your being behind them. We will be coming off US 68 by Hopewell Crossing. The road by the tracks leads to Guest Yards. At this time of day, there shouldn't be very many foreign railcars sitting there."

Guest yards was where they parked railcars from other railroads while waiting for forwarding instructions.

"They will set up in front of the cars. If they are smart, they will be set up on top of a boxcar to give them a clear view of the area. We will drop you off at the stockyards, so you can work your way up the tracks and climb onto a boxcar. You should either have a straight level shot or have the height and angle on them."

Looking at it that way, I hoped for a straight, level shot.

"How long do we have?"

"One hour, so let's move."

Mum, Dad, and I loaded our gear into the trunk of the Buick and took off. Dad had brought a suitcase, but I didn't know its contents. They dropped me at the stockyards, and I worked my way up the tracks. I stayed on the west side of the right of way. When I was near Guest Yards, I moved into the woods and kept moving.

I was cutting it close. I checked the time when I was at the base of the first boxcar. I had five more minutes to be in position. I had strung my bow and put on my armguard when they dropped me off at the stockyards, so I was ready. When I got to the top of the boxcar ladder, I peeked over the edge and realized I was in a surprisingly good position.

As Mum had predicted, they were set up on top of a car. It was three cars ahead of me so that the shot wouldn't be more than seventy-five yards. That was well within the ranges I had practiced. They were lying prone with sandbags for the rifle and focused on the scene in front of them.

I heard a car coming. Dad turned the car and parked it at a right angle to the road. Mum got out and stood behind the engine compartment, so she had that huge engine between her and gunfire.

Dad stopped, looked around, and started walking forward. I hadn't been able to see him, but a man had been standing at the base of the railcar. As he walked forward, I could see he was holding Mary. She was very still.

I was in an awkward position. I was standing on a ladder with no backstop behind me. There was no way I could draw my bow in this position. I had no choice but to climb over the edge and stand on top of the car. I had just drawn my bow when a steam engine whistle blew. This caused the spotter to turn towards me.

I didn't hesitate. I let loose the arrow at the sniper. It took him in the side at his armpit. As I bent the bow again for another shot, the spotter grabbed for the rifle. By the time he had it and raised to his knees to aim the rifle, I fired once more. It was a center-mass hit. Both arrows, at such close range, buried themselves into their feathers.

This only left the man with Mary. He hadn't heard the action on top of the railcar. I strung another arrow, but it would be a long shot. When Dad got close, the man set Mary down and pulled out a pair of handcuffs. As soon as the man was far enough away from Mary that I wouldn't hit her, I let fly, but I missed. It didn't matter because there was the crack of a rifle.

Mum didn't miss it.

Dad was already moving; he picked up Mary and headed for the car. I spent a minute and retrieved my arrows. They were very distinctive. It was easy to pull them through. There was no question that the guys were dead. I had no feelings at all about killing them. They started it. We finished it.

I picked up my missed arrow as I went to the car. I was relieved to find that Miss Mary was asleep. It looked like she had been given a sedative and missed all the excitement. That was a good thing.

I was left with Mary in the car. Mum and Dad took the suitcase and went to the bodies. They dragged the one on the ground to the railcar below the sniper and spotter. The car was empty. I knew this because the doors on empty cars were always left open for some reason. It was a struggle, but they got him into the car.

Dad climbed on the roof and pushed the two bodies over the edge. They wrestled them into the boxcar. Both Mum and Dad were inside the car for what seemed like a long time. When they did come out, Dad closed the door.

I could see him fiddling with something, so I suspected that he still had some of the lead seals they used to show the car was full and the contents had not been disturbed.

Dad was carrying the suitcase with him. This time it seemed heavier than before. He put it in the trunk after pulling an ax and a hammer out of the luggage. We drove over to the pond where water was collected for the steam engine boilers. He got out and, after looking around, threw the ax and hammer into the middle of the pond.

We then drove over to a single parked car on the edge of the large field. The keys from one of the guys worked. Dad followed us home, where Mum and I got into the Buick. I drove, following Dad.

We went as far as Springfield, where Dad left the car he was driving downtown with the keys in the ignition and the driver's window down. Springfield was not a crime-ridden city, but that car would be moving again within hours.

From there, we drove to Dayton. The plane and the rest of our family were waiting for us. Mum went into flight operations and made a long telephone call. When she came out, she told Dad we would be going to Washington. When we got on the plane, Dad retrieved the letter he had written to Mr. Monroe.

As we were taking off, Mary woke up. She looked around. You talk about a confused kid. The last thing she knew was a bad man grabbing her in the front yard while she was taking her Barbie doll for a walk. He had made her drink some water, and then here she was.

It was absolutely for the best.

After we were airborne, I was invited by Mum and Dad to join them in the lounge. We sat around the table and examined the documents and other items that the men had on them. They had matchbooks, movie ticket stubs, and other items that Mum called pocket litter. These were used to support their cover stories.

Mum labeled slides that were from my chemistry set. I asked her about them. She told me they had taken fingerprints of each of the guys. That didn't make sense, as the police would fingerprint the bodies when they found them. I verbalized that thought.

"Rick, you are making assumptions. First, you assume the police will find the bodies before they decay, and second, they will have fingerprints."

That seemed strange. Where would their prints be?

After going through it, Mum and Dad concluded they were East Germans. I asked them what they based that on.

"There is nothing wrong. Only the Germans pay such attention to detail," Mum told me.

I would like to take some of the classes she has been through.

"So now what?" I inquired.

"We send a message, or more to the point, you deliver a message."

"Why me?"

"You are still a minor. If something goes wrong, you won't have as many problems."

"Who am I delivering the message to?"

"To the Russians and Germans. You will leave a present at the Soviet Embassy. We have to convince them it isn't in their best interest to attack the families of agents."

"What am I going to deliver that will convince them?"

"When we arrive in Washington, we will be met by a person from the CIA. They will have an envelope which will contain pictures of the families of the heads of the KGB, the KGB North American Directorate, and the East German Stassi."

"Pictures of their families will scare them away. How will they know to take it seriously?"

"You won't be going into the embassy; you will be throwing three bowling ball bags over the wall surrounding their embassy."

"What's in the bowling ball...oh, I see."

Now I know what Dad was doing with the ax.

"Why did Dad need a hammer?"

"He pounded a stake through each of the wounds. The arrows leave distinctive damage. It has been eradicated. Further confusing the issue, the bodies will be far away when they are discovered. By the way, we will have to destroy the arrows you retrieved."

Chapter 21

The flight to Washington didn't take more than an hour and a half. Upon landing at the private aviation terminal, a man approached Mum and handed her an envelope. In turn, she handed him a roll of the film along with the slides and pocket litter. I assumed the film was from her small Minox camera. She examined the envelope's contents and must have been satisfied.

Dad had retrieved three bowling ball bags, which I recognized as formerly belonging to us boys, from the large suitcase. Mum unzipped one of the bags and stuffed the envelope inside. The stranger offered to take the now empty suitcase, but Mum declined. She was pretty forceful in doing so.

I was escorted to a taxi, which I suspect wasn't a normal cab, and driven to the backside of the embassy of the USSR. The wall was only about eight feet high, so I could easily throw the bags over. From there, it was back in the cab, back to the airport, and wheels up to California.

Once on the plane, I fell apart. The events of the last day were too much. My sister was kidnapped. I had flown across the country and killed two men to get her back. Suddenly, I was so tired I couldn't see straight.

I slept most of the way to Burbank. When I woke up, only Denny and Eddie were awake. When they saw me open my eyes, they came over. I held up my fingers in front of my mouth. I then used the restroom, peed, and washed up. The water felt good against my face.

When I came out, Mrs. Hernandez was awake and reading, so I gave her a small wave as she looked up but didn't stop and talk.

The boys and I went up front, where we cadged a snack from the stewardess. She told us that this was the easiest flight she had ever worked. After she went back to her station, Denny commented on

Mary's disappearance. Obviously, while he knew that something had happened to Mary, he didn't know the details.

He was smart enough to know we wouldn't be traveling like this unless it was a seriously big deal. I let him fish for the story, but when he wouldn't give up, I finally told him he would have to ask Mum or Dad for the details.

Eddie was more philosophical, acting more his age. He lived in the now and was flying on the neatest airplane ever for the first time. I knew this because he told me. He also had his tour of the cockpit and had flown the jet airplane!

We joked around about his flying. From how he told it, he had flown so low that he could pick daisies, did loops, and flew upside down. Of course, he may have been exaggerating.

This nonsense helped keep the memories at bay. It is not pretty to see people die, no matter how much they deserve it. How Dad was able to use that ax, I couldn't fathom. Maybe if I have children, I will understand.

Mary woke and came out to the lounge table. After the stewardess helped her use the restroom, she climbed on my lap. I noticed she was wearing a plastic set of stewardess wings.

"Mary, aren't you going to be a princess anymore?"

She replied, "Silly, of course I am. After my job at the drive-in, I will be a stewardess. I wonder whether they will let me wear roller skates on the plane."

Our flight attendant Cindy told us that it would be a great idea. Her feet always hurt her after a long flight.

Denny butted in and asked how the movie was going. I filled him in on where we were at. Suddenly, I had a very attentive stewardess. She was probably ten years older than me, but that didn't seem to deter her. I was polite but steered her away as much as I could. I could see where this would get old quickly.

I was saved by both Mum and Dad waking up. They sent the other kids to play in the back of the plane. Cindy gave them a deck of cards with pictures of all the TWA fleet. A very noisy game of Go Fish started on the floor in the aisle of coach class.

Dad asked me how I was doing. I told him I was okay but kept remembering the event.

"Rick, don't call it the event. We can talk plainly among ourselves. It was a hostage rescue where you and Peg killed people. Don't try to hide it where you can talk plainly. We were there; we understand. The human mind has to process things and file them away.

"Do you remember having something upsetting happen and replaying it in your mind repeatedly until the memory had softened? People have mental issues when they try to hide it from themselves and then keep replaying the incident without softening it. Now it is like a broken record; the same song over and over.

"You have to let time change the memories to where you can accept them. They will always bother you because you are not a psychopath, but you will have to smooth them over.

"You did it with those guys in Colorado. You can do it here."

I thought for a moment, "In Colorado, it happened so fast that it didn't seem real. Here we planned it out first and then did it. The first was a reaction. This seems like murder."

Mum replied, "Rick, you're right. We murdered them. Now, what was our alternative? Let them murder Mary? Let them torture and murder your dad? This was kill or be killed. This was war. There was no warped malice or profit motive here, just the need to take a life before ours was taken. Now you know what war is like."

"I don't think I like war."

"The only person I have heard of liking war was General Patton, and sometimes I wonder if he was put down for that reason," Dad replied.

I knew Mum had a past with MI6. How did Dad know so much about keeping sane in a violent world?

"Well, you guys owe me something for this."

"What?" asked Dad.

"A new bowling ball bag."

That caused laughter, actually too much laughter. I then realized that events affected Mum and Dad as much as me. For some odd reason, that made me feel better.

We had to return to our seats for landing. I was still tired. It was ten o'clock California time when we deplaned. Once on the ground, we realized a fundamental mistake. Where was the family going to stay? Luckily, Chatham had a listing of all the major hotels. Dad called and got lucky with a three-bedroom suite for the family and a single for Mrs. Hernandez.

While the family went to a limo that Chatham had summoned, I took the suitcase that Mum had held onto. I asked her about it on the plane. She didn't want to turn over any physical evidence to anyone.

When I got back to my apartment, I was to put all my clothes into it. She and Dad already did that. The first chance I got I was to take the suitcase down to the sub-basement until we could figure out a safe way to destroy it and its contents. I would add the arrows that I had retrieved.

I was to join them for dinner tomorrow night at the hotel.

By the time I got to my apartment, I was exhausted. I was smart enough to set the alarm. I now knew what jet lag was like. That and what an adrenaline rush would do while staying up for thirty-plus hours. I fell asleep trying to figure out the number of hours.

Chapter 22

I woke to the alarm. My greatest desire was to turn over and go back to sleep. Setting the clock on the other side of the room proved to be a good idea. I had to get out of bed to turn it off.

By the time I had done my exercises and started on my run, I was feeling really crappy but awake.

Dick, who had joined me enough, said it best, "Rick, you look like hell. What's going on?"

"Dick, I'm not certain what I can share, if anything. I will tell you it was bad. I have to talk to my parents first."

We would have to come up with a reason for my sudden trip to Ohio and the appearance of my family. I also suspected that someone chartering a 707 on no notice for half a dozen people would not go unremarked in the community.

I think Mum would describe it as needing a cover story. I never thought I would use a term like a cover story in context.

My absence was remarked at the studio, but no one made a big deal about it. I only said it was a family emergency and dropped it. People respected that.

Even Mr. Monroe, who stopped by to see me, didn't inquire more than, "Is everything all right?"

When I replied, "Yes," he let it go.

The only scenes I had to appear in didn't require much acting, which was lucky as I felt brain-dead all day. When my eight hours on set were finished, I went directly back to my apartment, which was a first. I was able to get in an hour's nap before I had to join the family for dinner.

Mum and Dad looked like I felt, pretty bad. The kids and Mrs. Hernandez were fine. Mrs. Hernandez was keeping the kids in line. This was the first time they had ever been to a restaurant this nice.

Before this, Islay's in Bellefontaine was at the top of the chain. They weren't acting up, but they were sure rubbernecking.

Earlier, I asked Dad about Mrs. Hernandez. It turned out she and her sister-in-law almost came to blows. She needed somewhere else to live and an income. We needed help for Mum with the kids and the new house and got along with her. It was a natural fit.

She was now on salary with us. Dad wasn't certain what her title would be as he was certain that there would be a nanny, cook, and head housekeeper along with maids and gardeners before it was over. I suggested the title of Chatelaine. He thought it was a possibility but thought that traditionally that would be Mum.

As our dinner continued, it was a little scary watching Mary. You could see her mind whirling as she noted the dresses women were wearing. My fears were confirmed when she announced to the world at large that the woman in the red dress was "a brazen hussy."

I asked, "Where did she learn that?"

From the way Mum colored, I had my answer. I was so glad that the woman was across the room and couldn't hear us. It didn't stop a few men at the next table from looking around the room. The poor lady only wore a dress that would fit in at a high school prom. Granted, I had never seen one cut that low.

We had plenty to talk about at dinner. Mum met with Sergio about moving into Jackson House early. He had a hissy fit, was how Mum described it. Our moving in will interfere with his artistic abilities. I asked Mum what she said to him to keep him on task.

"I handed him my file on him. His real name is Ronald Hampton. He is married with two children and lives out in the Valley. He poses as gay, as that is expected around here. He better get over it if he didn't want me to expose him as a straight married man. We are moving in."

"What did he say?" I asked.

"How soon would we be moving in? I have already ordered beds, mattresses, and bedding to be delivered on Thursday. Tomorrow I will look for some basic furniture for a family room and a TV. We are going to put a rough kitchen in so we can do some cooking, but most of our meals will be out."

From living arrangements, we transitioned to how we needed to keep a low profile. While it would be impossible to keep completely out of sight, we would not advertise our presence. The hotel had us under another last name, Mertz, I think.

Dad had selected it because he was a fan of Ricky and Lucy.

Speaking of Dad, he had a copy of the newspaper with the weekend box office standings for *Sir Nicklaus*. It was a runaway success with a box office three times what was predicted. It probably wouldn't win any awards, but I would make good money and Mr. Wayne a whole bunch. Maybe he would ask me to do another movie.

We called it an early evening. We were done catching up with the events of the last week with everyone, well, everyone, but Mary. She was wide awake and raring to go. She had figured out we were where they made movies, so she was ready to go be a princess, stewardess, and movie star on roller skates.

She had on her tiara and stewardess wings. At this rate, she would be on the silver screen in no time. That gave me an idea. I asked Mum and Dad if they could bring the kids to the set tomorrow for a tour. I told them we only had two days of shooting left, so it had to be soon. Of course, Denny, Eddie, and Mary were all for it.

My parents were a little slow to come around. They were going to be busy setting up Jackson House and the many loose ends the sudden move had created. However, they both agreed. I think they wanted to see what went on making a movie as much as the kids. It was a given Mrs. Hernandez would accompany them. She was now a member of our family.

I slept like a log that night. I picked up a book and set it right down. I was still making up for the weekend. Thursday morning was a wonderful day in California. Even in Ohio, spring was breaking out, but this was better. It felt good to be out running early. I think I was back to normal.

The first thing I did at the studio was to go see Donna. I told her my family would be here around ten o'clock and could she arrange for passes and bring them to my set?

She told me she would take care of all of it. My voice must have carried because Mr. Monroe came out of his office. He wanted to know if things were okay now. I told him they were and that my parents would be here later with my brothers and sister for a tour.

He said he would be happy to join them.

I was on the set, and we were getting ready to do a village scene. I had expected my family in at ten; now, it was almost eleven. The littles came onto the set to assume their positions around Mr. Fitzhugh for a story session where he would be giving a message for Robin.

One little was giggling in a familiar giggle. Mary was making it to the silver screen! Then I realized that Denny and Eddie were also in the crowd of kids. They were all in costume. They had been on time but had been in the makeup and costuming. I looked around, and there were Mum and Dad, Mr. Monroe, and Mrs. Hernandez.

I was so glad that my part today was only several lines about receiving the Old Man's orders and being on my way to rescue Maid Marion. Of course, I flubbed my lines, and it took seven takes. So much for showing off how good I was.

In the meantime, my brothers and sister were little pros. They played their parts as just some of the kids in the crowd perfectly. They had to pay attention to Mr. Fitzhugh as he told a story. He was a natural storyteller and would make up his stories on the spot. It riveted all the kids. In the movie, all you would hear is an occasional word.

I expected Mary to stand up and announce that she was a princess stewardess, but she did as requested. After the scene, she got into a Ring Around the Rosey game with the other girls her size. When it came to "all fall down," I noticed the cameras were still running. Our director never let a good scene go to waste.

Mary had already taught the other girls an English version of when they all fell down. Instead of falling on the floor, they all did a curtsy. Eddie, in turn, the boy in the center, bowed to all the girls. At that point, they all giggled and ran away, leaving Eddie all alone.

Eddie looked around, then shrugged his shoulders and walked away. As he did so, I heard, "Cut." I wouldn't be surprised if that made it into the movie's final cut. It had no point but was cute. It also meant that my brothers and sister were now members of the Screen Actors Guild. That was fast work by, I guess, Donna.

We were going to join Mr. Monroe for lunch in his private dining room. Mum excused herself to make a phone call. We had just settled in when she rejoined us. You could tell Mr. Monroe was dying to ask what had caused Dad's and my sudden trip to Ohio.

He didn't ask directly.

He stated, "It must be expensive to charter a 707."

Dad nodded his head. That wasn't going to go far. Then Mum dropped a bombshell.

"I just talked to London. The KGB has quietly let them know that the newly promoted head of their North American Directorate tied his hands behind his back and committed suicide by shooting himself in the back of the head."

My Mum could be ornery at times. You should have seen the look on Mr. Monroe's face!

She then continued, "Sam, that is much of the story as you will probably ever know. So please don't push it."

All he could do was nod his head. The man must think our whole family is daft.

He regained his composure and changed the topic of conversation to *Sir Nicklaus* and its box office receipts. This strong showing of a movie right after the successful board meeting left him in a good position. Because of that, he asked me if I minded him opening negotiations with Mr. Baxter to sign me to a two-year contract.

I would receive a weekly salary from the studio plus whatever I would receive from the production company. This was to ensure that I wouldn't sign with another studio and would guarantee me some work. They would want me to do something for all the money. They would keep me busy doing publicity and stand-in work.

I responded that it sounded very good on the surface but that I would have to look at all my options. Who knows, maybe MGM was about to offer me more. You would have thought I had driven a dagger through his heart.

"Rick, how could you consider going to work for Leo?"

I chuckled, "Gottcha."

Dad asked Mr. Monroe, "You want me to smack him?"

"Jack, let me get back to you on that. If he keeps it up, yes."

"Okay, I will consider your offer, and no matter what, there won't be a contract with another studio. If I don't take your offer, I will be open to working with other studios, but no contract, I promise."

"Rick, what if I sweeten the pot?"

"How?" I asked with suspicion.

"Oh, maybe like screen tests for your brothers and sister."

I looked over at Mum and Dad; they both shook their heads no.

Mum spoke up, "We need to talk this over before anything else happens. We have had too many changes this week to consider anything else right now."

"Fair enough, the offer for screen tests still stands, even if Rick doesn't sign a studio contract.

Chapter 23

After lunch, the family headed out to make additional arrangements for living at Jackson House. I went back to the set. I had originally not been scheduled for this afternoon, but with being out Monday and Tuesday, I had to make up some scenes. I noticed that when we had to go an hour past my eight hours, Mr. Fitzhugh was not in sight.

We went to the Hamburger Hamlet for dinner. Nina and her dad joined us, so it was quite a group. Mary and Nina instantly became best friends. They both agreed that most boys stink but that I was okay.

When Nina asked Mary how her day was, Mary held her hand to her brow and said, "It was so tiring. The director made us work so hard. The lights were so bright and hot I could hardly stand it."

All of us, Nina, sympathized with her, but the boys thought it hilarious. The boys were more interested in cheeseburgers and fries.

Mary went on to announce that she now would only be a princess at teatime and a stewardess when she was flying. It was all so tiring. We agreed that was a big load for her to carry.

Toward the end of dinner, Mum brought up a new subject.

"Rick, you weren't at the house with us today. We decided that it would be impractical to stay there now. The electricity and plumbing will be off and on, plus the entire kitchen has been torn out."

She continued, "In light of the recent Russian developments, we feel safe again, at least for a while. We are going to move back to Bellefontaine to finish the school year and will return at the end of summer vacation to live here permanently."

I read between Mum's lines. She still wanted to be in a house that had a safe room and a guard at the entrance. That meant she was concerned about our safety in the future.

I asked Dad, "Have you made any decisions about the guard service?"

He replied, "The current service is only for night watchmen. They are not bodyguards. I'm looking for a bodyguard service to take over the family's security. Rick, we have much to be concerned about between your fame and your mother's and my past. Your mum has asked for recommendations from her contacts."

Eddie had to tell me about the new house. Mary and Denny quickly joined him. It was big! It had elevators! It had a tower! Each kid would have an enormous room! You get the picture. Wait until they learn about secret passages.

One thing that surprised me was that Mrs. Hernandez was going home with my parents, and she would be staying in my old room. While the family was in England later this summer, she would supervise the packing and the move. She would also arrange for shipping the two cars and that beautiful Chris Craft boat.

Nina was unusually quiet at the end of the meal.

She told me, "It is hitting me that I will be going to Europe while your family comes here."

"We both knew this day was coming," I told her, "but it is hard when it happens. This is the second time I have been parted from someone I cared for, and it doesn't seem to get easier. Besides, who knows what the future will bring?"

She cheered up a little at those words. This was my last week in Hollywood for a while. Tomorrow was the last day of the *Bandits of Sherwood* shooting. The cast party will be tomorrow night. Because of all the kids, it would be an early evening for most of us. I suspect the adults would go until the wee hours.

That put me off on another train of thought. What would I be doing next week? I vaguely thought I would be heading back to Ohio after this movie ended before I set off to New York to find a ship.

How were my parents getting home? If I went with them, where would I stay since Mrs. Hernandez was taking my room? Did I have a home with my family anymore?

It turns out, in a way, I didn't. I asked Dad where I would stay if I came home with them. He had a furnished rental vacant that I could use. It made the most sense but left me feeling cast out.

It must have shown on my face because Mum told me, "Not so sad, it's the old Hawkins house across the street from us. I can watch what you get up to from the front window. Now for some odd reason, it made me feel better that my Mum and Dad could keep an eye on my coming and going.

After dinner, I took Nina home via our favorite parking spot. When we arrived, the police were finishing their hourly round, so we had some time to ourselves. For some reason, while we necked for a while, neither of us acted like we wanted to go further.

We talked quietly about what the future would hold for us. While we both had bright futures in front of us, there was a good chance there would be no us. This was sad but not the end of the world.

Certainly, we had gone together for the last five months, but it hadn't been a grand passion. It certainly wasn't a Romeo and Juliet-level romance, which was just as well. Neither of us felt like dying.

We started laughing about how silly that would be. We exchanged one last kiss and promised to keep in touch when we could. I took her home. Would I ever meet my love?

After dropping Nina off, I returned to the hotel to talk with Mum and Dad. We decided that we would fly back to Ohio on Saturday. We were getting spoiled. Dad had talked to Chatham Aviation about using a smaller jet plane. They could fly us privately for almost the same cost as commercial first class for all of us. We agreed this was the way to go.

Chapter 24

The next morning was another fine day, and I arrived at the studio for the last of our work. It turned out I only had one retake. There was one distant shot where Junior was wearing a gold necklace. When they moved into the over-the-shoulder view, he didn't have it on as though the viewer were seeing what I was seeing.

After that shot, which required nine attempts, we were done. Everyone kept breaking into laughter. It was like the last day of school.

Even the director screwed up by yelling "Cut" too soon.

We finished up by lunchtime when the director made the time-honored announcement, "And that's a wrap."

There would be two parties, one on the set for everyone, but mostly the littles, and then one later for adults only. I will be attending both.

We had many hundreds of still pictures taken by the publicity group during the filming of *Bandits*. I got together with the photographers and paid them a little extra on the side to make certain there was a picture taken of me with each cast member.

I presented every child actor with an autographed picture of them and me together. I also gave everyone a gift-wrapped squirt gun. Several of the parents made a point of thanking me. I don't think they were sincere. I wonder what they would have thought of the gifts I could have given for a movie that was just going into production called *Seventy-six Trombones*.

I didn't count Sharon Bronson or Bill Bixby as child actors. I will give them their presents later. I ran into Mr. Fitzhugh. He was smiling. We shook hands, and I sincerely thanked him for understanding the movie's needs and still protecting the children.

He told me he had been thinking of retiring from his job but held off because he didn't have any hobbies to follow into retirement.

He had a screen test next week for another part. He may be retiring really soon! This was the most fun he had had in years.

At his office, going to the studio had been considered one of those jobs to avoid. Now they were fighting to see who could go to the studios. Who knew, you might get discovered?

I wished him the best of luck and to break a leg. I walked away smiling. I would rather deal with a government employee like him than the lady who was going to whisk me into protection for my good.

I wonder what she would think of my adventure earlier this week. She would probably try to get me banned from the state.

Later in the evening, I went to the ballroom of a local hotel where the cast and crew party was being held for the adults. There I gave certificates for the time on a shooting range, bowling, golf, or a pedicure, your choice of one. I was surprised about who took what.

I cut out as early as I could after making my rounds. Mr. Monroe was there, and he related his recent conversation with my agent, Mr. Baxter. His exact words were, "That bastard Baxter is trying to skin me alive."

I smiled and moved on. That was Mr. Baxter's job.

There was the usual talk of upcoming movies and possible jobs. A gratifying number of people expressed pleasure in working with me. I know that they were planting seeds for the future, but at the same time, they thought I was someone whom they could work with.

I went back to my apartment and went directly to bed. I didn't try to read. For some reason, I had been tired all week. I was glad that I would be sitting on an airplane for most of the day instead of working on my hand-to-hand combat. I completed my brown belt requirements, but it would be sometime in the fall before I could start on my black belt.

Saturday morning, we went out to Chatham Aviation. We were surprised to see the 707 waiting for us. Since Dad had talked to them early enough in the week, they were using our trip to position the plane on the East Coast on Monday morning. I didn't ask how much it was costing.

One nice thing about the warning was the food service was much better than the last trip. This time we had a choice of steak or chicken dinners. I had a steak, of course. There were also two stewardesses, and I ran into what was becoming a too-frequent problem. One of them practically offered herself to me on the plane.

Now I'm vigorous enough to get excited by the thought but not so stupid as to try something like that in front of my family. What were we going to do, go to a restroom at the back of the aircraft? Paint me romantic or whatever. That just isn't my style.

We landed in Dayton with a limo waiting. We stopped in Springfield for dinner at a small restaurant. Somehow Islay's in Bellefontaine, which had been the peak of our dining experience, didn't cut it anymore.

We arrived at our Bellefontaine home at around eight o'clock. By the time I had settled in and made my bed across the street, it was time to go to sleep.

Sunday morning, I was able to run my old route around the airbase. I did notice the pull on my legs from the hills. The high school track I had been running on for months was flat.

At lunchtime, I went downtown to Don's, but it was practically empty as it wasn't a school day. I went home and goofed off with Denny and Eddie for the rest of the day.

Dad went down to Jackson's Newsstand and bought the Columbus Sunday paper. On the inside pages, there was a story titled "Vampires?" It seems a railcar was opened in Chicago because of a horrible smell. Inside they found three headless, handless corpses with wooden stakes driven through their hearts.

I wonder? How could that have happened?

The story continued; reporting the investigation had been turned over to the FBI as the car had crossed several state lines. I doubt the CIA would volunteer any information, and why would the FBI even think to ask? We were okay if they didn't get back to Bellefontaine and no one had seen Mary's rescue.

If the truth came out, public opinion would be on our side, but the law would not. We were vigilantes of the worst sort. I wasn't going to worry about getting caught, and as far as killing those guys, I hadn't lost any sleep. I had slept a lot and was just catching up.

Next week I could meet with all my Bellefontaine friends and go to the Boy Scout camporee for the weekend.

Thinking back over the last week, I wondered how we got through it. Rescuing Mary, flying to California and back, planning an immediate move and then not doing it, saying goodbye to Nina, my brothers and sister being in their first movie, and wrapping up the same movie. How did my family and I stay sane?

Chapter 25

Monday morning, I realized that I had to change a few things in my living arrangements. I was used to getting up, doing my exercises, putting coffee on, doing my daily five miles, taking a shower, and then enjoying my first cup of coffee.

To start with, the furnished house that I was staying in wasn't furnished with any dishes or a coffee pot. I would have to go across the street to Mum and Dad's, which wasn't a big deal unless it was raining, which has been known to happen in Ohio frequently in the spring.

On those sorts of days, I would pass on running and settle in with my coffee. So high on my list for the day was to find a coffee percolator, plus stop at the A&P to buy and grind a bag of beans.

Since it was a nice day, I could run. It felt good, but I still had a burn in my legs from the hills. There was a difference between running on flat ground as I had in California and the hills in Ohio. I would have to incorporate hill running when I returned to Hollywood. I bet I could run in the park next to Jackson House.

After my run and shower, I went over to Mum's, hoping there would be coffee on. There was also a surprise. My publicist, Susan Wallace, was sitting there with a man I didn't know. She quickly got up, shook my hand, and then introduced me to William Coleman. After the introductions and I gratefully accepted a full coffee mug from Mum, I asked, "What's going on, Susan?"

She laughed and handed Mum a dollar. "You win. He forgot."

"Forgot what?"

"While you were working on *Bandits of Sherwood*, I wouldn't disturb you, but after that, we would start working on your image."

"You're right. I had forgotten, but did you have to follow me to Ohio?"

"Yes, I did. Where will you be after the next two weeks?"

"Off on my summer vacation."

"Can I go with you?"

"You know it's starting on a ship," I replied.

"What happens after you get back?"

"I hope to begin work on another movie."

"That is why I had to follow you to Ohio."

"Oh."

There ought to be a law about using logic on a person before they have their first coffee of the day.

"Susan, I get your point. Now, what is William's assignment?"

"He will follow you everywhere for the next two weeks taking every picture he can. We need to develop a catalog of pictures and then use them to illustrate the story we want to talk about, Rick Jackson."

"You make me sound like a product you are advertising."

Susan looked at Mum and grinned. "He catches on fast. Rick that is exactly what you are, a product, and we have to brand you."

"What do you mean?"

"How do you view John Wayne?"

"He's an American hero."

"How do you view Jerry Lewis?"

"He is a slapstick comedian."

"What about Anna Romanov?"

"Elegance personified."

"They all have successfully branded themselves. You will never see John Wayne playing a bad guy, Jerry Lewis in a dramatic role, or Anna Romanov in a silly comedy. Now, we have to come up with the Rick Jackson brand."

"When you put it that way, it makes sense. I can see that once I make a brand selection, it will restrict the parts I can accept."

"As you get older, we can rebrand you as needed. That is the biggest hurdle of any child actor, getting the audience to accept that they have grown up and are going in different directions. It has been the downfall of many young actors to try to rebrand themselves in their public life rather than their screen life.

"They feel that by acting like an out-of-control adult, they will be accepted for adult parts. They forget the out-of-control image causes them to be considered a poor business risk. Once they start down that path, it is hard to turn back. It can be done but at a great price. Look no further than Sharon Bronson."

"So, you are telling me that I must have a current brand and keep my eye on how to transition to the future."

"It's not as hard as it sounds. Your first two movies and public reputation have set you up as an All-American boy hero type. If you always play those parts, you just have to grow up and be the All-American hero type."

Mum interjected, "His problem will be growing up."

"Thanks, Mum!"

I turned to William, "So how do we do this?"

"Pretend like I am not there."

"That's kind of hard."

"After the first hour or so, you won't notice me. These are to be candid shots, so there will be no posing."

Susan asked, "What are your plans for the day?"

"I don't have any appointments. I thought I would say 'Hi' to some people at school and then make stops at my accountants and stockbroker."

"That's the sort of day we want to record. You are living a normal life."

I accepted that comment but wondered how many fifteen-year-olds stopped in at their accountants and stockbrokers.

Susan continued, "I have several messages for you. Frank Sinatra wanted to let you know he would be happy to do another duet with you. He is making a fortune off 'Brothers'. It is still number one, you know. There is a good chance you will end up with a gold record."

"The other message is from John Wayne. He wants me to tell you that *Sir Nicklaus* is surpassing his wildest dreams. Considering it was a fill-in project for *The Cowboys*, it is doing better than anything he has made in a long time. He attributes a lot of it to you and would be pleased to have you in his future movies."

"Please tell Mr. Sinatra, 'Thank you for your kind words'."

Then tell Mr. Wayne, "I would be delighted to work with him on any of his projects."

"I gather you don't care to work with Mr. Sinatra again."

"I am not a singer, and I didn't care for the contempt that was shown by how 'Brothers' was put together. I got the publicity that I was hunting for, and he is getting the money he wants. I'm not sure that his image is one that I want to be near in the future."

Mum gave a small shake of her head at the last part of my comment. I had taken that as far as I could, maybe a little too far. Since Susan didn't explore my comment on Sinatra's image, I was probably okay. I only had circumstantial evidence. Time would tell.

Chapter 26

Susan let me know that I would be going to Columbus on Wednesday for two events. I would be spending time at Children's Hospital with critically ill kids and then meeting with my Ohio fan club.

This is the first time I heard of an Ohio fan club. I asked Susan about it.

"As you may or may not know, most fan clubs are creations of your publicity group. We find a willing person in an area, appoint them president, put announcements in school papers, or wherever the local thinks we can attract members. Anyone who requests an autographed picture from the studio of you is then automatically enrolled in the nearest club and sent all the information.

"We keep track of the numbers and use them as evidence of your popularity. Some very few entertainers like Elvis have their own true spontaneous fan club. That is where someone writes to you and asks how to form a local club. We call those Real Fans."

"I haven't gotten any letters about fan clubs," I replied.

"Silly boy, the studio set up a post office box for you. You are receiving a bag of mail every day. Most of them are requests for autographed photos. There are about five marriage proposals a day. Your hate mail is fairly low, and there are no actual death threats yet."

"Death threats?" I dumbly asked.

Mum sat up and took notice. Dad continued to sit there looking sleepy-eyed, drinking his coffee.

"Goes with the territory. It is almost a badge of success, if you will. If any seem serious, we turn them over to the local police if we have a postmark."

"What do you mean, serious? I would think any death threat would be serious."

"Would you be worried about someone threatening to kill you if you ever went to Moldova?"

"If I remember my geography correctly, that is inside the Soviet Union."

"You got it; now, would you be worried about that threat?"

"As far as I know, I will never go there in my life, so no, I wouldn't worry about it."

"That's my point. Now, if it were postmarked Bellefontaine, we would inform you, the police, and anyone else who we could think of."

Dad spoke up, "I would like to see every death threat, no matter where it comes from."

Mum had a startled look on her face at Dad's words. Something was going on there. I also realized that Dad was now sitting upright and looked anything but sleepy.

"As a parent, you have that right. I will arrange it," replied Susan.

She continued, "On Thursday night, there will be a special showing of *Sir Nicklaus* at the Holland Theater. I have brought one of your costumes for you to wear. You will be out front on a stage. For a donation to the high school band uniform fund, people can have their picture taken with you."

I looked at William, who was sitting there quietly.

"Will you be taking them?"

He just shook his head no.

Susan explained, "We have hired Hadley's, a local studio. It would be too much work for one person who will develop them immediately. They should be ready by next Monday for you to autograph. This way we also spend some money in your hometown. That always helps with your reputation."

I realized I had much more to learn about this business than I thought.

We chit-chatted for a few more minutes. I shared with the group how horrified Susan had been at the thought that she may have to live in Bellefontaine. Dad, who had dropped back into his normal laid-back demeanor, chuckled and asked her, "What about now?"

"Jack, I won't lie to you. I'm not cut out for a small town. I would go nuts here."

We continued for a few more minutes; then, William and I stood to take off.

Mum stopped us, "Before you go anywhere, Rick, check your Boy Scout uniform and that Civil War one to see if they still fit. The pants might be okay, but the shirts probably won't fit."

She was right. The Civil War shirt was tight but would do. The BSA shirt was way too tight. My chest size had expanded from all my exercises and workouts. The pants were fine. My waist was the same, and I hadn't grown any taller.

Of course, William had to take pictures. I told him he was a smart ass. He laughed at me. I would have to stop at J.C. Penney and pick up a new shirt. It was a little irritating as the fabric wouldn't be as nice as my special-order shirts. Oh well, Denny would have some nice shirts later. I would try and sweet-talk Mum into dropping the old shirt and new one at the tailor's and have them transfer the patches.

My first stop was at school. It was strange driving my second T-Bird, but fun. Since I wasn't a registered student, I had to stop at the office and sign in. I planned to see Coach Stone, my old golf coach, and let him know that I probably wouldn't be coming back to Bellefontaine High School. Then I wanted to see Mr. Donaldson, my shop teacher and business partner in the faucet business. If possible, I would like to say hello to Mr. Hurley and Miss Bales. Those two teachers had the most influence on me while at BHS.

First, I would have to see Mr. Gordon, our school principal, to get permission to be there. I went directly to the office. Luckily, it was during the first period, so kids weren't changing classes. At the office, I wasn't recognized at first. They paid more attention to William than me. He had this big camera hanging around his neck and several bags full of flashbulbs and film.

It didn't take Mr. Gordon long to come out of his office. He acted pleased to see me. He looked at a schedule when I explained why I was there and told me that Coach Stone and Mr. Donaldson would be free next period. He knew they both went to the teacher's lounge at that time. I had never been in the lounge but had looked through the door; it had comfortable-looking chairs and a cloud of smoke.

The teachers would take a smoke break there so they wouldn't set a bad example for the students. The only problem with that thought was that the smoke was usually so heavy that the door would be propped open, and anyone walking by in the high school's main hallway could see a teacher smoking.

Mr. Gordon walked me down to the lounge with my photographer in tow. William was right. I forgot he was there unless I saw or heard a flashbulb go off. I don't know how many pictures he could take, but he was loaded down like a pack mule.

We only had to wait a few minutes before Coach Stone showed up. We shook hands, and the first words out of his mouth were, "Will you be back next year?"

"I'm afraid not, Coach. I think I will be in California for the foreseeable future."

"That's a shame from my point of view, Rick, but I wish you the best."

"I appreciate what you taught me while I was here."

"Will you be turning professional at any point?"

"I don't think so. I make better money in the movies, and I don't feel a need to prove my golf game is world-class."

"Well, it could be world-class if you kept it up. You might play in some celebrity tournaments and possibly even make it into the US Open as an amateur."

"Now that is a thought, Coach. I'm not certain how I could find the time right now, but it would be good publicity for my career."

We then spent a few more minutes talking about the school golf team and its chances this year. We both agreed they would be particularly good in their league but not go far in the state tournament.

Mr. Donaldson came in, so Coach and I finished up. Mr. Donaldson was extremely happy to see me and told me how he and his brother were doing well since I had given them their first orders.

"It put the shop on the map, Rick. We now have twenty-two employees and are looking for more good people at the factory. We are prototyping for several companies now, and they all look good. Plus, your being fair with us on your first product has left us in very good shape."

"I'm so glad to hear it, I don't have anything going on right now, but you will always be my first choice for this sort of work."

We chatted for a while. What I hadn't noticed was the traffic jam as students changed classes. Kids were coming to a dead stop at the door to the lounge to get a look in. Mr. Gordon closed the door so the kids would move on. After about ten more minutes, I wanted out of there. Talk about an advertisement for not smoking!

Mr. Hurley and Miss Bales wouldn't be free for another two periods, so I returned to the office in time to run into Mrs. Hadley, the teacher in charge of the Drama Club. She made over me like crazy, as though she had never told me I could never be an actor. I took it in and politely thanked her for her comments. Of course, she always knew I would be a "Star". Her quotation marks, not mine. If I stayed another five minutes, I was certain to find out that she was the one who had discovered me.

Mr. Gordon, who had been escorting me the whole time, interrupted me and asked me to come into his office. He didn't object when William accompanied me.

When the door was closed, he said, "Rick, she is a good teacher, but I do regret the day I asked her to take over the Drama Club. Thank you for putting up with her."

He went on, "That's not what I wanted to talk to you about. Unfortunately, your presence here is disrupting the school day. You were busy talking to people, so you didn't notice the crowds in the hall. I imagine detention will overflow tonight because of kids being late to class.

"I'm afraid I'm going to have to ask you to leave the grounds. Not because of anything you have done, just because of who you are."

This was the first time anything had happened because of my fame. I didn't like that my movements were now restricted because my presence was disruptive. At the same time, I did appreciate his point of view. In two days, they would be starting their final exams; this wasn't a time to disrupt the school day.

"I understand, sir. I will leave as soon as you and I are done."

"Don't get me wrong, Rick. We are proud of you and what you have accomplished. At the same time, I have a school to run and children to educate. That seems to get harder every year as more requirements are imposed from the state and federal levels. I don't know what we would do if we didn't have strong parental support from most of our homes."

I had never given that a thought. At our house, whatever trouble I got into at school would cause me grief of some sort at home. Like when I had a detention, I was on garbage duty for a week. My mum or dad was always checking to see if I had done my homework until this year when I surged ahead. Even then, they periodically checked to keep me honest. Even in California, the Sunday night call had inquiries about my schoolwork.

"We would love you to come on occasion, but it would have to be a scheduled event. I must ask, will you come back here next year?"

"No, sir, this isn't for general publication, but my family is moving to California. We bought a house out there and will move there after our summer vacation. Even then, I won't be in a regular classroom. If I'm making a movie, which seems probable, I will be in a studio classroom. Other than that, I will have a private tutor. I can't stand the slow pace of a classroom anymore. I completed a year of school in three months by working hard. If I can, I would like to do the tenth and eleventh grades next year."

"I can see you doing that, Rick. I encourage you. The only reservation I have is your socialization. Some of high school and even college is to teach you how to be an adult in a fairly safe environment."

"Right now, I'm learning how to be an adult as a live-fire exercise."

I hadn't thought those words through. As they came out of my mouth, the scene on top of the railcar at Guest Yards flashed through my mind. It was only a second, but it was disconcerting because it was so vivid.

I asked Mr. Gordon to give my regards to Mr. Hurley and Miss Bales and took my leave.

Chapter 27

From school, William and I went downtown to my accountant's office. On the way, William asked me about garbage duty. Though the way I said it, it was different from taking the trash out. I explained that garbage disposals were illegal in Bellefontaine, like most small towns in America. It was felt the food scraps would damage the city sewer system. Most cities like Los Angeles and their suburbs allowed them.

When I moved to California, I was fascinated by the InSinkErator in my apartment. It sure beats taking the scraps out to a garbage can that had been sitting in the hot sun. By the end of the week, it was a stinking liquid mess. When you lifted the poorly fitting lid, there would be a mass of maggots. It was hideous. If we hadn't done our homework, we would be told the only job we could get was on the back of the garbage truck. This was a different truck than the trash truck, which didn't seem that bad.

At the Grimes accounting office, I met with Robert Junior and Roberta. William sat in the corner of the office and didn't take any pictures.

Money-wise, I was in excellent shape. Ignoring the stocks and bonds, I was worth over a million dollars. This didn't consider the value of Jackson House, which was still up in the air. After our modifications and upgrades were put in, the county would send a property tax appraiser out to re-value for tax purposes. It wouldn't matter to me. Mum and Dad intended to buy the house in their name as soon as they could realize the cash from the sale.

Roberta Grimes asked me what I thought of them opening an office in California. In turn, I asked her what they had in mind.

She blushed and told me, "Well, it is me thinking of moving to California, so I have a chance to find a husband."

This set off all sorts of red flags in my mind.

"Why California to find a husband?" I inquired.

"I would prefer a mature, successful husband. They are hard to find around Bellefontaine. When a professional man returns to Bellefontaine after he graduates, he always brings a wife. The pickings are mighty thin around here."

That was a relief to hear. It didn't sound like she was gunning for me. Fifteen, and I was afraid of gold diggers.

"Well, if you go there, it makes sense for you to have your office near ours."

"Your dad has bought an office building. Do you think he would have space that I could rent?"

Her dad spoke up, "Rick, the family has spoken of this. Unfortunately, Roberta is right about finding a professional man in Bellefontaine; you either have to catch them in high school and hang on or forget it. Some eligible bachelors are around, but I don't think they are up to Roberta's standards."

Boy, this all was new to me, a family thinking and planning things like marriage through. I thought it just sort of happened.

Her father continued, "Also, we don't see our business being able to support all the family members with our Bellefontaine clients. We need an office in a big city, and this seems like a good way to start. We will financially support the new office; it isn't Roberta going out on her own. Besides, I hear the winters in California are better than here."

"That much is true. May I use your phone?"

Of course, I could. I dialed home.

"Hi, Mum. Could I speak to Dad?"

"Dad, do you still have space in your new office building?"

I knew full well he did, as he wasn't planning to advertise the space until the building was almost ready.

"Oh good," I said as I winked at Roberta. "Are you paying a commission to people who find you occupants?"

"Great, you owe it to Roberta Grimes; she has a lead on someone who needs space. Here, I will let you speak directly to her."

She talked for a while, explaining the Grimes family plan, leaving out the better-husband-hunting-ground part. When she hung up, she was smiling as she repeated Dad's statement, "One of these days, Alice, pow, right to the moon."

We got a chuckle from that.

After that pleasant conversation, I walked over to the James Daniels broker's office, followed by my ever-faithful companion. William looked at me funny when I called him Tonto, then laughed as he got it.

Bill Schwab was in and saw me after finishing a telephone call.

He said, "Let me make one quick call to put an appointment back slightly. It's not that important, my haircut at Beer's Barbershop.

He dialed the five digits and told Merle he would be running late.

"Now, Rick, what can I do for you?"

"I'm in town for a few days, so I thought I would check in and see how I'm doing."

"Aren't the quarterly statements we send enough?"

"They tell me how I have done. I would like your thoughts on where the items in my portfolio are going."

"Fair enough," he said as he pulled a file out of the filing cabinet behind him.

We went through each stock and discussed in general how it was doing. The Eisenhower recession had ended officially, and the economy was bouncing back. Ike had switched the economy from spending on the military to spending on infrastructure like rural electricity and was now easing restrictions on "No Down Payment" loans. It was going from guns to butter.

There was no end in sight for the economy, at least for the next ten years. Now was the time to invest in the stock market, at least according to Mr. Schwab. He was probably right from what I read in the daily paper and my economics self-study. He then talked to me about some short-term opportunities he saw.

I informed him that since I couldn't track my portfolio daily, I had no interest in short-term opportunities. I wanted to buy and hold for the long term. I asked him if he could live with this.

After a pause, he agreed. I was proud of myself. I had never used the term I had read about, churning, but I had let him know that he wasn't going to make a fortune from me at my expense.

I also made a mental note to ask Mum to look into Mr. Schwab. I may be overreacting, but what else would he do if he were willing to churn my account to make money? I knew "they" were out to get me. The only question was exactly who are "they"? From Russian spies to teenage girls, I seemed to be a target. Those faraway days in the eighth grade didn't look so bad right now.

The current value of my portfolio was two and a half million dollars, which on a personal basis was great. On a space mission basis, it was nothing. How was I going to make serious money, like several hundred million dollars?

It was well past lunchtime when I finished with my broker. William and I stopped at Islay's and had milkshakes.

William asked me something out of the blue, "Rick, do you think your dad would rent me office space?"

"I don't know why not, but why would you need it?"

"My business is larger than you might think. I have three other photographers working for two darkroom technicians and me, plus an office manager/secretary."

"Oh, I thought you were a one-man show."

"Not even close I'm thinking about hiring two more photographers. That is why I need a larger office. Also, I would like to open a walk-in studio for family pictures."

He got a little grin, "That Roberta is sure cute, isn't she?"

Now I'm dense at times, but when you hear a cute girl say she wants to move to California so she can find a husband who is around thirty and professional, and there you sit with a thirty-year-old successful professional photographer, it is easy to put two and two together.

"Yes, she is, William. Are you trying to get a head start on the rest of the California boys?"

"Yes, but I'm not a California boy. I grew up in West Jefferson, Ohio, right outside of Columbus. I would like to find a small-town mid-west girl."

"Do you want me to say anything?"

"No, I want nature to take its course."

From Islay's, we walked over to J.C. Penney, where I was able to pick up a shirt for my Boy Scout uniform. Of course, it was a man's size, and after that, we walked around town, William taking pictures as we went. Monday afternoons weren't busy around town, so walking back and forth across the street was easy.

When we walked down Opera Street, I realized the *Bellefontaine Examiner* was just around the corner, so I stopped in on the chance George Weaver might be in. Fay, the newspaper secretary, announced me to George, who bounced out of his chair to shake hands.

"Ricky, I heard you were in town. I was going to stop by your house this evening. What's up?"

"Nothing George. I was taking a walk and found myself here and thought I would stop in and say hello, but now that I think of it, my publicity agent Susan Wallace may have wanted to be here. You being a reporter and all."

I grinned as I said that to give no offense. Mr. Weaver had been one of my biggest fans all along.

"I talked to her earlier today. She told me if I could catch you, I could interview you."

"Consider me caught."

From there, I spent a pleasant hour with Mr. Weaver recounting my California adventures that could be talked about, which was a little weird if you thought about it. It was my Bellefontaine adventure that had to remain a total secret.

At that point, Mr. Weaver asked me if I had heard the FBI had been in town. I told him no. What was going on? He told me they were following up on the Vampire Murders. They had been all over the train yards, especially Guest Yard, but had found nothing. That may have been because of all the rain they had last week.

Something must have crossed my face because Mr. Weaver all of a sudden gave me a searching look. He must not have found what he wanted because he shook his head as though to clear it and changed the subject.

Even so, he kept looking at me as though he were trying to figure something out.

Finally, he said, "I've heard it said that the Viscountess did some nasty stuff during the war."

I looked him straight in the eye and said in a dead-level voice, "You can't even imagine how bad it would get if someone attacked our family or did something really stupid like kidnapping Mary. No, you may not quote me on that."

"I see," he said slowly. "Is everyone alright at your house?"

"We are fine, thanks for asking."

"Good, I'm happy to only print good news about your family."

"Thanks, Mr. Weaver. We will always consider you a friend. Now it is time I got moving along."

Chapter 28

On the way home, William mildly said, "You forgot I was there, didn't you?"

"Yes," I sighed, "I did."

"I know there was a subtext to that conversation, but I don't know what and don't want to know."

"Thanks, William. You have the making of a friend of our family."

"Could you get your dad to pay me a commission as you did for Roberta?"

I laughed. "I will see what I can do."

It felt like a heavy weight had come off my shoulders.

When we got back to the house, William went across the street to use the telephone there, which Dad had maintained for me. Susan Wallace was out doing whatever publicity people do.

I took the opportunity to tell Mum and Dad about my day, starting with school, the accountants, the broker, Mr. Weaver, and finally, my last conversation with William. I left nothing out.

Dad thought I had overreacted about Bill Schwab. He had a very good local reputation, but it wouldn't hurt to keep things straight. Mum had the best tidbit.

"After you left Grimes, I got a phone call from Roberta. She wanted to know about the photographer accompanying you." All three of us grinned at each other. We could hear the wedding bells.

As far as Mr. Weaver went, Mum and Dad weren't concerned.

As Dad said, "This won't be the first story lead that George has decided not to follow up on. He has several national bylines because of this family. He isn't going to start guessing games when the FBI has been and gone."

Mum added, "I had a call from London. The CIA told the FBI that this was a Russian job that went bad and that Ike had signed off on sealing the files."

"You must have some pull with MI6, Mum."

"I have some, but I think this had more to do with Eisenhower not wanting to get your dad riled up."

I must have looked lost at that comment.

"Remember the Patton investigation. Your dad is viewed as a stick of dynamite waiting to go off. Only that one crazy Russian was willing to try something."

I looked at Dad. He had a big grin.

"The secret is I have nothing on anybody, but they all are afraid I do and don't want to be exposed. They must think if I die, there will be a document release. There is absolutely nothing because I didn't pay attention to that log when I found it. I just set it aside to review the next day."

Mum added, "We have talked this through many times. There must have been other names on that log besides the Russians. We just don't know who. They left us alone as long as we were content to keep a low profile in Bellefontaine."

"So now what?" I asked.

"We do just the opposite. We keep such a high profile that if anything happens, there will be all sorts of questions."

I don't know why I thought of it, but it came to me. "When you go to Switzerland this summer to check out that numbered account, you should leave documents for release if anything should happen to you. You now actually know about the Russians and their attempt, plus the US authorities going along with a cover-up. Their covering up is giving you the lever they thought you had all along."

Dad looked at Mum and said, "He is a chip off both our blocks!"

Mum also asked me if I had tried on my uniform shirts. She didn't give me any grief about getting the shirt to the tailor.

Later that night, I started a heavy novel. A new author, George Webber, in trying to discover himself, writes about his hometown of Libya Hill and reveals many a truth that may have been better left unsaid. He alienates the town and his family. He flees after numerous death threats. After visiting New York, Paris, and Berlin, he ends at peace with himself and returns to America renewed but does not return to Libya Hill. It took me several days to read, and I felt like it had mixed messages, but I was beginning to appreciate the one in the title.

Tuesday started well. It was a wonderful spring day, and I enjoyed my run. My legs still pulled, but not as much. I called each of the Toms' houses and asked them to meet me at Don's after school to catch up on things.

After that, I called Mark Downing in Detroit to see how things were going for him. He told me they were going great. He had added two new salesmen and signed three new distributors. He was using the newspaper flyer idea to move old, slow-moving inventory through reduced pricing. His banker was happy to see these items move. For a while, they had value, which counted towards his line of credit. They had money tied up.

He let me know that Miss Romanov's signature pieces were flying off the store shelves. They were having a hard time keeping up. He was considering expanding the workforce. Life was good.

He wanted to know if I still felt the money should be put back into the business. I told him that my cash flow was more than enough so continuing to put the profits into the business worked for me. He wanted to buy new lathes for the tool room. They were the current bottleneck in production. I replied that I wasn't looking for a large annual dividend this year. If he didn't need the money, it was fine with me.

Mark made me slow down and hear what his proposed changes should do to the company's financial condition. If the plans came together as projected, the company would grow thirty percent this year and twenty percent the following. His main concern was putting experienced supervision in place. He was interviewing almost daily.

After I hung up, I thought how lucky I was to own part of this business. The most amazing thing was that I understood his financial terms. I couldn't put the company's big picture together in my head, but I understood the individual bits and pieces. Thinking of the big picture, I reflected that DF would go as the housing market went. Since the projections for that were sky-high, things looked good for the company. Now, if people just bought hairdryers.

After my phone calls, I did the logical thing. I went to see what Mary was up to. I should have been able to guess. I'm just too big for the chairs she uses for her tea parties. It was still fun; she was so serious and yet funny at the same time. William took many pictures of Mary and me as we played with the camera. I cannot imagine what it will be like around our house when she starts dating. With any luck, I will be living elsewhere.

We had toasted cheese for a late lunch. Then I went to the basement and lifted weights for a while. Our set was puny compared to what I had been using at the studio. I shortly gave it up as not worth the effort.

Since it was such a nice day, I went for a ride up around Indian Lake with the T-Bird's top-down. I was driving by my Uncle Wally's house and saw him out in the yard, so I stopped to say hello. One thing you can say about Wally, he is consistent. He glad-handed me like I was his favorite person in the world. Red flags went up in my mind. Wally treated you like this when he wanted something.

Dad had observed a long time ago that Wally always had a money-making scheme. It involved your money, someone else's work, and him getting rich. This time was no different. For a mere fifty thousand dollars, we could start a chinchilla ranch. He knew a guy who would sell us fifty breeding pairs; he also had a line on a twenty-acre lot with the right buildings. All we would have to do is build the cages, and the money would come rolling in.

I told him I thought that was a wonderful idea and that I would talk to my parents as they controlled my money until I was eighteen. He said, great, nice seeing you, and went into the house. I guess he didn't have much hope that Mum and Dad would release the money. I would have to tell them that I had thrown them to the wolves.

William wanted to know if he was like that all the time.

I told him, "His whole life, and he has never made a dime from his schemes."

I drove around until school was out and then went to Don's. I was sitting there when Tom Morton and Tom Wilson showed up. They had gotten my message. I told them burgers were my treat. We loaded up with burgers, fries, and shakes. It took us about twenty minutes to talk about what had happened in Bellefontaine during the school year. William sat in a corner by himself and only took a few shots of us guys.

It wasn't much, a few couples coming together and a few partings but none I cared about. The biggest news was Rita Harrison was moving to Columbus for the school year. The rumor was that she was pregnant. Pam Schaffer from the Drama Club had dumped Sam Shepard after their play was done. I think I had heard that before, but it showed what sort of a person she was.

After Bellefontaine topics quickly wore down, they started quizzing me about life in Hollywood. There were many things that I couldn't tell them, but what I could share amazed them. I tapered off as I realized if I continued, I would sound like a braggart.

In a way, I got lucky; the rest of the school kids started pouring in from their after-school activities. Very quickly, I was surrounded by more teenage girls than I had spoken to in the last year. It was obvious they all wanted a trophy called Ricky. I like to hear how good-looking I am as much as the next teenage boy, but this was getting too thick. It didn't help that William was snapping pictures like crazy.

I said goodbye to the Toms and fled the scene. Even then, several followed me to my car and wanted a ride. I told them my license didn't allow me to carry passengers. They could see this was a bare-face lie as William got into the car, and I drove off.

This was twice today I had to lie to avoid a problem. I didn't like the feeling. I had to learn how to tell the direct truth without hurting people's feelings, that or not to worry about their feelings. That wasn't the sort of person I wanted to be, either.

When I returned home, Mum informed me that Mr. Baxter had called and would I please call him back, no matter what time it was. I called him immediately. He had finished negotiations with Mr. Monroe and thought he had a workable package for me.

Basically, for signing with the studio, I would receive twenty-five hundred dollars a week. That about put me in shock. I recently read that the average male wage earner makes five thousand dollars a year. The contract was for two years, with a renewable option.

That money was only to keep me from working for other studios. If I performed in a movie, that would be a separate negotiation with the production company. My weekly salary would continue with Warner Brothers even while I worked on a movie. If another studio wanted to hire me for a movie, then they would have to negotiate with Warner Brothers to use me and then with me to appear in their film.

It sounded like a fantastic deal to me. Mr. Baxter told me it was the best one he had ever seen.

"Rick, usually the studio bean counters quash a deal like this. You must have made some friends in the office there because there were no arguments."

"My Dad and I will sign that deal as soon as we get it."

"It is being sent special delivery, and you should have it by next Monday."

"That's great, and thank you for all your work on this."

"My pleasure, Rick. The word always gets out on a deal like this. It will help my reputation as much as yours."

I finished reading the novel about the young writer before falling asleep.

Chapter 29

Wednesday was another great spring day. After my exercise and run, I stopped across the street for coffee. I had to get a coffee pot if I was going to be here awfully long.

Susan Wallace and William Coleman were waiting for me. Susan had arranged a limo for the day. I knew the driver, John Sullivan. I asked him if this limo had been won or lost recently. He told me that now it appeared to be racehorses, as Mr. Maverick had won several recently. We laughed about that. Susan and William were too polite to ask, and I was too ornery to tell them what we were talking about.

Well, that lasted until Marysville, and I broke down and told them how John and I never knew if there would be a limo, or if so, which one, as they were used as stakes in a poker game. They thought it was funny when they figured out the owner and gambler's name was Maverick. They roared.

We laughed until John told them that a writer had done extensive interviews with Mr. Maverick about his great-grandfather, who was also a gambler in the Old West. "Do you think...no. It couldn't be," said Susan.

"Maybe it is the basis of the story rather than facts," said William.

"I don't know. Mr. Maverick and his brother were named after their great-grandfather and great-great-uncle, Bret and Bart." In the rear-view mirror, Susan and William couldn't see John's face, but I could. He winked as he delivered the last line. They were still wondering if the TV show brothers could have been real people.

Now, if they had grown up in Bellefontaine, they would have known there was no Mr. Maverick. The taxi company was named Maverick, like a little lost cow, the only taxi company in a town of its size in Ohio. Mr. Barnes, the founder of the company, was told he was a maverick for trying it, so he named the company that. I bet

John Sullivan had been waiting to tell this story ever since the TV show became popular. I wasn't about to spoil the fun.

The fun stopped when we got to the Children's Hospital. Those poor kids, many of them wasting away with cancer. I had on my Western clothes from *Sir Nicklaus*. A special showing of the movie was made at the hospital two days before. They had set it up in their cafeteria area, and the kids were brought in, in wheelchairs.

I talked to each child and left them with an autographed photo that Susan had brought. I was doing okay with them until a little boy said he was sorry that Susan wasn't here to see me. She had liked the movie.

I asked him where she was, and he calmly told me, "She died yesterday."

I couldn't take it. I had to excuse myself for a few minutes and go to the men's room. Yes, I did cry. These poor kids were all under a death sentence, and yet they carried on. When we left, I was torn. I never wanted to see anything like that again.

Yet I told Susan, "We have to visit places like this whenever we can."

The rest of the day was cheerful and good for my ego. We went to the Christopher Inn in downtown Columbus. It was the only round hotel I had ever seen. The Rick Jackson fan club was meeting there. I had seen a list of the officers, so I wasn't surprised when Judy King welcomed me with a big hug.

She introduced me all around. There were fifteen girls and two boys. I figured the boys weren't there because of me. I mean seven girls to each boy! There was the usual picture-taking with everyone's camera. Susan had given me free passes to the movie, which I found strange because they had all seen it, but they were thrilled to get them. One girl told me she had seen it four times and couldn't wait to go again. Don't these people have a life?

I noticed Judy was still wearing that ring on a chain around her neck. I asked her how her boyfriend was.

She answered slowly, "Not so good right now. You might say lipstick on his collar has told a tale."

"I'm sorry to hear that. What are your plans for the summer?"

She was going to be working at Cedar Point as a lifeguard. She asked about mine. I told her I would be signing on as a deckhand on a tramp steamer in two weeks to work my way to England. I didn't realize that everyone was listening to us until the questions started.

That took us half an hour beyond our schedule. We finally were able to break away and leave for Bellefontaine. Susan gently told me I shouldn't have revealed my plans in public. I was glad she was gentle because I was already calling myself a fool for doing it. I knew as soon as I opened my mouth that I had made a mistake. We just had to hope that no one blabbed before I left.

It was late by the time we got to my newest home, so I went straight to bed and slept.

Thursday morning was another good morning. It was as good a day as any in California. California just had a lot more of them. I had an easy morning. There was nothing scheduled until the special showing of *Sir Nick* in the evening. With everyone but Mary in school, there wasn't anyone to entertain me. Dad had gone down to his office to look over the rental books. Mum and Mrs. Hernandez were getting ready for the trip to England.

They wouldn't be going until August, but they were still checking out clothes to take and discussing what to pack. I don't understand women and trips. I just throw my shaving kit and some underwear in a bag, and I'm ready to go. Maybe I will understand all their preparations someday.

I decided to take Mary to the swings at Mary Rutan Park. It wasn't far, and it was a nice day, so we walked. An hour pushing the swing and turning the merry-go-round was work. The teeter-totter was fun. I weighed so much more than Mary that I would just stand beside it and move it up and down. She would never get her feet on the ground if I sat on it. I tried the slide once. Let's leave it that I am too big to fit anymore.

I threatened William with his life if he ever released a picture of me on the slide.

Mary had played so hard that I had to carry her partway home. She was also getting cranky. That kid needed a nap! By the time we got home, she had fallen asleep on my shoulder. When we got home, I took her straight to her bed. Lying there asleep, she looked like a little angel.

Mum asked William if he had pictures of me carrying Mary and tucking her into bed. He did, and she wanted some for the family album.

After lunch, I drove down to the tailor and picked up my Scout shirt. They had done a good job as expected. As my British friends would say, I looked like a Christmas tree with all my different colored badges. I always wondered why we differed in that respect. Even our respective militaries were that way. The British wore few badges, and the Americans many. It must have something to do with the British way of understatement.

We had an early dinner so that I could get down to the Schine's Holland Theater. I loved that old place. I wish that someday they would refurbish it. There were windmills high on the sidewalls that turned and clouds that moved across the ceiling. I never saw them move, but it must have been neat when they did.

When we arrived, they had finished setting up outside. A large flatbed was towed into place by a semi-tractor, and two sets of steps were put in place. People paid at the bottom of one step and were assigned a number after signing in with names and addresses. They would climb the steps where I would be waiting. A goofy Western scenery backdrop was in place. Hadley's had cameras and lights in place.

People would have their pictures taken with me. Then give their number to the photographer's secretary to ensure the pictures would end up with the right people. They would then descend the other set of steps. I wondered if we would make enough money to buy any band uniforms.

Of course, as soon as I got there, I was put up on the trailer for light checks. This was old hat to me, so I patiently endured the fussing. Susan even arranged for a makeup person. Heaven forbid I do not look my best. Well, I did understand the need. I was more bothered by half the town watching me having makeup applied. Well, maybe not half the town, but those three small boys would tell everyone that Rick wore lipstick!

Columbus Avenue between the theater and the courthouse was closed. The city officials working on a short timeline arranged a street carnival. Service organizations like the Jay-cees, Lions, Kiwanis, and Rotary had dunking booths, and basketball throws to raise money. Even my Scout troop had a recruiting booth.

I made a point of stopping by and talking to my old Scoutmaster Mr. Geist. I thanked him for all the help, gentle guidance, and downright shoves he had given me in the last three years to get me to Eagle.

It was the foundation of many skills that led to my success. I also let him know that I would be going to the camporee separately and staying with the staff while I was there. He wished me well. As we stood there, they signed up three boys who wanted to join Rick's troop.

I shook hands with the boys and told them I expected them all to make Eagle. They all nodded their heads solemnly. Their parents even wanted to shake hands. All the time, William was taking pictures. I didn't even notice until one of the parents asked if they could have copies. William made notes and promised them he would send them in several weeks.

At six o'clock on the dot, we started taking pictures to raise money for band uniforms. I had been hoping to raise enough money to outfit one kid at one dollar per person. The uniforms cost around fifty dollars each. The Bellefontaine High School Marching Band had sixty-five members. If there were five people in the photograph, it would be five dollars. We also would take any extra donations they wanted to give.

After five grueling hours as busy as any on the movie set, we finished. At one minute per shot with an average of three people per shot, that was one hundred and eight dollars per hour, which would be nine hundred dollars or eighteen uniforms. I was happy with that number.

I was confused at the end when it was announced that three thousand two hundred and fifty dollars had been raised. It seems I committed to doing a little fund matching. As the band director was making this happy announcement, I looked over at Susan. She winked at me.

Oh, the fix was in all along. The band would get new uniforms even if only one person had shown up. It was a good cause, and I liked our school's colors of red and black. It also saved me from having to sit through another showing of *Sir Nick*.

Halfway through the evening, I had one surprise. My Columbus, Ohio fan club had rented a bus and came for pictures. They were chaperoned by Mr. and Mrs. King, so I know who paid for the bus. Judy was close in the picture, like right up against me, and I noticed she didn't have a ring around her neck anymore. I wondered. We didn't have time to talk, and they were gone when we finished up several hours later. It was a school night.

I was too wound up to read when I went to bed later. I had a hard time going to sleep. Every time I closed my eyes, I could see flashbulbs going off.

Chapter 30

Friday was the big day. I had been waiting for this camporee all year. I was so adrenaline-charged that I think I set a record on my run. I still couldn't run fast by football standards, but I did very well for me. I wondered what my life would have been like if Coach Crowley had said I was fast enough to play football.

I was ready to leave by ten o'clock, two hours early. William and I had lunch. I only had to pack my uniforms, shaving kit, and sleeping bag. I realized that William didn't have a sleeping bag and offered to take him to the Army-Navy surplus store to buy one. He laughed and told me he was roughing it. He made a reservation at one of those new Holiday Inns. Susan was staying at the same hotel, so she would take him there and back in the morning when he was done for the day.

Wimps! I hoped I wasn't like them when I was old as they are. They must be thirty!

The car was loaded. I put my gear in the back seat. This included my pistol, which I checked to make certain it was unloaded. It was, and I finally laid my sword on top. I was looking forward to wearing it around camp. Being fifteen is good.

I put on my Civil War uniform for the trip. This weekend, my main job was to liaison between the Scouts and the 6th Ohio Volunteer Infantry. William rode with me. Susan was driving separately as she had mysterious publicity things to do.

They were at least mysterious to me, as I hadn't bothered to ask. She knew her job, and I didn't, so I would stay out of her way. I would know what she had been up to when it was time. At least once a week, she updated me on her activities. So far, there had been nothing to give cause for concern.

It was another lovely day, so we rode with the top down. At a stoplight in Urbana, I received a hard look from a deputy sheriff. I pulled away, and the next thing I saw was a red flashing light from his gumball machine. When I pulled over, I realized that he looked faintly familiar. He asked for my driver's license.

He perused it and finally handed it back.

"I thought it was you. Do you remember me giving you a ride last summer when you were hitchhiking?"

Now I knew where I had seen him before. We talked for a few minutes. William took a picture of us together and got his home address.

The deputy, John Dougherty, had recognized my picture when it first came out and had followed my career. I told him that I would follow his career now. He would be sheriff one day. He told me he had been there and done that. He liked being a deputy. It seemed like he had been doing it forever but still enjoyed it. We shook hands, and I was on my way again.

We had to stop for gas in Springfield. I got out of the car just in time to see a man backing out of the service station with a shotgun aimed inward. I never hesitated. My sword was on top of my gear in the open backseat. I grabbed the hilt and pulled the sword from its scabbard. Today the sound of a shotgun being pumped will give rise to fear. The sound of metal on metal as a sword is being drawn is scary in a more primal way.

The sword sang as it came out of the scabbard. It got the attention of the guy with the shotgun. He never had a chance. He was turning when I brought the flat of the sword down on his head. He dropped straight down, none of those Hollywood scenes. Another man came out of the store, facing me with a revolver in hand.

I knew fear for real as he fired. I also learned that accuracy goes all to hell when firing under pressure. He missed. He almost lost his hand as I brought the sword down on his gun arm. Like that, the whole event was over. I was fast; William was faster. He had shots of both actions.

While we waited for the local police, I got the shakes. The owner of the station brought me a Coke and some chips. "I was in the 6th infantry in the Pacific. We were involved in island clearing. I used to get the shakes after an action."

He thought it was cool that I was wearing a 6th infantry uniform. Different war and outfit, but still, it was the 6th. Of course, William was there with his camera. The owner assured me his copy would be on the wall of fame in his VFW post.

We had put rough bandages on the guy whose hand I had almost severed so he didn't bleed out. The guy I had whacked on the head was coming around but was so groggy that he didn't know where he was. He had to have a concussion.

The police called ambulances and took statements. They all examined my sword with great interest. I had wiped it clean before they arrived. They debated seizing it as evidence but decided it wasn't used in the crime, so it wasn't needed. I would have been brokenhearted if they had taken it. A crime scene photographer showed up and took plenty of pictures. He and William hit it off and exchanged stories.

I was informed that I might be called on to testify in court. I would face that day when it happened. The local reporter showed up. He heard about it on his police scanner. I gave him a very brief statement. He didn't recognize me as the actor, and I didn't enlighten him. He didn't even ask why I was traveling with my photographer.

At least he recognized that my uniform wasn't normal, so I explained about the camporee. The headline would probably be Eagle Scout hacks up robbers. I had dealt with real professional reporters; he was the worst I had run across.

I think the police knew who I was, but they played it straight. As the reporter asked his few questions, one of the cops winked at me, so I knew their opinion of the reporter. I gave the policeman a smile and a small shake of my head.

After all that hoorah, the camporee, while not dull, seemed a lot tamer. On arrival, I was checked in as part of the 6th OVI Headquarters Company, so I would be camping with them. They used large tents that you could stand up in and had cots. Talk about camping luxury. There was even a shower tent. I was told as an officer I didn't even have to help haul the water.

Later I realized these people didn't rough it or haul water. They had a small water buffalo set in place, and it fed into a small propane water heater.

As soon as I set my gear down, I was ordered to present myself to General Tolson. He was in his glory with his brevet rank of general. Enough re-enactors had shown up that he could assume the rank. He had the full uniform and was all smiles.

He had me accompany him to a Scout staff meeting. There we pored over the maps to see where our units were to camp. I received the assignment to visit every unit to make certain they were set up in the correct area and to see if they needed anything.

After that, I only stood still and rested when the flags were lowered at camp. Everything came to a halt wherever we were, and we saluted the flag as it was lowered. Other than that, it was run, run, and run. I stopped by my tent and took that danged sword off as soon as I could. It was beating me to death.

The duties kept me busy for the rest of the evening. There was only one unit that had problems. A cavalry unit from Virginia was set too close to a rifle range. The horses were used to gunfire, but too many hours too close would stress the animals. It took a couple of hours to find a spot that worked and to arrange an exchange with the unit camping there.

It was a Boy Scout troop that we had to move. They were a little resistant at first until the Virginians promised all twelve of the boys there that they would give them a ride. When that offer was made, the Scoutmaster yielded to a superior force or accepted the bribe, your choice.

That ended my day well past midnight. I was exhausted. They could have been firing those cannons, and I wouldn't have heard them.

Chapter 31

Friday morning, I was up before reveille. Now Boy Scouts don't do that, but Civil War units do. Even though I was wide awake and had my first cup of coffee, I still jumped when that bugle started playing. So did about five thousand other people, most of whom had been asleep.

We had a steady stream of Scoutmasters and assistants after that through the camp. Not one expressed nostalgia for reveille. General Tolson realized that his troops were gravely outnumbered and decided there would be no sunrise reveille tomorrow or Sunday.

There would be "To the Colors" when the flag was raised, "Retreat" when the flag was lowered, followed by the "National Anthem" and "Taps" at lights out, but no "Reveille". It didn't matter to me since I was up, but if I had forty boys in my charge, I would want them to get their sleep out.

It was Saturday and the day started earlier than planned. The opening ceremony was to be at 9 a.m. After that, the events would start. The only problem now was that the boys were all dressed and ready to go by eight o'clock.

The Virginia Cavalry unit took matters into their own hands. They mounted up and did an impromptu raid on a Union encampment. I think it was a group from Michigan. Well, that started the day. We had boys running around following the riders, others helping the Michiganders wave shirts to keep the horses out of camp. When things got exciting horses would tend to take care of business.

I found out later that the count of horse apples inside the tent ring would be decided later. If there were none, the defenders won. Each horse apple inside the ring counted as one defender lost. Each apple found outside the ring counted as a rider down.

Why no one was trampled is hard to say. For the record, the Michigan unit held off the Virginians, but as some other general said, it was a close-run thing. Some of those horse apples may have been thrown out of the tent ring by hand.

It took a full hour to settle things down. I could tell from the looks of the Boy Scout executive staff they were beginning to regret the entire adventure. I could have told them anyone willing to dress up as a Civil War soldier was still a kid at heart. They just had bigger toys.

Anyway, we had the opening ceremony on time. All went well with the speeches. I received some recognition as a Boy Scout hero and as the official liaison. The first was a compliment. I wasn't certain about the second.

The day went by on schedule; after that, every boy who wanted to got a chance to fire a black powder rifle. Cannons would roar on occasion as they were demonstrated. There were the usual boy competitions such as knot tying, chopping a standard-size log in half with the fewest strokes, rope bridge and tower building, along with other fun stuff.

I was roped into a demonstration almost by accident. I had a breather and was watching an officer showing the arms manual for swords. It was different from what I knew about sword fighting. It looked like a choreographed dance. Someone in the crowd recognized me and yelled that I could do better.

I shook it off, but the crowd of boys started chanting "Ricky, Ricky." The officer handed me a sword and beckoned me into the ring. I was glad the sword edges were rounded and the end blunted.

All this time, since last night, William had been following me, snapping pictures. He went crazy now, snap, snap, snap.

I limbered up with my sword. I didn't know what to expect. We both were tentative when we started, but I soon had his measure. As long as we went by his manual, he did well. I hadn't learned from a manual. I was taught by the descendant of a long line of bloody Scots and Irish. Sammy Dawson taught me how to kill with a sword, not to parade around like a bloody fool, as he put it.

As soon as I realized the quality of the swordsman, I was facing, I took it to him. It was a short fight ending with him on his back and my sword at his throat while he choked out, "Yield."

How was I to know he was considered to be the master swordsman of both the Confederate and Union re-enactors? He was not a happy camper and stalked away without shaking hands.

Right on time, President Eisenhower showed up in his parade of limos and Secret Service agents. He arrived at the reviewing stand and started the required political handshaking. He did greet all the adults there as he could. He was scheduled to make remarks over a loudspeaker to the entire camp in an hour.

When he saw me, he walked up, and while he shook my hand, he drew me into a hug. He wanted to know how my parents and Mary were after our recent ordeal. He wanted me to pass a message to Dad.

"If you ever need help, let me know."

He also had a message for me, "Good shooting with that bow. It took the FBI a while to figure out what killed them. I assume it was your Mum with the rifle."

I just nodded yes.

'Rick, you have a unique set of parents. They make James Bond seem like an amateur. It appears you are taking after them. There are a lot worse role models."

With that semi-cryptic statement, he moved on. I knew about Mum, but it appeared Dad might have some things about him that I wasn't aware of.

There was a Civil War re-enactment. It was not based on a real battle; it was a typical battle. There were over a thousand soldiers, six hundred Union and four hundred Confederate. They put on a show. I was lost in the moment with all the noise, sound, and fury. It wasn't real. For one moment, I thought of it as real, and it was horrid. So many were falling, and this was nothing compared with reality. I hoped there would be no war in my lifetime.

At "Taps" that night, I felt melancholy like never before.

The next morning the sun was shining, and all was right in the world. The entire camp cleaned up and went to church services. After that, units would tear down, clean up, have their site inspected, and leave for home. By one o'clock, it was quiet. All the scout troops and re-enactors had left.

The camp staff performed one last walkthrough. I shook hands with General Tolson. He let me know that he had been promoted to his rank permanently by the groups present since the general had proven he could run a good encampment.

He did admit they had to rethink the horse-apple wars. I learned later that was the last one ever fought. It became known as the last great battle of the Civil War, and if you were on-site, you had bragging rights. They even talked about a special medal, a horse apple hanging from a ribbon, but nothing came of it. That would have been cool.

The general informed me if I wanted to stay active, he would promote me to captain and appoint me as an aide. I had to decline because of my schedule, so we shook hands and parted company.

William captured a picture of me in full uniform saluting the general in his full regalia. For some reason, the media picked up on it for its Sunday supplements. I suppose the fact that Susan sent the pictures and the story to every news outlet in the country helped.

We left for home. William's duty was done for this week, but I suspected I would see him again in the future.

That night I read a book about failed leadership. A group of British teenagers survived a plane crash during World War II. They picked a leader Ralph because he could blow a conch horn. That seemed to be a weak method to me. When Jack challenged his leadership, Ralph didn't rise to the occasion, which led to disasters.

I hoped I would do better in life.

Chapter 32

Monday started beautifully and just got better as the day went on. Spring and early summer in Ohio are some of the best weathers anywhere. High summer is nasty. Fall is great, winter not so much. It was a pleasure to get out and run. As I was running, I thought about my last year. I had been running since the middle of last September. I averaged five miles a day, at least twenty-five days a month. That worked out close to one thousand miles.

Fifty pushups and sit-ups a day for the same period worked out to over ten thousand. I couldn't even guess how many tons of weight I had lifted. It certainly explained the difference between most of the freshman class and me. I had noticed how the guys looked when I visited the school last week. Many of them had grown taller, but most of them were still gangly. Very few were filled out like I was, and none were as big overall.

There was also a difference in how everyone moved. The freshmen boys seemed clumsy to me. I suppose it was all the working out, learning the sword, boxing, and hand-to-hand combat, but I was smoother in my movements. They were jerky at times. I was fluid. I got my full growth early and grew into it through all my work. I had a full-grown man's body. They were still children.

Now the girls, that was different. They had grown up and out. Oh my.

After that bit of introspection on my physical appearance, I finished up my run, cleaned up, and crossed the street for my morning coffee. That was another change in my life. I was addicted to caffeine. I wasn't worried about it, but it was certainly a change.

Susan, my publicist, was waiting for me. She wanted to discuss the events of the weekend, particularly the gas station holdup. The question is how to use the story. In the case of the Springfield report, there was no story. She had been down to Jackson's Newsstand (no relation) and picked up the morning paper from Springfield.

The report had three lines about how a gas station robbery had been interrupted by a young man long enough for the police to arrive and subdue the robbers. I don't consider myself a publicity hog, but that was unfair. I stopped them cold!

William worked overtime using the Hadley Studio to develop his film from last Friday's holdup. He had a series of shots that were almost a stop-frame action. Since it was broad daylight, he was able to keep clicking rather than worry about flashbulbs.

The picture series started with my sword swinging at the back of the guy's head. I even winced at the one showing contact. The following showed me moving towards the guy coming out of the store as he turned his weapon on me, and then I was almost severing his hand from his arm. The timing was such that the picture caught flame coming out of the barrel as the revolver fired.

I wouldn't be surprised if he lost that hand. Later, I would learn that he did.

After much discussion in which my parents took part, we could see no downside to letting the real story get out. In a way, it made my branding issue easy. I was going to be the clean-cut All-American Boy.

While I didn't feel like a goody-two-shoes, I was pleased that I would have a clean-cut image. Well, actually, I already had that image; this reinforced it. I even brought that up in the conversation, and we discussed how I could avoid the goody-two-shoes part of the equation. Being clean-cut was one thing. Being a prig about it was another.

We made various jokes about what I could do to keep my image realistic. Drugs and alcohol were out. Speeding tickets were okay if it wasn't driving recklessly. Susan was all for a series of girlfriends, but that left me cold.

I was all for the idea of sex, but not for a lot of girlfriends. Go figure. Of course, I didn't say I was all for sex. I mean, Mum and Dad were sitting there.

Mary came in and listened while we talked about what I could do that was socially inappropriate to keep my image realistic. She even had a suggestion. I could pick my nose in front of people. Mum gave her a talk every time she did it, so maybe that was bad!

William asked Mary if she wanted a picture of her in the newspaper picking her nose. She liked the idea of her picture in the paper. She didn't like the idea of the picture being put on the front of the refrigerator.

"Mum, that would be gross," was her reply.

"So don't pick your nose in public."

Mary brightened a little at that. She could pick her nose in private.

"And always use a handkerchief."

Her face dimmed a little now. She would have to remember to carry a handkerchief. All these rules! Poor kid, life was hard.

Back to my problem, there was little mild anti-social behavior I could get into that helped me look good, but not too good. This was getting to be weird talking about what I could do wrong so I wouldn't look too good. This image thing was harder than I thought.

Mum finally got everyone's attention.

"This is Rick. We are talking about the guy who had the fire department called over a squirt gun fight. Don't worry about him. He will screw up all by himself."

"Gee, thanks, Mum."

She smiled sweetly at me and said, "You're welcome."

Some battles can't be won.

It was finally decided that Susan would invite George Weaver out for lunch and give him the story. That is where I learned that you could never go wrong feeding the media. Part of it was they were underpaid, a part that their hours and assignments were so irregular that they missed many meals.

According to Susan, the only problem that was created was that they were like puppies. Feed them too often and they follow you home.

Mr. Weaver must have wondered when I laughed when he showed up exactly at noon. We had a casual lunch then the interview started. Mr. Weaver and I had a routine down now. He would let me tell my story completely while he made notes of follow-up questions. My answers would lead to more questions. Finally, he would give feedback on my story as he understood it. I would then clarify the points he made. It was very efficient, at least for us.

William provided Mr. Weaver with a set of negatives of the robbery pictures. I don't know why I couldn't call Mr. Weaver, George, but I couldn't do it.

As we were finishing the interview, the telephone rang. It was Mr. Baxter. We haven't received the contract yet. It would probably be in the afternoon mail. He was calling on an entirely different matter. He needed me in California tomorrow!

I was being asked to audition for a part in an upcoming teen movie set in California. It would have me as a surfing dude meeting a girl just getting into surfing. There would be the usual I hate you sort of start finding its way to true love. She would think I was a worthless surf bum when I was the heir to a large fortune and taking the summer off from working on my engineering degree.

I would think she was a society snob from the east slumming with us California types. She was a nice girl who was running with a stuck-up crowd, and she had more money than all of them put together.

It turns out our parents had been best friends when they were younger. They had thought it would be great if when we grew up, we got married, but life had separated the friends. This was all one hundred percent believable, at least in Hollywood.

The untitled movie was to start filming in September, so the timing was great. What sealed the deal for me was Sharon Bronson being asked to star opposite me. We both would be playing eighteen-year-olds, making me three years older and Sharon three or so years younger. I guess, on average, we were eighteen.

That meant I had to high-tail it to Dayton to catch a flight. A phone call to TWA came up with a five o'clock flight, which gave me four hours to get to Dayton. They had an opening in first class.

It didn't take me long to throw some gear together in an overnight travel bag. I planned to fly today, audition tomorrow, and fly back on Thursday.

I stopped to say I was leaving. I'm glad I did; Mum had the mail. There were two letters for me and one for my parents from John Wayne. The contract from Mr. Baxter had arrived. I opened it. Not only was the contract there but a letter from Mr. Spiller, our entertainment lawyer. Mr. Baxter knew we would want Mr. Spiller to look at the contract, so he sent it over to him first.

While it was in dry lawyer talk, what it meant was, "You would have to be crazy not to take this deal."

I signed where I had to immediately. Dad signed and said he would get it in the mail. I asked him why. I was going that way. That sort of took us all back for a moment. Our lives had changed.

The letter to my parents from John Wayne was from him to let them know he was having a housewarming gift delivered to Jackson House. He told me I would recognize it as the horse trough used in *Sir Nicklaus*. He figured Dad might find it handy. The other boys laughed till Dad explained that they would fit in it also.

The other letter for me was in a familiar flowing script. It was from Judy. I put it in my pocket, deciding to read it on the plane. I didn't have anything to read with me and would probably go nuts on the flight.

Chapter 33

I drove to Dayton in my Ohio T-Bird. I thought about speeding, but it might cause me to miss my flight. Still, I chuckled at the thought of getting stopped for speeding so soon after the conversation this morning. Somehow, I didn't think Mum and Dad would be happy no matter what it did for my image.

After arriving at the airport, I raised the top and left the car in overnight parking. It cost more in the long term, but it was worth the inconvenience of getting out of the airport. It was one more change I noted in my life. Last year, I wouldn't have dreamed of paying for a flight, much less not being concerned about paying more for parking.

That made me think of my Ohio T-Bird and that I would be using my California T-Bird tomorrow. I know I had over three million dollars with more coming in, but for some reason, the thought of the two T-Birds made me realize I was rich by most definitions. What got me was until this minute, I had never given it a thought.

Susan had done her job and notified the airline a star would be on board. Her term, not mine. As soon as I checked in, I was taken to the Ambassador Club to wait for my flight. A photographer was in place to take pictures of me as I boarded the flight. I wondered what William would be doing the next several days. Maybe he would call Roberta.

I was boarded last on our brand-new Boeing 707. As we boarded, I saw the plate on the door frame that said it was built in 1959, so it was only months old.

A stewardess helped me settle in for the flight. Settling in, in this case, meant she made certain I knew how to work my seat belt by helping me. She seemed to take longer than necessary. I'm not certain what smoothing my shirt over my stomach had to do with tightening the belt, but she seemed to feel it was needed.

She told me this was the first flight of a 707 from Dayton to LA and that I should feel excited to be on a plane like this for the first time. I made the mistake of telling her it wasn't my first time on a 707 from Dayton to LA.

"That can't be. It has only been in service for a week."

"I flew on a charter," I replied. I knew that was a mistake as soon as I said it. This young lady had shown she liked my body. Now it was my wallet she was interested in.

She asked probing questions about being on a charter flight, but I continued to evade her. I blamed it on the studio. Her eyes got big at that, and then the coin dropped for her.

"You're Ricky Jackson, the singer and movie star!"

Oh boy.

"Your mother is a British viscountess," she gushed.

"May I have a Coke after we take off?"

"Oh, you can have anything you want," she replied.

I don't think she meant the double entendre because she blushed the deepest red I have ever seen. That faux pas made her quiet for the rest of the trip. She served my meals and drinks but otherwise left me alone.

Once we were airborne, I opened Judy's letter. I noticed it had SWAK on the back flap like she always wrote. I'm sure it didn't mean the same as it used to. Probably just a habit of hers.

Then again, the letter surprised me. She told me how much she enjoyed our brief meetings in Columbus, then again in Bellefontaine, and that it was a shame we hadn't any time alone. She went on to tell me that she had broken up with her boyfriend. He had been dating other girls behind her back. I thought he had to be crazy.

She went on to say that she knew that we couldn't be a couple with me in California and her in Ohio, but she would like to take up writing like we used to. It was nice to have a friend her age who would understand how bad the teen years were.

I had no problem writing Judy but didn't understand the teen years being bad. I was having a great time. That gave me pause. I *was* having a great time. In the last year, I had come so far, inventing, acting in two movies, learning to speak another language, and even being on two records.

On top of that, I could defend myself. I owned part of a bathroom fixture business and two T-Birds. Who wouldn't like my life?

Parts of my life had been grim. I killed four different men, two bank robbers and two kidnappers. Plus, there was the bank robber wounded by an arrow and two wounded with my sword. I don't know if helping capture rustlers was a plus or a minus.

On the plus side, I had pulled a woman and child out of a burning house and saved a cowboy in a cattle stampede. There was that Gate's boy I had pulled out of the water and those people in the car wreck in Bellefontaine. There was that rabid coyote on the movie set, but the one I was saving was me.

Those types of things change a person. I could see the differences between my friends and me when we ate at Don's. They were concerned with ninth-grade kids. I was facing real life. Maybe I was bragging, but I was facing it well.

I reread Judy's letter. She didn't come out and say it, but it was obvious she still had hope for us. After thinking about it, I realized that I wanted the same as her. Keeping in contact with letters was a thin thread, but it was all we had, so we would use that.

These serious thoughts must have shown on my face because no one disturbed me on the whole flight. We arrived at LAX around eight o'clock, and I was back at my apartment by nine. I took a taxi to the Burbank Airport to retrieve my California T-Bird. The keys were with flight services.

My audition wasn't until eleven o'clock, so I had time for my normal routine on Tuesday. Dick was surprised to see me on the track. We had the place to ourselves as high school sports were done for the year. I brought him up to date on our plans.

In turn, he told me that he and Janice were moving to Wall House on the first of June. I told him it was a shame that I wouldn't be around to help with the furniture. I don't think he believed me.

Before I went to the studio, I stopped at Mr. Baxter's office and handed him the signed contract. He told me he thought I might bring it with me if we received it on time. He wished me luck with the audition. He thought it was mine to lose as they had specifically requested that Sharon and I try out.

They saw rushes from *Bandits of Sherwood* and liked the chemistry between Sharon and me. I think that was a stretch because *Bandits* didn't have that many serious scenes.

I arrived at the studio, and it seemed like a homecoming after a long absence, which was strange as I had only been gone a week.

There was a small sound stage set up for our reading. Sharon and I were to do it together. If it worked, there would be no other tryouts. If it didn't, they would start calling others in.

Sharon was waiting there. We hugged each other and started reading through the script that was waiting. I realized it wasn't a script. They set a scene and where they wanted it to go, and we had to improvise from there. This was strange.

After some very quick introductions, which promptly went out of my mind, we went right to work. We were allowed to practice a scene several times until we felt comfortable, and then they turned the cameras on.

I don't know what they thought of it, but I thought it was fun. In one scene, Sharon had to be formal with me, and I was to misinterpret her actions, thinking her a snob. From there, she would turn up her nose and walk away, proving to me she was a snob.

Sharon started with, "Mr. Charles Dawson, if you were a gentleman, you would have held the door for me."

"I'm sorry that you feel that way. As you may have noticed, my arm has been injured while surfing, and I don't have the strength to open the door."

"I'm sorry you hurt yourself in such a plebian manner."

"I'm sorry that your nose is so high that you can't see past it."

"Humph," she grunted as she turned and walked away, nose in the air.

Not very impressive dialog, but the delivery was spot on. She came across as a snob and me as a clueless surf bum. They kept us at it for several hours. By the time we were finished, we both were a little punch drunk and carrying on something fierce. At one point, we had to argue, and we both got into it so much that we had hardly any lines. It was all foot-stomping and throwing dishes. It got very lively.

When the director yelled cut, we both looked at each other in disbelief. We weren't acting. We were having a fight, what about, I had no idea, but we were fighting.

Mr. Baxter had been sitting off to the side with the producers all this time. Since he was representing both Sharon and me, he had a lot riding on this. As Sharon and I were walking out, he gave a discreet thumbs-up.

Sharon and I were both on an adrenaline high from performing. It seemed more like an impromptu stage performance than a movie reading. We went over to the commissary for a late lunch.

Chapter 34

After we had settled down a little and quit replaying scenes, I asked Sharon if she had gotten back together with her parents. She had. She gave me credit for the going-to-church idea. It took her three weeks, but they finally invited her to sit with them. After church, she went home with them for lunch and told them her whole story since starting *Bandits*. She probably gave me too much credit.

I changed the topic to my conversations with Susan Wallace about my image. I told her the concern was that I would look like a goody-two-shoes. I had to do something a little risqué but far from over the top. I told her speeding was the only thing we could come up with, but that seemed lame to me.

She replied, "You need to be seen out with a Bad Girl."

I must have looked a little lost.

"You know a girl with a reputation."

"But I don't know any!"

At that point, she leaned over and rapped my head with her knuckles.

"Hey, Bad Girl right here."

It finally sunk in, "I thought you were trying to change your image."

"I am. I think we would offset each other if nothing else. It would keep people guessing. I'm not saying we should do anything except be seen at dinner several times. The tabloids will take care of the rest."

I was starting to get it. We need to talk this over with Susan, but it might work."

Sharon continued, "We could let your and Susan's media contacts know in advance what is happening. After the others all jump to the wrong conclusions, they could set the record straight and look on top of things. That would get us extra mileage. I'll also bring my parents in on it, so they know there isn't a problem."

"What about Bill? Are you guys dating?"

"It never got serious. We drifted apart. I think he was more interested in his comic books than me."

"A guy his age reading comic books?" I inquired.

"He digs that superhero stuff."

"Whatever turns him on, I guess."

We were getting up to leave when Mr. Baxter caught up with us. He had good news.

"They thought you guys were great. They wanted to see how you reacted together and how natural you were. That last bit where you pretended to argue put it over the top. They want to start negotiations."

Sharon and I exchanged glances. We both were excited about this.

"Great, Mr. Baxter. Try to get points for me."

Sharon wanted to know what I meant. Of course, she knew what points in a movie were. She hadn't even asked for them before as part of her payment. When she learned how much *Sir Nick* and *Bandits* owed me, she wanted to try the same. We came up with some rough numbers on the spot for Mr. Baxter to start with. As he put it, we will start asking for an arm and a leg and be satisfied with a couple of fingers.

I told him he had better do more than that, or I would give him the finger. I can't believe I said that.

He just laughed and said, "I will try to drag a leg or two back home."

He was late for another appointment, so he took his leave. Sharon and I continued our small talk for a while.

"Rick, there are all sorts of rumors about you and your dad chartering a 707 a week ago and bringing your family back here for a few days and then going back to Ohio after a short stay. The gossip columnists are trying to find out what went on."

"They will have to keep trying."

"Is everything okay?"

"Yes, it is, and that is all I can say."

"Okay, but it has been the talk around town. People have called me wanting to know if I've heard anything."

"That should be easy because you haven't."

"It has been. I was curious myself."

"Sharon, I would tell you if I could, but it involves my parents, and it is not my place to say."

At that, we dropped the subject. We did talk about our summer plans. Sharon intended to have a low-key summer with her family. She desperately wanted to reconnect with them. Staying at home with them would keep her away from the LA crowd that had encouraged her bad habits. It seemed like a reasonable plan to me.

For some reason, she didn't think my summer plan was reasonable at all. She thought my signing on as a deckhand was irresponsible and dangerous. How could my parents let me do such a thing? She almost lost it when I told her it was Mum's idea.

"What sort of a woman is she, endangering you in this manner? Doesn't she know it is a hard world out there?"

How could I tell Sharon that Mum was one of the hard people out there and that she was trying to prepare me for life as she saw it?

I tried to downplay the danger. She wasn't having any of it.

I finally had it and told Sharon, "My family has a different perspective on things than most normal American families. Look up my Mum and Dad's war records and see that we don't fit the profile of a safe middle-class American family."

I hurried along, telling her I was joining the family in England and would probably get to meet my godmother, the Queen. This news was enough to steer the conversation away from danger and my family. I would have to get better about not giving things away. I came too close in this conversation.

I would be in trouble if a real reporter started in on me. Of course, I couldn't say "no comment" to a friend.

We parted ways after that, promising to keep in contact over the summer as we could, and fingers crossed on the movie.

I stopped by Mr. Monroe's office, but Donna told me he was tied up in meetings all day. I did sweet talk her into scheduling a limo ride to LAX in the morning, so I wouldn't have to leave my car in long-term parking. Giving it a moment's thought, I made the pickup spot at Jackson House. I would leave it in the garage there for the summer.

After that, I went to the stunt area and lifted weights just for something to do. Few people were around. Those that were told me they had read that I was up to my old tricks. The story about the gas station robbery made the national editions.

I was tired of hearing, "Don't bring a knife to a gunfight."

First of all, it wasn't a knife. It was a bloody long sword; second, you use the tools you have, not the ones you wished for. While I thought this, I didn't say it. It wouldn't have helped. They were being smart-asses, and they knew it.

I left the studio, went home, and cleaned up. School had let out, so I gave Nina a call. She wasn't home; she was staying with some girlfriend, so that was out. I wish I had called yesterday when I found out I was coming here.

Instead, I went to the Brown Derby for dinner. It was a quiet night there, so I finished a meal and went for a ride. I finally ended up near Jackson House, so I went there and walked through the place. The same guards were in place and recognized me, so no problems with getting in.

The place was a mess. It was in the beginning phase of redecoration. The kitchen had been ripped out and now looked enormous. It was always big, but as a space, it was truly large. I wandered all around, peeking in every room. I realized once Mum knew I had stopped by, she would have a hundred questions. Of course, I would only have twenty or so answers.

I even went to the top of the tower. The view at night was fantastic. The lights over the LA basin were sparkling and brilliant. It almost made up for the light pollution hiding the stars. I remembered how bright the night was from my nights on the road last summer.

I returned home and went to bed. I had returned all my library books, so I had nothing to read. I was like a junky without his fix. Still, I didn't lay awake very long.

Chapter 35

I was up early and ran. Dick wasn't even out yet. He showed up at the track as I was finishing up. I told him my car would be in the garage at Jackson House, and the keys would be with the guards if he needed to use it.

He didn't think he would, but it was nice to know. He wished me a good summer, and I took off.

At the guard gate, I left the keys and wrote out a note permitting Dick or Janice Wyman to use the T-Bird all they needed. In the garage, there was even a car cover. It was for a larger vehicle, but it worked. The limo was pulling in when I arrived back at the front of the house. That pretty well described my trip home to Ohio.

Everything was on time. The only irritant was a guy sitting next to me on the flight. He continued about how it would be easy to commandeer one of these flights and hold it for ransom.

I don't know how Cooper thought he would get away, so until he did that, he was wasting his time. He tried to tell me he would use a parachute, but I pointed out the way the doors worked on these planes, he would smash against the side when he bailed out.

He didn't like it but had to agree. I tuned him out as quickly as I could. Safe to say, we would never hear of him again. When we got to Dayton, my car was where I left it, so it was an easy drive home. Since I lost three hours coming west to east, it was past dinner by the time I arrived.

Mum had saved me a plate of spaghetti, so I was okay with the food. If she hadn't set it aside, the crew would have devoured it. It looked like Denny was starting a growth spurt like I had last year.

Susan and William were there. I think they moved in. I found out they had moved in across the street with me. I took the opportunity to share what Sharon Bronson had said about needing a Bad Girl. That started a spirited discussion, to say the least.

When Susan finally got what Sharon meant into her head, she started considering the possibilities. She liked the idea of having our newspaper and magazine contacts in on the story upfront. It was an absolute necessity that Sharon's parents be aware of what was going on as we were seen together in public. Reporters would be certain to call them to try to get an outraged quote.

All Sharon and I would have to do would be seen at dinner a couple of times, and the rumor mill would take care of the rest. When asked, we would both deny which would be true. But we would deny it in a planned fashion. I would answer the questions in an evasive way. Sharon would take the attitude of "So what if we are?" I was underage, so it would draw attention quickly.

The whole thing would start in September after the new movie started. That was if we could negotiate a deal. The "romance" between Sharon and me would only last several weeks. We hoped it would raise questions about me. While I would still be viewed as the heroic type, at least on screen, I wouldn't be considered a goody-two-shoes. After it played for several weeks, we would sit down with our media types and give a full interview with all the parents sitting in.

I made a mental note to let Judy and Nina know what was happening as it started, so I wouldn't have my head handed to me.

While we were discussing all this, a young lady had been sitting at the end of the table coloring.

When we were finished, she came out with, "I think I will be a Bad Girl Princess."

We all looked at each other.

Dad shook his head and said, "Why me, Lord?"

There wasn't anything else to say.

We retired for the night. I reread a favorite about Major Martin of the Royal Marines and Operation Mincemeat. Now I know where Mum's term, pocket litter, comes from.

Thursday morning, it hit home that the school year was coming to an end. I had finished my morning run and was having coffee with Mum when Eddie and Denny came in and sat down. I asked them why they weren't getting ready for school. "School doesn't start until nine o'clock this morning. All we have to do today is hand in our books."

Just like that, it hit me. My ninth-grade year was over. This was weird. School finished months ago for me. I remember other years that during the last week of school, I was giddy with excitement that school was over, and I could be free for months. It seemed like a vacation would be forever.

I would have no responsibilities or expectations. Things certainly changed. First of all, a summer with no expectations would be boring in the extreme. I had to be doing something. Last year, I was rich because I had saved several hundred dollars from a paper route and lawn mowing. This year I was rich by any standard you could name. I was a multi-millionaire!

I didn't want to be lying around, letting the days pass, reading every waking minute. I wanted to be out there doing things. It wasn't reading the stories. It was living the stories.

There was a knock at the door. It was Sergeant Woodruff of the Bellefontaine Police. Dad invited him in like he had been expected. They sat and drank coffee talking about events around town. Mum brought in a half-awake Mary. Mary woke up when she saw a policeman at the table.

The sergeant ignored her and kept talking to Dad.

After a few minutes more, he stood and said, "Well, thanks for the coffee, Jack. I have to get back to work."

"What are you doing this morning?"

"There is a Bad Girl on the loose. We have to catch her and take her to jail."

"Oh, good luck."

And that was when I watched Mary from the corner of my eye. Her head jerked up when she heard the policeman say he was going to put the Bad Girl in jail. Her eyes were as big as saucers. She quickly looked down at her cereal.

After the good sergeant left, Mum, Dad, and I all kept straight faces. This was one of those stories that would be retold in future years. I would love to tell it to Mary's children many years from now, but I bet Mum and Dad would beat me to the punch.

There was one outcome. We never heard another word about her being a Bad Girl Princess.

I spent the day getting ready to go to sea. The plan was that I would fly to New York tomorrow and sign in at the Seaman's Union Hall. I had my union card, so it was good to go. There were so many ships in and out of New York that I would be gone in a couple of days.

There were no child labor laws once you were on the high seas, so I would be legal once we cleared New York harbor.

Mum gave me my elusive British passport. It was interesting to look at. It was much larger than my blue United States passport. It was black. The outside stated "British Passport}, then below it, the "United Kingdom of Great Britain and Northern Ireland". The inside cover stated, "Her Britannic Majesty's Secretary of State Requests and requires in the Name of Her Majesty all those whom it may concern to allow without let or hindrance and to afford the bearer such assistance and protection as may be necessary."

That was so cool. The next page listed me as The Honorable Richard Edward Jackson.

She also gave me a money belt that I could wear around my waist. It wasn't very thick so it wouldn't be noticeable. Inside were ten one-hundred-dollar bills and ten five-pound notes. There were also ten United States quarter-ounce ten-dollar gold pieces. She warned me that they were worth the going rate for gold, not just ten dollars.

There were coin slots in the belt where they would sit against my back. I tried it on. With a shirt tucked in, you would never know it was there. It wasn't uncomfortable nor restricted my movement, so it was a winner.

I also had my United States passport, two hundred dollars in smaller bills, and my union card in a leather billfold. There was also my trusty Buck knife. I thought about something longer with a locking blade. They were illegal in the US, so I thought better of it. Guns were completely out.

No captain wants an unknown armed crewman aboard. If caught, I would be lucky if they waited for the next port to put me off. The union sent me a brochure with my card spelling out the rules pretty clearly. Once I was at sea, the captain was the law. Judge, jury, and executioner if need be.

Dad picked up a seaman's duffle bag from the Army-Navy store. I packed five sets of work clothes along with my shaving kit. I had also picked up another pair of Red Wing steel-toed work boots along with four pairs of leather gloves. I thought I was ready to go to sea.

It was a quiet evening at home. Mum fixed pizza, and we all played Monopoly. Even William set his camera aside and joined in. Mum and Mary took the honors. I asked William as an aside if he had talked to Roberta when I was out of town.

It so happened that they met at Islay's for coffee while I was in California. Since she wouldn't know anyone when she got there, he had volunteered to help her get her bearings. I asked how they had gotten together. He told me they had run into each other accidentally when he had to run down to Hadley's to pick up some film. Mum winked at me, so I knew it wasn't as much of an accident as he thought. Guys, we never have a chance.

I went to sleep without reading anything. I was tired and wanted to go to sleep so I could start my new adventure.

Chapter 36

In the morning, the whole family was up to see me off. Hugs and kisses all around. A Maverick limo driven by John Sullivan picked me up on time.

I sat up front with John on the ride down to Dayton. I asked him how the betting of horses was going. He told me Mr. Barnes was frustrated. He had won a trotter, so he took it to Scioto Downs in Columbus and entered it in a five thousand dollar claiming race.

It won and was promptly claimed. It seemed the horse was valued at ten thousand dollars. Not only was he out the money, but he also didn't have a horse to bet. He would have to buy one. That was funny.

John dropped me off in Dayton. Unlike my other trips, the airline hadn't been warned that they had a star on board. I still flew first class, but it was a quiet trip for me. With my rough clothes, people probably wondered what I was doing up front.

One stewardess recognized me from a previous flight, but other than a discreet, "Welcome aboard, Mr. Jackson," she didn't make a fuss.

It gave me time to think on the way to Idlewild. If my ninth grade were a book, it was ending without a bang or any large resolution of problems. It was like living in that way. It went on. Very seldom were there events that brought everything to a neat conclusion. Even death usually leaves a lot of loose ends in a person's life. My school year was no different. There were a lot of things that happened but no dramatic conclusions. Maybe that was for the best.

Upon arrival, I retrieved my seabag from the baggage area and caught a cab to mid-town Manhattan. I was staying at the Waldorf Astoria. They treated me like everyone who came to town had a seabag instead of luggage. The bellboy had his hand out for a tip as usual. I had a dollar ready which was over-tipping, but he carried that bag for me, which was heavier than any suitcase.

I took a long walk and ended up at Times Square. I must say they have a lot of lights. I thought about buying a ticket for a play on Saturday but decided I would rather sightsee.

By the time I got back to the hotel, I called it a night.

Saturday morning, I woke up at my usual time. Last night, I inquired at the hotel about running, and they recommended Central Park, so I tried that. It was fun, and there were certainly interesting people out and about.

After that, I had a large breakfast and found the union hiring hall by the Port of New York building. It was a lot like the oil rig hiring hall in that the people waiting for a job looked like the dregs of the earth. Many were sleeping on benches as though they had been there for days.

I checked in and was called almost immediately. I presented my card, and the guy behind the desk read it like it had a secret code embedded. It did. He excused himself and came back with a supervisor.

I thought, oh boy. Now I have trouble. Instead, I received a hearty handshake.

"Mr. Jackson, it is nice to see a real worker apply. I know you haven't been to sea, but your two other unions have given you an excellent recommendation. At times, we are ashamed of the people we have available to ship out. It hurts our reputation, and captains don't even bother to pick up crew here. Now, what are you looking for?"

"I would like to be on a cargo ship for two months ending up in or near England."

"Other than that, you have no preferences?"

"I don't know enough to have any."

"How about a trip to South America, then work your way back up the African coast? Ending up in Spain in late July, it is easy to get to England."

"That sounds perfect. I'll take it."

"You realize as you are new at this, you will have every scut job on the ship?"

"I understand. It's the experience I'm looking for."

"Good. We will sign you on the *Pride of Liberia*; we owe her a good crewman, so this works great."

He told me it was leaving from the Red Hook terminal on Sunday evening. He gave me a pass to get onto the pier.

As I turned to leave, he whispered, "Tell your Mum Mr. Lucky was glad to be of service."

I nodded my head and got out of there. So that is why it was so easy. And I worried that my image was too clean.

I went shopping that afternoon. At F.A.O. Schwarz, I found a *Sir Nicklaus* lunch box. I bought three of them, one for each of the kids. Of course, the boys wouldn't use them, but it was fun anyway. They even had a *Sir Nick* Barbie doll out. I wondered if I was getting any money for this. I did pick up some items the boys would like and, of course, the doll for Mary.

For Mum and Dad, I made a stop at Macy's and picked up matching sweaters for them. It seemed like they were going to be the big thing in the fall. I went to customer service, and they were helpful. They wrapped everything, including the toys, for shipment to Bellefontaine. For a few dollars more, they even took care of the shipping. What a store!

On the way back to the hotel, I was walking close to the street. Two women were about to step off the curb. They looked to their right but not at oncoming traffic to their left. A taxi was speeding at them as they stepped off the curb. I grabbed both of them barely in time. The taxi jammed on its brakes and veered to the left, causing another cab in the next lane to clip it.

Both vehicles came to a stop with no further damage and no apparent injuries. In good New York tradition, drivers jumped out of their cabs and started shouting at each other.

I still had both ladies by the arm. It was a young lady and another who could be her mother. The young lady was about my age and had the bluest eyes I had ever seen. Her hair was a pale blonde, and her eyebrows were so pale it looked like she didn't have any. Her complexion was perfect. Her figure was very full in a good way. I stared too long because the older lady tugged at my arm.

As I let them go, a man came running up, "Lady Pamela, are you alright?"

As they turned to him, I walked away. This was my vacation, and I was out of the hero business for a while. There were a lot of people on the sidewalk, most stopping to view the commotion, so I was able to make my escape.

I made an early night of it.

I ran in the morning in Central Park. Then I made a call home to let them know all was as scheduled. I did tell Mum about the comment from the union supervisor.

She told me, "Rick, I didn't ask for anything. That is how tight these people are on the docks. Please make no mistake about it. They control them."

We both agreed that it didn't upset any balances. I told them to expect a package from Macy's.

From there, I checked out of the hotel with my seabag and took a cab to the Red Hook Terminal in Hoboken, NJ. There was no problem when I arrived. The purser on the *Pride of Liberia* was expecting me, so it was an easy transition. He had me sign the ship's papers and took my American passport. For its safety, he said. I figured it was to prevent me from jumping ship.

I confirmed that I was leaving for Spain at the end of July. That was fine and what he had been told. He had a hand show me where I was to bunk.

After the guy showed me my bunk, he took off. I heard a deep voice behind me.

"It looks like we have a new toy, guys."

The ninth grade was over, and my "vacation" had started.

Chapter 37

I turned quickly, ready to fight for my life. Standing there were three sailors. The one in front was a scrawny little guy with the biggest muscles on his arms I had ever seen.

"Had you worried, didn't I? Name's Jim Kendrick but my friends call me Popeye."

As he said this, he stuck out his hand for a shake. It felt like holding onto a steel bar when I grasped his hand. He didn't play any games. He just shook my hand and let it go. If he had wanted, he would have me on my knees in no time.

Kendrick went on, "This here is Bo Grady and Steve "Patch" Johns. Both are able-bodied seamen. My job is to get you squared away. Let's go to the galley, and I'll fill you in."

I felt enormous relief as I realized I not only wasn't about to die but was getting some direction in my new job. As they headed to the galley, I acknowledged that I had willingly walked into something over my head and that I was scared. It hadn't sunk in until the fear started to lift.

On the way, Popeye explained they were part of a four-ship company fleet and had their ways.

"People think sailors have a common ranking system and keep watches all the same on every ship. That's not true. While the Navy's are standardized, even they differ from each other. I would much rather serve with the British where you get an issue of grog than with the US Navy, which is teetotal."

"Here, our watch system is straightforward. Each watch is four hours, and the first watch starts at midnight and runs until four a.m. There are eight bells to a watch, one every half hour. After the first half-hour, it is one bell. At the end of the four hours, it is eight bells. We do overtime on a full watch basis of four hours or a dog watch of two hours.

"How did you end up here anyway?"

This question was asked as we arrived at the galley and poured coffee.

"I signed up at the hiring hall, and the agent asked if I minded this voyage. He owed the captain a favor of a sober, physically fit crewman. Since it got me to Spain at the end of July, I said yes. By the way, what is the name of this boat? I was told but only remembered the berth location."

Popeye laughed at me and replied, "This is the *Pride of Liberia*, and you sure are a green one. This *ship* has had some pretty sad crews in the past, but we seem to be okay now."

"Uh, what is the difference between a boat and a ship?"

"A ship can carry a boat, but a boat can't carry a ship. It is a matter of size. That isn't even a one hundred percent definition. Ocean-going fishing boats can be pretty damn big, but they are still called boats. Same for ore carriers on the Great Lakes. Some are bigger than us, but they are still called boats. For most of us on the ocean, a ship can haul a boat on board, but not the other way around."

"Thanks. I see I have a lot to learn."

"As long as you learn before your ignorance kills you."

I felt comforted by that thought.

We had a cup of coffee in the galley while Popeye explained the ship.

Popeye explained that the *Pride*, as he called it, is a fifteen-thousand-ton general-purpose cargo ship. It was four hundred and forty-one feet and six inches in length; its beam was fifty-nine feet and four inches. Two triple-inverted quadruple expansion engines powered it with two oil-fired boilers. It carried ten thousand and eight hundred-fifty-six tons deadweight with a crew of forty-eight.

What I learned from this was this is a big ship. The look on my face must have shown my non-comprehension because Popeye laughed and told me it would come to me over time.

"Let's get you squared away to work. First, I will show you how to arrange your cabin, and we will check out the gear you brought."

My cabin turned out to be about twice the size of a single bed. I could fit in it and turn around, but that was it. It had a small fold-down desk, cabinets, and drawers to stow my gear, even a small "head". It was equipped with a shower. The toilet was in the shower. I figured I could shower and shave while doing my daily business.

I'm still fifteen.

Popeye checked my gear out while I was putting it away. He approved of the work clothes that I had brought. My steel-toed safety boots caught his eye, worn and scuffed as they were.

"Had these for a while?"

"Yes, sir," I replied.

"Well, they tell a good story. You are willing to work. And I work for a living, so don't call me sir."

"Yes, s—" I started but cut myself off. "Yes, Mr. Popeye."

Popeye flicked me in the back of the head with a finger that felt like an iron bar.

"It's Popeye," he growled.

"Got it, Popeye."

My head smarted.

"Now that we understand who I am, let's talk about your work. I'm starting you out on our third watch, which is 8 a.m. until noon, then the fifth watch which is 4 p.m. to 8. Any overtime you are asked to put in will be on the fourth watch, from noon to two or four, depending on how long we need you. You can turn down overtime, but most sailors need the money. I would recommend you as the new guy you work when asked.

"I'll work all I'm asked, Popeye," I responded as I rubbed my sore head.

"This voyage isn't long enough for you to make able seaman, but we will get some of your tickets punched. Starting tomorrow and the third watch, you will be chipping paint. We might let you have a paintbrush when and if you get good at that. The fifth watch will be spent checking out containers in the cargo hold. Things shift all the time down there, so the tie-downs and chains have to be checked constantly."

It sounded pretty comfy to me. I had helped remove wallpaper and painted many an apartment, and it was fairly easy to do.

Popeye took me to the bridge, where I was introduced to Captain Jonas Grumby, First Mate Ben Cartwright, Second Mate Henry Warniment, and Third Mate Tony Banta.

They were all pleasant to me, but you could see I was just another sailor to them.

I woke in the middle of the night to a thrumming that went completely through the ship. I realized that we had cast off and were underway. I dropped right back to sleep.

Chapter 38

I woke up at my usual 5 a.m. The previous day I had checked out the deck with the thought of running in mind. Popeye told me it was okay but to always be cautious if it was rough weather. It would be easy to go overboard.

It would take about ten trips to go a mile, so I decided that I would only do a couple of miles a day for the voyage. I would pay for it in my conditioning later, but you could only go in a small circle for so long.

The deck had a coating so that it wasn't slippery, and there was good lighting all the way around. The lighting was so good I could run at any hour of the day or night. After my run, I felt tightness in my legs and realized that running on steel decking was different from anything I had ever done. I would have to think about this. Maybe it wasn't a good idea to run at all.

I did get in my pushups and sit-ups before running, so it wasn't a total loss.

Popeye collected me for my first watch at sea. We weren't that far at sea as the coastline was visible to our right. I wore my safety helmet, safety glasses, steel-toed boots, and gloves as instructed. Popeye gave me a bright orange vest to wear so other workers could see me easily.

Chipping paint wasn't the same as sanding a wall in a house. This paint was layers upon layers from many paintings. It was bubbled and cracked and a general pain. It took a hammer and chisel to chip away the loose flakes. I asked about using a power tool, but it was explained that an electric drill with a steel wire brush would weigh about ten pounds, and I would last about half an hour before my arms fell off.

I wondered if the drill weight could be reduced using plastic housing but forgot about it in the excitement of starting my new job.

That excitement lasted all of five minutes. After that, it was work. It was boring work. I tried to convince myself that I was making the ship better so it would last longer. By the end of my four-hour shift, my arms felt like they were about to fall off. I was wondering if I could find any plugs to pull to sink this cursed vessel.

When Popeye collected me, he commented that I had done a lot of work.

"Good job Rick. You cleared more than I thought you would. Did you take any breaks?"

"No, am I allowed to?"

"Ten minutes is okay, or if you need a trip to the head. You mean I didn't tell you that?"

"You must have forgotten it."

Popeye smirked, "I seem to forget to tell every new guy on his first shift. I find out what they are made of really quickly. You hung in there. As I said, good job."

I would have hit him, but I couldn't raise my arms that high.

When I returned to my tiny cabin, I cleaned up, took a nap, and then went to the galley for lunch. Lunch consisted of cold cuts set out to make your sandwich. They were quite good.

After lunch, I wandered around the ship, learning the layout. Some crewmembers were playing basketball on the main deck, but after watching for a while, I moved on. My arms were feeling a lot better by the time my next watch started. I met Popeye at Cargo Hold One as instructed, all geared up.

Popeye handed me a large flashlight from a rack near the hatch.

"When you go below, always grab a flashlight in case you have to go into an enclosed space. Sailors have got into serious trouble by not being able to see what they were around."

He also handed me a short iron bar he called a belaying pin.

"We use this to tap on ropes and chains to check if they are tight. This isn't a belaying pin as used in the old sailing ships, but the name has continued."

We climbed down into the cavernous hold. Crates of every size and description were stacked from the deck to the overhead. They were tied down with rope or chained into place.

"Rick, if this would shift in a storm, we would be in bad trouble. We have to check these constantly. The way the ship moves, things work loose all the time. I will show you how to tighten things up, but you never come down alone and never work with loose cargo by yourself. It will get you dead quick."

We worked our way around the hold. I pounded on ropes as I went. I found one that had some give in it when hit. Popeye double-checked and agreed that it needed tightening. Using the iron bar as a turnbuckle, we refastened the wooden crate.

As we went on, I marveled at the sheer number and sizes of the containers in the hold. I asked Popeye how they ever figured out what went where.

"That's the hardest part of my job. As bosun, I'm in charge of the deck, which includes bringing all the cargo on board with the derricks and stowing it in the hold.

"It takes experience to get it right. I have to check everything onshore, then tell the longshoremen what order I want it in. Of course, they want to do it the easiest for them, so I have had several discussions on the issue. Nowadays, they do as I say."

As he made these remarks, he held a massive arm up and made a fist.

As we worked our way around the hold, I thought about all the labor that went into moving the cargo. They had to unload it from a truck or railcar and then reload it on a ship. Once it arrived at its destination, the process was reversed.

It dawned on me that it had to be loaded on a truck or railcar in the first place. In some cases, it was hauled from the factory on a truck to a rail station, by train to the ship, then from the ship to a truck onto another railroad, then onto another truck. Each container had to be handled five or six times. It was a shame they didn't have a huge container that could be loaded at the factory and then opened at its destination. That would cut the amount of handling tremendously. It would also give a uniform container size, making loading decisions easier.

I needed to give this some serious thought.

From New York, we coasted down to the mouth of the Delaware River and turned upstream. Our next destination was Baltimore to pick up more cargo. It would save a lot of miles and fuel by using the Delaware Canal to go from the Delaware River to the top of Chesapeake Bay. This was better than going clear down to the mouth of the bay and coming back up.

We picked up a Delaware Canal pilot before entering the canal. The pilot was a guy named Noah Ireland. Popeye said the guy had been doing it as long as anyone could remember. He thought he must be a hundred or so, but that couldn't be.

We would change pilots at the Delaware/ Maryland state line. The Maryland pilot would take us on to Baltimore.

While we were going through the canal, we passed a restaurant near Chesapeake City. It was Schaefer's Canal House, a local landmark. It was within feet of passing ships. The restaurant would always announce the names of any passing ships and their listed cargo. They picked this up from radio communication between the ship and the pilot.

This evening a young lady and her family were having dinner there. They were celebrating her Air Force general's father's second star. They were seated next to the window and had an excellent view of the passing ship. Cheryl Hawthorne saw a sailor standing on the deck. It looked a lot like her old boyfriend, Rick Jackson, but it couldn't be. He was now a movie star in Hollywood.

She mentioned this to her parents, but the ship had passed the restaurant by the time they looked.

Her mom Cynthia said, "You liked him, didn't you?"

"Yes, I did, Mom. I think he was my first love."

Her dad, Major General James Hawthorne, asked, "Shall we tell your new boyfriend Bill about this?"

"Dad, I think we can pass. Thank you."

In the meantime, I was standing on the ship's deck, wondering if I would meet any girls on this trip. Girls were more on my mind all the time.

Chapter 39

The next day, as we loaded cargo in Baltimore, I continued chipping paint, and at the same time, I paid attention to the loading. Not only was it time-consuming, but it could be dangerous. A cable broke while they were hoisting a crate aboard. The wooden box broke into pieces when it hit the deck, and its contents, some sort of machine, smashed to bits. Luckily, no one was under it.

This gave me more reason to think of some sort of large container. As I was thinking these thoughts, a short trailer was pulled onto the dock. Most trailers were forty to fifty feet long. This one was only about thirty feet. The trailer doors were opened, and longshoremen began unloading some fragile-looking boxes by hand.

I thought it would be neat if they could have just hoisted the entire trailer aboard. A light bulb went off. Why not have a container that would sit on a frame? You could load the container at the factory, load it onto a special frame that the semi would pull, move the container to a railcar directly, then onboard a ship, and not touch the contents until it arrived at its destination.

That afternoon I started making a list of the design issues. I came up with the height, width, and length of the box, the weight that it could hold, and hard points to lift from. Later I asked Popeye how much dead weight one of the cranes onboard would lift. He told me almost a hundred thousand pounds or fifty tons.

I remembered hearing that an over-the-road truck could take forty thousand pounds or so, so there was plenty of room to work with.

I dashed off a letter to my patent attorney with sketches of my idea. I asked him to draw up an NDA for Paul Samson, the mechanical engineer. I wrote another letter to Paul listing out the idea and asked him to investigate what size and materials would be best for a container as described.

We were in the dock long enough for me to have them mailed. I didn't go off the ship, as we didn't have liberty in Baltimore, but Popeye got the purser to drop them in the mail for me. Popeye thought they were letters to girlfriends. He joshed me about sending two of them.

Popeye did look at the addressees as he handed them to the purser, one letter to a lawyer and another to an engineer. That was one strange kid they had on board.

From Baltimore, we sailed to Miami. I had more time to think while chipping paint. I wrote a letter to Dad explaining my thoughts. The cargo container would be the easy part. We needed a truck bed to hold the container. Once at the ship, there wouldn't be a problem rigging it to bring it onboard or to offload.

The problem would be at the other end, where they had to haul it to its destination.

With that in mind, I asked Dad to look into purchasing a small truck line that specialized in trans-ocean shipping. We would need one that has customers who have many small containers. This was for the American side of the equation. To further complicate matters, we would need to buy a truck line or at least plan with one at the point of delivery to have the special trailers available.

There was also the matter of return loads on each container. The containers would have to be marked and sent to the correct destination, but I figured Dad's railroad experience would come in handy. They had to identify and track every railcar, so it had been done before.

It was two weeks before my family would fly to England, so Dad would have time to set things in motion. I didn't know where to find the needed truck line, but there must be a method. Some business brokerage or freight association would probably be able to help. I put that suggestion in the letter and hoped it would work.

After we left Miami for Havana, I mentioned my hunt for a truck line to Popeye. At that point, Popeye knew I was strange. He took me to the purser. The purser dealt with the freight companies that delivered their cargo to the dock. A freight forwarder handled that, but the purser paid the bills, so he knew what was going on.

Purser Sam Simpson came up with a thought.

"There is one small trucking firm we used to use in Baltimore. On this last trip, another one was chosen, and I asked why. Narrow Freight is in financial trouble, and they were hesitant to use them."

"Thanks, Mr. Simpson. You don't happen to have any contact information for them, do you?"

After some rummaging around in his files, the purser found an old invoice with the company's contact information. I copied it down and thanked the purser profusely.

Popeye was curious about what was going on and asked me directly.

I thought for a moment and asked, "Would you mind signing an NDA?"

"What in the seven hells is an NDA?"

I explained it to Popeye. While I did, Popeye looked a little pop-eyed. You could tell he thought this kid was strange!

"Sure, I wouldn't have anyone to tell anything to anyway."

Later I wrote up one the best I could from memory. I certainly had seen enough of them in the last year.

Popeye signed it, and the purser witnessed it as a Notary Public. As Simpson witnessed the document, you could tell he was bursting with curiosity but resisted asking what was going on. There were four copies made, one for Popeye and three for me. I would mail one to my patent attorney and two to Dad.

Once that was out of the way, we walked the deck during the short cruise to Havana. Popeye was about dancing as the details unfolded.

"You can make this happen? This will change our entire business. What were days in port will become hours! The longshoremen will hate it at first, as many will lose their jobs. At the same time, shipping costs will go down, so more will be shipped, recovering many of those jobs. On the plus side, it will be a lot easier job.

"Rick, this is going to take real money to get it going. Do you have access to real money?"

At this point, I told Popeye my story. To say Popeye was amazed is putting it mildly. When he heard that I was working my way as a deckhand while the family flew to England, he about busted a gut laughing.

"Your mum is one tough bird. She reminds me of a girl I dated in England during the war, Sybil Newman."

"I have an Aunt Sybil Newman."

"Your mum's name wouldn't be Peg by any chance?"

"Yes, it is."

"She ended up marrying some MP officer?"

"Yeah, she married Jack Jackson."

"Boy, it is a small world. I came within a hair's breadth of being your uncle but got put on the Murmansk run, then we had to make a run to the Pacific, and we never caught up again. Who did Sybil end up marrying?"

"She didn't. Word in the family is that some sailor broke her heart, and she has been alone ever since."

Popeye left rather abruptly.

Chapter 40

When we docked in Havana, I was informed that we would be in port for several days and that I could go ashore. I jumped at the chance. Instead of going to the bars and houses of ill repute with the others on leave, I hired a taxi to take me on a tour of the city.

My taxi driver complimented me on my Spanish. While I was out, I bought some stamps and posted a letter to Mum telling her about a certain sailor.

After being shown most of the city, I paid up and dropped off at the main shopping plaza. I bought a tourist trinket to send home to the family, but nothing significant caught my eye. I stopped at a small restaurant for lunch.

While waiting to be served, I observed the other diners. One group, in particular, caught my attention. They appeared to be Cuban Army and Russian soldiers. They were having a good time like old comrades in arms. Several of the soldiers were involved in trading unit patches.

The patches looked interesting. The Russian ones had rockets on them.

While I was eating, most of the soldiers left, including all the Russians. Remaining behind were two of the Cuban soldiers who had been trading patches. They had a stack of them in front of them and were having a low discussion.

I could hear scattered words. I picked up enough to realize that they were discussing selling the extra patches and were trying to decide how much to charge. I took a chance and approached the men. They named some sky-high prices when they realized I was interested in the unit insignia. After some spirited negotiation where I was called a thief and worse and I cast aspersions on their manhood, a deal was struck.

For twenty dollars US, I was now the proud owner of the unit and rank insignia of the 43rd Guards Missile Division of the 43rd Rocket Army of the Soviet Union. Upon leaving the restaurant, I purchased envelopes and more postage to send the patches to Mum for safekeeping. I also suspected she would be interested in what was happening in Cuba these days. Relations between the US and Cuba have been deteriorating ever since Castro came into power.

Before I dropped the patches in the mailbox, I had second thoughts. I would mail them from the ship's next port of call, Buenos Aires. I took another taxi back to the ship.

Unknown to me, I had been followed all day.

After I boarded the ship, my tail reported that the American sailor was just a kid out for the afternoon. The tail had elected to wait for me outside of the restaurant so he wouldn't have to buy a meal. This way, he could eat cheaper elsewhere and pocket his per diem. He didn't see me make my purchase.

Once back at the ship, I remained on board for the rest of the stay. Two days later, we sailed for Buenos Aires on June 16. Two days after that, we ran into a developing low-pressure trough. It hadn't been forecast, but according to Popeye, who kept track of news from the bridge, it was building rapidly and might be a problem.

The barometer was 29.8 inches of mercury and falling. He had all hands battening hatches and checking all the cargo lashings. He had ropes put up between all open areas that would still have to be accessed under heavy seas. I thought this was total overkill as the skies were clear and sunny.

The next day bands of rain kept coming over the ship, and the seas became heavier. I didn't have motion sickness problems, so I thought it was neat. The barometer readings were now 28.5 and still falling. The wind out of the east was now coming in gusts.

I asked Popeye what would be happening.

"We are going south as fast as we can. Right now, the captain thinks we can cross the path of the storm before the main body catches us. I'm not certain about that. This one seems to be moving mighty fast."

"What can we expect if we get caught up in it?"

"I hope you don't find out. If it gets bad, we will have to turn and drive into it, so we don't get struck by the waves broadside and capsize. It is moving too fast for us to turn and run in front of it. Going south by east is the best we can do. Going due south would have us on land. We need to round South America's northern edge before turning completely south. That means we are running directly into the storm right now."

"How bad will it get?"

"Pretty bad. I have seen some nasty storms in my thirty-some years at sea, but this might be the worst of them all."

"What should I be doing?"

"First, go to your cabin and stow anything loose. Then come back here and help with the galley. Cookie is making a bunch of cold food because there is a good chance he won't be able to cook for a few days."

I did all that. In the meantime, the storm-clutched ship started to roll and pitch in ways I hadn't experienced before. It also started to make sounds. There would be creaks and moans. They started high-pitched like the ropes and lines of the ship were thrumming under tension.

As the day progressed, the sounds deepened as though the entire hull was alive and twisting. At this point, all we sailors could do was stay inside the ship. Water was bursting over the prow in such waves that anyone venturing out would be swept away.

We couldn't even talk to each other over the roar of the wind and water, and the ship's groans.

At one point, Popeye leaned over to me and shouted into my ear.

"I just felt our turn. We are running directly into the storm now. The captain must be afraid we will broach if we try to cross its path anymore."

The ship was running into the teeth of thirty-foot and higher waves. It would rise as the wave came under it and then crash back down as the wave passed them. I was beginning to wonder if the ship would break in half.

As I thought it couldn't get any worse, it did. The ship went up on a wave, and then it felt like the whole ship twisted as it lurched sideways. I thought for sure the ship would break up when we hit the bottom of the wave's trough. It didn't.

As I sat there, I began to realize how those guys in the first wave on D-Day felt. There was nothing they could do about what was about to happen. All choices were gone. All they could do was endure and hope to survive.

The trough was the scariest moment of the storm. It took another six hours of battering before it started to ease, but it was never as bad again as when the ship almost corkscrewed into the waves. There was a good chance that we would have gone under, but we didn't.

When things were quieter, Popeye asked me, "Are you still glad you've become a sailor?"

I replied in a shaky voice, "Sure, piece of cake."

Popeye was chuckling, "You would be more convincing if you still weren't shaking."

"My God, Popeye, how close did we come from breaking up?"

"Too damn close for my liking. That was by far the worst I have been in. Now let's go up to the bridge and see what we need to do."

When we got to the bridge, there was a very bleary-eyed watch crew. The captain had been on the bridge with all the mates for the entire storm. Now things were settling down. They wanted to restore order and get some sleep.

The biggest problem facing the ship was the radio room. The equipment wasn't as secure as they thought and had broken free from its brackets. Unfortunately, the radio officer, "Sparks", was in the room at the time. He had a broken collarbone, right arm, and severe concussion.

The captain and mates tried to figure out how to restore communication, but none had any real experience. I listened for a while and then spoke up.

"I have a ham radio license; would you like me to see if I can get anything to work?"

The skipper shrugged his shoulders and replied, "Sounds like the best deal going. Give it a try."

I went to the radio room behind the bridge. It looked like the place had been worked over with a sledgehammer. I returned the equipment to its apparent places. The microphone was beyond salvage. The transceiver, while dented, came on when I powered it up. I could send and receive but had nothing to convert the signal to voice. I checked out the antenna. By some miracle, it was intact.

I rummaged in the closed cabinets and found a varnished wooden box. A Morse code key was set up, which must have been fifty years old. Now, if I could remember what I learned in Boy Scouts, I was in business.

After hooking it up, I sent CQ, CQ, CQ. This is KC69ATM calling any station. My dits and dahs were slow, but I picked up as I worked at it. I would never be professional, but at eight words per minute, I would be able to get the job done.

Nothing came back at once, but after several attempts, I got a return. It was a land-based operator in Sao Paulo, Brazil. After exchanging call signs and locations, I signed off and went back to the bridge.

"Skipper, we can send and receive in Morse, but that is it. Do you want to compose a message?"

"Hold on for a minute."

As he spoke, the skipper wrote out a message for me to send.

It read, "Lost radio. Sparks injured. Going to Caracas VZ to replace radio and get Sparks to a hospital. End Captain Jonas Grumby, *Pride of Liberia*."

It was addressed to the shipping company's headquarters.

My CQ was returned by an operator in Puerto Rico who said he would relay the message. I let the skipper know the message was sent. I was told to take over the radio duties until further notice.

I continued straightening up the radio shack. Sparks was in the ship's small infirmary. I would be bunking in the radio shack until we docked in Caracas. I set up an alarm so if a message started coming in during the night, that would wake me.

I had been in the shack for three hours and was getting bored as I scanned the airwaves when I heard my call sign. There was an incoming message from the owners. They acknowledged our difficulties and confirmed Skipper's actions.

It took thirty hours of steaming, but we made Caracas with no further issues.

Chapter 41

Once we docked in Caracas, arrangements were made for the ship to be surveyed. It had been under terrible stress during the storm and had to be structurally checked out. Breaking down and having to be towed at sea was one thing. Breaking in half was another.

During this period, the crew was allowed shore leave. Immigration officials checked out our passports, which were left with the ship. We were given temporary identity cards to allow us to go from ship to shore for our brief (hopefully) stay.

Popeye and his friends gave me a taxi tour of the city. My conclusion at the time was that Caracas wasn't a place I would care to live. I would refer to it as a hole. I did take the opportunity to mail the letter to Mum with the Soviet patches.

After that afternoon foray ashore, I elected to stay in the dock area. It was large enough that I could run, which I did twice a day. It felt good to stretch my legs. Popeye thought I was crazy.

On the second day, a replacement radio officer came aboard. He had been flown in from headquarters with several large packages containing new radio equipment. I helped him set it up and then was out of the radioman's job. I was back to working as an ordinary seaman. This was okay with me as I wasn't hunting for a new profession.

We were released on the third day to return to the sea.

On the morning tide, we sailed for Buenos Aires.

I found out that I had been promoted. Instead of chipping paint, I was allowed to paint the surfaces I had chipped! The only good thing about it was that I was able to give serious thought to the container business as I thought of it. I concluded besides owning a truck line and having arrangements with a shipping company, I should also invest in a company to manufacture the containers.

I would also have to find some way to convince ports to put in special areas for the moving and storage of the containers along with special handling equipment.

Then there was the question of what would be needed at a railroad yard to handle containers. Many questions had to be answered along the way. I hoped that I could call home from Buenos Aires and catch my parents before they left for England and get a progress update from Dad.

Several days later, when I finished my evening watch desperately needing a shower, I was caught at my cabin door by Bo and Patch.

"What have we here, Patch?"

"Looks like a slimy Pollywog to me, Bo,"

At that point, they roughly grabbed me before I could protest. They began removing my shirt and pants.

I was about to start physical action when Patch said, "Now we have to dress you to appear in front of King Neptune."

That was weird to me for a moment. Were they planning on throwing me overboard? Then it dawned on me we were crossing the equator sometime during the night. I relaxed as they stripped me down. They turned all of my clothes inside out. Then they let me get redressed, with everything on backward.

I was taken to the galley/dining area. There a bearded King Neptune, in a glorious robe, crown, and trident, waited along with his court. Popeye, in a ragged robe with paper stars pinned onto it, wearing a tacky false beard holding a bent homemade trident with a crown made of a hand-cut strip of aluminum, awaited with a similarly clad court.

"So, this slimy Polliwog who wants to become a Shellback has answered our subpoena," roared Popeye.

"Is that true, Polliwog?"

I stammered out, "What subpoena?"

"You deny you received a subpoena?"

I began to realize I was in deep. "Sir, maybe I didn't recognize the subpoena."

"We must get to the bottom of this. Administer the truth serum."

Patch brought forward a bottle of a foul-looking concoction and said, "Open wide."

I thought, in for a penny in for a pound, and opened wide. Patch poured a generous dollop into my open mouth. I would've screamed if I could. My mouth puckered up and burned like the fires of hell at the same time.

I was gasping for breath when King Neptune asked again. "Did you receive a subpoena?"

"Yes, sir," I gasped in a mangled voice.

"You lied to my court. Whip him!"

Bo and Patch brought out cut-off lengths of fire hose and pummeled me about the neck and buttocks. They didn't hit me hard at all. By this time, I had enough wits about me that I screamed in mock agony and pain anyway.

"Help him with his pain," said Neptune.

Bo had me open my mouth, and Patch cracked a raw egg and poured it into my mouth.

Next, Neptune said, "He needs to kiss the Royal Baby's Belly."

The Royal Baby was Third Mate Tony Banta dressed in a huge diaper. I wondered what the black stuff that Tony had smeared on his belly was. I quickly found out it was axle grease as I got a mouth full.

"Introduce the Royal Court to the new Shellback. My Queen is Her Highness Amphitrite."

The queen looked suspiciously like First Mate Ben Cartwright to me. Then I was introduced to First Assistant Davy Jones, who looked a lot like Skipper Grumby.

"Now, for the beauty contest. Let the slimy Polliwog judge the contest."

Women came out, well, men in drag, poor drag. I recognized the ship's engineer, a deck steward, and a deckhand among the six candidates. I wondered how I would decide which of these "women" was the most beautiful.

"It is a hard task we have put before this slimy Polliwog. Let us help him. Administer the truth potion. That way, none of these women can accuse him of being false in his reasoning."

At that point, Patch raised the loathsome concoction. He winked at me as I slowly opened my mouth. As it poured in, I realized the contents were different. It was Coca-Cola!"

I not only swallowed it, but I also went for more to quench the burning.

"Ah," cried Neptune, "there is a real sailor."

After I finished drinking, I pointed to the huge Ben Cartwright. "The winner," I croaked.

Neptune awarded a crown for the winner to wear. It looked suspiciously like one from Burger King. Then Neptune raised his trident and declared it time to dance. The portable record player in the galley had a 33LP with tangos playing.

Sailors danced with sailors, all doing the tango. What amazed me was that they were good! More than good, they looked like professional ballroom dancers to me, and I had seen them in Hollywood on various sets. There was controlled violence in their movements that was downright scary. It looked like blood would flow.

Neptune (Popeye) came over to me and asked me to dance. I was plain weirded out by this.

"What is going on, Popeye? What sort of people are you?"

"Aarrgh, Rick! You don't know about Buenos Aires?"

"I guess not."

"In the old days, the bawdy houses would have long lines. To kill time while waiting, the customers would dance. Now since they were all men, they had to do manly dances. I think you agree that the tango is manly. Those days are past, well, in most places, but the tradition still exists. Now the tango is performed openly by men in rougher bars."

"There are now tango contests at these places. The men are just practicing. We don't want to shame the ship. Speaking of shaming the ship, you dance, don't you?"

"I haven't danced the tango very much, only a few lessons at home."

As I thought of those lessons, I remembered Mum and Mrs. Hernandez exchanging funny looks about where the tango came from. Now I understood.

Popeye proceeded to teach me the tango and practiced with me two hours a day for the next week as we sailed to BA. Looking back later, I would consider the whole voyage as a surreal experience. But that was later. Now I was dancing the tango with a bunch of sailors in drag and having a good time.

After several energetic hours of dancing, Neptune dismissed his court. The court seemed a bit unsteady from all the punch they had been drinking, which Popeye had warned me to avoid. This was fine with me as I was trying to put the fire out in my mouth with bottle after bottle of Coke.

Neptune told me, "We will finish the ceremony on the morrow when you have made your crossing."

Chapter 42

The next morning was different. The same crew assembled as the previous evening, except they were dressed in their normal wear.

Captain Grumby brought out a document and read it aloud to the assembly.

"Imperium Neptuni Regis

To all Shellbacks Greetings:

This is to Certify that Richard Jackson, *SS Pride of Liberia*, was duly initiated into the Solemn Mysteries of the Ancient Order of the Deep. And made a worthy Shellback in our Royal Dominion at Latitude 0000, Longitude 0040,1959.

Neptunus Rex

Ruler of the Raging Main

Official:

Jonas Grumby

Captain, *SS Pride of Liberia*

The Skipper then took the document, dipped it into a bucket of seawater, and presented it to me. He then presented me with another document showing me to be "A Member of the Spanish Main" for sailing the Caribbean.

Afterward, I had a cup of coffee with Popeye, who I would think of forever as King Neptune. I expressed my surprise at the Spanish Main title.

"I had read about the Equator Crossing but not the Spanish Main."

"Rick, I am also a member of the Spanish Main, the Realm of the Czars for crossing into the Black Sea, the Order of Magellan for circumnavigating the world, Order of the Sparrow for sailing all seven seas, the Order of the Blue Nose for the Arctic Ocean, the Order of the Red Nose for the Antarctic, the Order of the Ditch for the Panama Canal, the Magellan's Strait-Jacket Club, the Order of the Rock for passing through the Strait of Gibraltar and the Safari to Suez for that canal.

"I'm also a Golden Shellback for crossing the Equator at the International Dateline and a Royal Diamond Shellback for crossing at the Prime Meridian.

"The only thing left for me is the Royal Order of the Purple Porpoise. To become a member, you have to cross the Equator on the International Dateline on a Vernal Equinox. I would love to do that dearly, but I don't see how it will ever happen."

We docked in Buenos Aires five days later on a Tuesday. This was a major stop for the ship so that we would be allowed time ashore.

After discussion, Popeye changed my work schedule to the evenings. This way, I could explore the city during the day, and another crew member could do the same at night. We probably would be exploring different parts of the city. An unspoken part of this was that Popeye had figured out my real age. My union paperwork said one thing, but Popeye's family knowledge had led him to seek out the purser and check my passport. The purser had never looked, and Popeye didn't enlighten him.

While at sea, they were not in violation of any laws. Only while in a US port, and they wouldn't be back to one with me onboard, so why worry? He wasn't about to let them strand his almost nephew in a foreign port!

I stopped at the American Embassy on Tuesday afternoon to pay my respects to the ambassador. Mum had explained I should do this while in port. Not that I would ever get to see the ambassador, but if there were problems later, at least they would know I was in the country.

A friendly Marine directed me to the correct desk at the American Embassy. There I was asked to fill out a brief form stating how long I would be in the country, where I was staying, and my method of egress. It was cut and dried, and there was no doubt the form would be filed and never looked at again by human eyes.

I also stopped at the British Embassy. Instead of presenting my ship's papers, I presented my British passport. This reception was different. That may have had something to do with my name being preceded by "The Honorable". The nice young Argentinian girl summoned a higher-level assistant. This gentleman welcomed me and had several questions about my stay. He made certain to tell me if I needed any dress clothing that it could be had at Harrods on the Calle Florida.

This led me to spend the rest of the afternoon exploring the shopping district in Calle Florida. I went from Plaza de Mayo to Plaza San Martin switching sides of the street as I worked my way back. I paused at Cathedral Station on Diagonal Norte Avenida to look at the original cobblestones.

I had an ice cream cone as I walked. Though it was winter, it wasn't a chilly day. After finishing my cone, I went into Harrods. I couldn't believe the price of leather goods. They were almost giving them away. When asked, a clerk told me that Argentina was one of the world's largest beef-producing countries. They had a large leather industry.

I ended up buying myself, Dad, and my brothers briefcases. I purchased Mary and Mum purses. Mary's purse was much smaller than Mum's. Harrods, for only twice the cost of the presents, would ship them for a small additional fee. By this time, I was in deep, so I told them to go ahead.

The purchase itself was different. With the help of a clerk, I picked out the items. The clerk then carried them to a cashier who used a system similar to Dee's in Bellefontaine to send the money upstairs. A receipt was returned, and then my purchases were taken to another clerk for gift wrapping. They were then taken to another clerk for packaging for overseas shipment.

I gave the address for Jackson House in California since they would be moved there by the time everyone caught up with the gifts. What should have been a half-hour shopping trip at the most ended up taking almost two hours. I couldn't figure out how the store could be profitable.

I also stopped at the post office to make an international call. I was lucky and caught Dad at his office in California. I found out that my idea for containerized shipping was proceeding nicely.

This included the patents, the design, and finding truck lines to work with. Dad told me that he started in Baltimore with Narrow Freight. They were for sale and at the right price. He had an offer tendered and expected it to be accepted.

His next step was to make a trip to Baltimore and meet with the Longshoremen's Union to make certain they understood that, while on the surface it might cut down on the individual crates handled, the cheaper rates incurred would increase the overall work available. At the same time, he would be selling the Port Authority on the increase in traffic.

He also was talking to a shipping line about what would be needed to facilitate using containers on their ships. The shipping line was The Scottish Lines, which just happened to own the *Pride of Liberia*. They were interested in a joint venture as the benefits were self-evident. The Scottish Lines also had a contact in Argentina,

Howell Freight Lines, who they had worked with and were willing to talk to.

Dad also told me to call Mum. She had several questions for me. As soon as I hung up, with the help of the international operator I then put in a call to Mum in Ohio. She picked up on the first ring. We chatted for a while about my trip. She thought my crossing the equator ceremony was interesting but told me her crossing was wilder. I decided I didn't want to know about it.

Mum then got to her real questions. It was about the Russian soldiers in Cuba. How many, how did they look, any and every detail I could give, which wasn't much. I asked her why all the concern.

"Rick, that division of the Soviet Army launches nuclear missiles. You have thrown the cat amongst the pigeons! I called my contact in London. The next day a courier from the CIA picked the patches up. Intelligence circles are frantic right now. If the Soviets attempt to put nuclear missiles in Cuba, we might have a world war."

"It won't come to that, will it?"

"It very well could. It depends on whether or not the American president will take a stand. Eisenhower wouldn't put up with it, but we don't know about his successor. This will take a while to play out. It takes time to build launch stands. They won't bring the actual missiles and warheads in until the last minute so that it may be after the next American election."

"Anyway, Rick, several high-ranking British and American officials give their thanks. There will be nothing official in our world, as there never is, but something nice might happen to you in the future. In the meantime, you are now on the American and British watch lists as someone who runs into interesting things.

"Now hang on. Your brothers are out, but Mary wants to say hello."

"Hi, Mary, how are you doing?"

"I'm good, and if you are going to buy me a present in Argentina, please make it leather. I understand that it is very inexpensive there. A purse would be nice."

"Squirt, how old did you say you were?"

Mary giggled at that and said that Mum had told her to say that.

"Good one, Mary. I love you and will see you in England."

"Okay, maybe you can shop for hats with Mum and me for when we go to the races."

"We will see."

That was my reply. What I was thinking was not if I could avoid it!

When returning to the ship, I found that chipping paint while others unloaded cargo was about the same as chipping paint while underway. Hard, bloody boring work!

Chapter 43

The next day after returning from a run around the port area, I was summoned to the purser's office. He had a letter from the British Embassy. To say the purser was curious was putting it mildly. I wanted to know its contents, so I opened it immediately. I did it carefully to preserve the embassy seal. It was an invitation to a Saturday night dance at the British Embassy. RSVP, dress Red Sea Rig required.

The purser asked me if I was going as I had handed him the invitation to read.

"I would like to, but I'm scheduled to work."

The purser hailed Popeye on the ship's Tannoy system. As soon as he heard the deal, he changed my work schedule.

Now I had to figure out what Red Sea Rig was. I remembered the man at the Embassy stressing that Harrods was the place to go for clothes. I figured they would know what was needed, so after cleaning up, I headed there.

After showing my invitation to a clerk in the men's department, I found out it meant a formal short-sleeved white shirt, a bow tie, and a cummerbund. That is the normal Red Sea Rig, so named because it was too hot in the Red Sea area to wear a jacket. However, since the embassy has had air conditioning installed, everyone wears the informal tuxedo set. That is a white jacket rather than a black one.

"Of course, it is no longer Red Sea Rig, but the embassy has never changed the wording on the invitations."

"Is it possible to purchase such an outfit in time for the dance?"

"Most certainly. There will be only a minor upcharge for the urgent tailoring."

I was getting an idea about the costs of minor upcharges at Harrods in Argentina, but I wanted to go to this dance. Maybe I could even tango. Though I didn't know if I could dance with an actual girl. I might break her.

I put in my work week and was ready to go on Saturday night. My shipmates were lined up at the gangway to wish me luck. The skipper, who had only recently heard of this event from the purser, was waiting at the top of the ladder. He shook my hand and told me he would like to talk tomorrow. He was a little curious about what sort of person he had on board.

I didn't know what to expect when I got out of the taxi but was able to follow the crowd into the main room. An usher asked for my invitation. I was placed in a line and was announced as the Honorable Richard Jackson, son of Viscountess Jackson.

I was surprised by the fact that people applauded my entrance.

I quickly came to find out it was because many of the older crowd knew Mum and Dad from the war. As I progressed through the welcome line, I was introduced to the ambassador. The ambassador made me aware of how much I was being watched.

"I understand that you are taking after your Mum. Do you intend to go into the family trade?"

"I'm not certain, sir, what the family trade is, so it is hard to announce."

The ambassador gave a small snort and replied, "With that answer, I think you already have. Welcome to Argentina. If we can be of any help, please let us know."

When I left the presentation line, I was immediately buttonholed by the American ambassador.

"Why haven't you stopped in at the American Embassy and given us a chance to invite you to one of our parties?"

This took me aback for a moment.

"Sir, I did, but unfortunately, I only presented my ship's papers, so I wasn't recognized."

"We just received notice this afternoon that you are a citizen who we should assist and keep track of."

Sometimes the devil makes you say things, or maybe it is the condition of being fifteen.

"Was that the CIA, my godfather, godmother, or the studio?"

Now it was the Ambassador's turn to be perplexed.

"It came through the intelligence channels. Who are your godparents, and what studio are you talking about?"

"Ike and Elizabeth are my godparents, and the studio is Warner Brothers. We sail on Monday, so I doubt if we will meet again."

I left a gasping ambassador behind me, trying to sort out who Ike and Elizabeth were. Warner Brothers was self-evident. After three steps, I turned.

"Mr. Ambassador, that was quite rude of me. My godparents are President Eisenhower and Queen Elizabeth. You had no way of knowing that. I showed up at the embassy with the papers of an ordinary seaman. There was no reason for your staff to know any differently."

This, of course, led to a conversation about my movie and singing background. It turned out the ambassador's wife was a Frank Sinatra fan. This led to further introductions. The band leader of the ten-piece orchestra was introduced, and before he could object, I was paired with the band's male lead singer to do "Brothers". We performed it, and I felt I did it as well as I ever had.

I was a little peeved when the lead singer, who hadn't been filled in on who I was, told me, "Don't quit your day job, kid. Not bad for an amateur, but you could never make it in the industry."

I had received a gold record for sales of "Brothers" before I left the US but kept my mouth shut. I had been a smart mouth once this evening and regretted it, so I decided the less said, the better. I would like to see the guy's face when he finds out.

I wandered about the room, being drug into various conversations about Mum. I began to realize that she and Elizabeth had been a couple of rounders during the war. They weren't bad, but they knew how to party.

I paused by a bevy of young Argentinian ladies. One, in particular, caught my eye. She was a slender, well-built blonde who looked like a teenager. I wondered if I could strike up an acquaintance.

They were talking in Spanish about Eva Peron. She died almost ten years ago, and they felt something should be done with her gravesite. Many people visited it, and it was looking a bit trampled. They thought putting a fence around it would be good and were prepared to raise the funds.

The discussion centered around what, if anything, they should put on the fence. The consensus was that she didn't want Argentina to be upset about her death or make a big deal of it. I commented in Spanish. "Say something simple, like 'Argentina, don't cry for me.'"

I took a chance with the blonde when they all looked at me.

"What do you think of it?"

"I think it is more than she deserves. Not all of us are Peronists."

"Oh, I'm sorry about that."

"Don't be sorry. You gave an honest suggestion to the question. It is a very good thought."

I introduced myself, which made all the girls giggle.

"Silly boy," said the blonde. "We heard you sing, and we know who the movie star and singer Rick Jackson is. We were wondering how to get your attention."

"Well, you have it. Now, what are your lovely lady's names?"

They went around the table, all giving their first names. The only one that I caught was the blonde Dorotea.

I took the opportunity and sat on an empty chair beside Dorotea.

One of the other girls said, "Oh woe is me. She has done it again. She always gets the best-looking guy."

It may have been because she was by far the best-looking girl present.

The band started a tune. It was tango. Dorotea asked me if I knew how to dance the national dance of Argentina.

"We won't know unless we try."

I proceeded to lead her to the floor.

If we had a week to practice together, we would have done better, but not by much. We flowed with the music. I was enough bigger than Dorotea I could move her at need. The song was long, and we both were sweating profusely when done.

When we returned to the tables, all the girls, including Dorotea, wanted to know where I learned to dance like that. I told them an old sailor on my ship had given me lessons. They laughed at that thought and wanted to know where I had learned.

I stuck with my story, which was the truth. I was glad they didn't ask where the old sailor learned the dance. I also made a mental note not to tell Popeye that I called him an old sailor.

Dorotea told me she was too warm and would like to take a walk outside. Since we were in air conditioning and it was a little warmer outside, I saw through this subterfuge and willingly went with her with high hopes.

My hopes were well-founded because she wrapped her arms around me and pulled me into a deep kiss as soon as we were off the veranda into the garden. We hugged tightly, so tightly I was afraid she might notice my involuntary reaction. She didn't seem to mind, though. We continued for a few minutes.

Dorotea pulled away and said, "Rick, it is too hot. Let's go swimming."

"I don't see a pool, and I don't have a swimming suit with me."

"We have one at my house. My parents aren't home. Haven't you ever gone skinny dipping?"

"Well, sure," I replied. I didn't think it was necessary to tell her it only had been with other boys and much younger ones.

At that, Dorotea hustled us out of the British Embassy through a side door to avoid all the goodbyes and possible questions. Her car was brought around by her chauffeur. This gave me pause. What sort of family was Dorotea from? All thoughts went away when she cuddled up to me in the backseat.

At her home, I realized that this was a different world. Just because her parents weren't there didn't mean the butler, maids, and for all I knew, the cook, gardeners, and security guards weren't.

I mentioned this to Dorotea. She told me not to be silly. The staff had practically raised her and would never give her away. This gave me concern; the staff had raised her? That sounded like another set of parents! However, that thought was lost as she towed me to the pool.

I removed my coat and set it on a cabana table. She told me to wait a minute, dashed into the house, and returned with a chilled bottle of champagne. If I had been thinking, I would have wondered about why a bottle was chilled and waiting in a bucket with two glasses. However, I was past all that. My thoughts were on Dorotea.

She started taking her clothes off and setting them on a table on the other side of the pool. It became a race to see who could remove their clothes the fastest. My cuff links and studs made me lose the race. I looked up and saw the most wondrous sight of my life, a fully grown, naked woman who was about to join me in the water.

I was taking a step towards the pool to dive in when Dorotea and I heard a car.

She said in a quiet voice, "*Madre Dios*, it is my parents. You have to go. Take your clothes and go out the back gate. Enrico, show him."

I was dazed by events, especially when an old man came out of the bushes. He was carrying a double-barreled shotgun.

"*Señor*, follow me."

I found my wits, gathered my clothes, and took a wistful look behind me, but Dorotea was gone. I followed the old security guard to a gate that he was in the process of unlocking.

"Get dressed, *Señor*."

I did it as quickly as I could. This meant the shirt was open, and the cuffs rolled up. That is when he discovered that I had missed my socks when I had grabbed my shoes.

The guard chuckled at my antics while dressing.

"The Frade women are hot-blooded, but the colonel is still careful of his daughter.

I asked, "The colonel, is he in your Army or Air Force?"

As soon as the words were out of my mouth, I realized how stupid I must sound.

The reply was serious. "No, *Señor*, he was in your Marines."

For some reason, I felt like my life should be flashing before my eyes. I finished tying my shoes and exited the gate.

"*Señor*, go four blocks to your right. There will be a taxi stand."

I was relieved when I found my wallet and papers in my inside jacket pocket. To lose them would have capped the night. I was in luck as a taxi was at the stand and immediately returned me to the docks. I was never so glad to see a ship as I was that night. Popeye was waiting at the top of the gangway. He smiled when he saw how disheveled I looked.

"Now, that is how a sailor should dress when he returns to the ship. Now, if you were singing and staggering, you would make able-bodied seaman."

I ignored him and went to my cabin.

After changing my clothes, I realized it was still in the middle of the last watch, so I went back down and told Popeye about my evening.

When Popeye heard the Frade name, he laughed.

"They are one of the most powerful families in Argentina. You better hope her daddy doesn't come looking for you."

Chapter 44

The next day Daddy didn't come hunting for me. Instead, he sent my socks back to me in a box. The box contained a note, the socks, and a brass shotgun shell.

The note stated, "We were told to be on the watch for you. Interesting things happen around you. I see they were correct. You can have the shell. I have plenty more waiting for you if you return to Argentina."

The wording of the note was familiar to me, almost identical to the British ambassador's. Frade wasn't British. Had I pissed off the father of a beautiful girl whose dad happened to be involved with the CIA in Argentina? I didn't think I would leave the ship to find out. I smiled as I thought of the beautiful memory I did have.

That was Sunday. We sailed on Monday. Our next destination was Lagos, Nigeria, to unload machinery, then Monrovia, Liberia. We were to drop off machinery and pick up a load of rubber, both liquid latex and solid blocks.

As I completed my watch by chipping paint which I was beginning to hate with a passion, I saw the skipper hitting golf balls off the fantail. I watched him for a while, and when the skipper came to a natural break, I asked him if he knew he was dipping his shoulder on his backswing.

"What do you mean, Rick?"

I demonstrated what I saw the skipper doing and what he should be doing. I worked with him until the skipper had a smooth, even swing.

"I gather you play golf?"

"A bit."

"Would you like to hit a few?"

"I would love to."

I took the skipper's position and ripped two hundred and fifty yards out one-off.

"That's good!"

My next swing put it out almost three hundred yards. They were estimating the distance, knowing how far out from the wave pattern made by the ship's prop.

"Where did you learn to hit like that?"

"I was the junior state champion in Ohio."

"Hmm, I have a golf match in Liberia with the managing director of the Firestone Plantation. Would you be interested in joining me? We always have some interesting side bets."

"I would love to. May I ask a question?"

"Sure."

"Golf balls aren't cheap, and you are hitting brand new Titleists into the ocean."

"When a container is damaged at sea, we notify the shipper, who in turn notifies the insurance company. In this case, the insurance company wrote off the golf balls because the packaging had gotten wet, so I was told to dump them over the side. That's what I am doing, one hundred thousand of them, one at a time. You can feel free to hit as many as you want. My clubs are kept in that locker over there."

During the voyage, the skipper made a point of crossing the equator at the prime meridian. Since I was the only one on board who hadn't made that crossing, they didn't make the same big deal as the first time. I was handed a certificate that stated I was a Golden Shellback. I was relieved. I still thought I had a funny taste in my mouth.

If I thought Caracas, Venezuela, was a hole, then Lagos, Nigeria, was the pit below the hole. I had never imagined that such filth and poverty could exist. I was glad I had those shots before the trip. Yellow fever and malaria were in the stories I had read. Here they were part of life. I had started taking my chloroquine pills when we left Argentina.

I had no plans to go ashore for the two-day stay in Lagos. There was not much to load or unload. Late on the first day, this plan was changed.

"Rick, we need you to come with us to the bank," said Popeye.

"What on earth for?"

"Your size. You are one big guy, and it will help discourage thieves."

"Do I have to change clothes?"

"Nah, the rougher you look, the better."

I joined the skipper and Popeye for the half-mile walk across the city.

Even getting off the ship was an eye-opener. At the end of the dock, there was a police checkpoint. There were four "policemen" there. They looked to be younger than me. Their uniforms were slovenly and their weapons leftover from the First World War were poorly maintained. As we approached the gate, an officer stepped out with his hand out. I figured that he wanted our papers.

Without breaking stride, the skipper handed the cop three one-dollar bills, and we moved on.

"Our costs in Buenos Aires were higher than expected, so we have to pick up more cash here," explained the skipper as we walked along. It's the trip back to the ship that is my concern. We are not allowed any weapons, and robbery is a way of life here."

I had been surprised earlier to learn that every ship had tens of thousands of dollars in its safe for transactions at various ports, so being a target of thieves was expected.

As we passed one stall, I slowed the group down.

"Wait a second."

I bought a walking stick about my height. It was solid, not a flimsy cane, more like I would have used walking the Appalachian

Trail or in the movie *Bandits of Sherwood* as a quarterstaff. I paid a dollar for it without haggling. Popeye told me I probably could have gotten it for a dime.

We didn't notice the man with a small camera following us. He would take snapshots of our journey occasionally.

The transaction at the bank went smoothly.

It was on the way back that things got exciting. There was a one-block stretch of street that didn't have much traffic. As we were in the center of the block, five men stepped out of an alley. By my standards, they were scrawny, and I could have taken any two or three in unarmed combat. But five men with knives were a different story.

"We will take the bag," said the leader, as he gestured towards the bank bag the skipper was carrying.

As quick as a snake, I went to the left and right with my stave and then to the center. Just like that, three men were down, the ones on each side with cracked heads and the one in the center with a sharp blow to the solar plexus. As I stepped forward, the staff was now a spinning blur like an airplane propeller. The remaining two decided that this was not their day and ran.

We made it the rest of the way to the ship in a rapid walk.

When we were back on board, the two men looked at me.

The skipper asked, "Where did you learn to use a quarterstaff?"

I hadn't told anyone about my recent past. I wasn't trying to hide anything. I just didn't want to make a big deal about it.

"I had the training for my part in my last movie."

"Sure, you did now. Where do you learn?"

"Let's get some coffee. This will take a while."

As my story unfolded, the skipper and Popeye kept glancing at each other. Finally, the skipper had to ask.

"How old are you?"

I must have looked uncomfortable as I replied, "Fifteen."

"Fifteen?"

"Yes."

The skipper put his head in his hands and said, "Why me, Lord?"

The Lord wasn't speaking that day, so Popeye answered for him. "That is great, Rick. I didn't get to sea until I was sixteen, and I know Skip here didn't make it until he was seventeen."

That took the wind out of the skipper's building ire.

"Rick, you told me you were the Ohio State Junior Golf Champion. When was that?"

I thought, in for a penny in for a pound.

"Last year when I was in the ninth grade."

The Skipper was now in a state of shock. If he tried to take me into a US port, he could see himself going to jail for a long time. This wasn't like before World War II.

Popeye broke in with, "Skipper, I know something about Rick's family. This is normal for them. His mother was made a viscountess for her actions in the war. She was a bodyguard to the then Princess Elizabeth."

"Oh, well, Rick, you will be getting the hell off my ship when we reach Spain. I appreciate what you did today, but I don't want to end up in a US jail for breaking the child labor laws. Actually, how did you get a maritime union card?"

"Heck, Skip, his godfather, would probably pardon you. I was there and saw Ike do the honors."

"Skipper, I think a series of assumptions allowed me a union card. I was a member of the Screen Actors Guild, which allows child membership. I used this to get my oil rig card. They didn't ask any questions, just wrote the SAG card number down, and then I used my oil rig card to get my maritime card. I didn't think anything of it, but I can see how it slipped through."

"I'm going to my cabin now and pour a drink," replied the captain.

Ashore, a man handed a roll of film to another. "You were right. Interesting things happen around him."

The next day we set a course for Liberia. As far as I was concerned, I would never be coming back to Nigeria.

It only took several days to arrive in Monrovia. From the water, the city looked wonderful. So did Lagos, so I was reserving judgment.

The skipper made several phone calls from the harbor master's office upon arrival. He returned and informed me that starting in two days he would be spending two days at the Firestone Rubber Plantation.

We were both invited to play golf at the company club, and yes, he had some serious money riding on the outcome of the match. Then there was a dinner reception at the Firestone Country Club that evening. The skipper continued that we were to wear Red Sea Rig, whatever that was.

I explained what that was and accompanied the skipper to a tailor that afternoon for a fitting. I also took my clothes. The tailor agreed to send my outfit out to a dry cleaner after making certain it was in first-rate condition. The skipper decided to have a white jacket made. They probably didn't have air conditioning, but he wanted to look like Humphrey Bogart did in Casablanca.

During the trip, I developed a very favorable opinion of Monrovia. At least it was clean with modern buildings. This was the future of Africa.

Chapter 45

I worked hard for the next two days. I had the chore of checking that all safety equipment was present on the ship, especially the lifeboats. Our next port of call would be in Spain, where they might have a Coast Guard inspection. I was given a checklist to fill in for each area. It was not physically hard, but being in the heat, especially between decks, was horrendous.

To make matters worse, it rained every day. When I asked about that, I was told this was the tropics. They grow rubber here for a reason. A rubber tree needs twenty feet of rain a year. They hadn't lost production due to the lack of water in recent memory.

On Friday evening, the skipper and I were picked up by a plantation car. Their driver wore the uniform of the Plantation Police Force.

I asked, "How large is this plantation that has its own police force?"

"Sir, it is over a million acres, and we have almost one hundred and fifty thousand people living on it. Twenty thousand men work there, and the rest are their families. Not only a police force, but we also have a fire department, hospital, and school system, not to mention several types of stores. The plantation has the only golf course in the country. Our airport serves all international flights for the country, though that is not saying much. Sabena has three flights in and out a week."

"Wow, I had no idea that it was that big. So being the managing director is a big deal around here."

"Mr. Dawson is a powerful and respected man. This plantation is the largest employer in the country and provides our hard currency for trade. They are opening up mines, but this is the money maker."

The plantation proved to be a thirty-mile, two-hour trip from the docks. I looked at the city closely as we went south through the heart of town. We passed a stately-looking compound that had signs indicating it was the British Embassy.

When we left town, it was a different world. There were thickly forested areas. They weren't a triple canopy like you would find in the Congo, but they were thick. Along the road in clearings were houses at least. I thought of the shacks with grass roofs as houses.

There were tall mounds of earth along the road. They were six to eight feet in diameter, narrowing down to a foot or so at the top. I asked what they were, and our driver told me they were termite mounds.

Women walked along the road with baskets balanced on their heads. I had seen this in *National Geographic Magazine*, but to see it in person was awesome. To top it all off, a group of young kids my age or older played in a stream. I saw several pairs of bare breasts. I was in Africa!

We arrived at the village of Harbal, which was a collection of huts. There was a gas station there. At least, I assumed it was. There was a table sitting out, with several two or three-gallon glass jars of gasoline, along with hoses and funnels. Our driver confirmed that was the case.

A set of stone pillars guarded the entrance to the plantation. Now instead of the jungle, there was row after row of rubber trees, miles of rubber trees as far as the eye could see. It was an eight-mile drive back to the guest house, with nothing but rubber trees to be seen.

Another set of pillars was at the entrance to the gatehouse. A small guard shack with a raised bar was next to the road. They drove through without stopping. The two guards saluted us as we went through.

The guest house was an elegant old brick structure. It consisted of a two-story main building with single-story wings. The wings contained the guest rooms. These were like small hotel rooms. Okay to visit but not to live in. The shower was different than those I was used to.

The showerhead projected out into the room. There was a ring suspended from the nonadjustable shower head. There was a two-inch high ring on the floor to catch the water, which went into a drain flush with the floor. It was a poor arrangement that left the room soaked.

The other difference was that the closet was locked, and I was given a key. It appeared the country was so poor that anything would be stolen. The staff was considered honest, but Mr. Dawson explained later that he didn't want to place temptation in their way. After changing into jeans and a golf shirt, I was ready to play golf.

They drove us several miles to the plantation country club. It was nothing fancy. It had a small pro shop which was self-help, a snack bar, and a large open area where events were held. Event meals would be catered from the guest house kitchen.

I outfitted myself with a set of clubs, a glove, balls, and tees, and I was good to go. I was assigned a caddie. I shook the young boy's hand and introduced myself. The young man very solemnly gave his name as Samuel Doe. Samuel was not much bigger than the bag he would be carrying.

At the first tee, all the other golfers made the normal excuses for why they wouldn't do well, new course, stiff knee, been a while, etc. The skipper and I were partners against Mr. Dawson, the plantation manager, and Mr. Washington. It turned out Mr. Washington was the Vice President of Liberia and a regular golfing partner of Mr. Dawson. This is when I found out that five hundred dollars was riding on the match.

I almost fell over when I found out. Since I had not played the course before and was only a kid, the skipper had negotiated me a five-stroke handicap. Everyone else was playing even.

The only part of the course that surprised me was the greens. They were not only not green, they were hard-packed sand. They couldn't grow the grass that would work on the green, so they just packed it down. It was like putting on concrete. It reminded me of a putt-putt golf course I had played with Judy.

That led me to wonder what she was doing these days. These thoughts also caused me to hook the ball from the second tee into the many rows of rubber trees which were out of bounds. That got my attention.

Because of that hooked ball, I didn't set a course record, but I did tie it, which led to a happy skipper. Counting my handicap, we won the match by ten strokes. Needless to say, the skipper took a lot of grief over his ringer. The skipper laughed them off.

They had taken him several times before, so he was just getting even. He gave me one hundred dollars of his winnings. I, in turn, gave twenty dollars to the eight-year-old Samuel Doe. I was informed this was a month's wages for a grown man, but it only seemed fair to me.

After the match, we repaired to the guest house veranda to replay the eighteen holes over a drink. I stayed with Coke, although I was offered anything I wanted from the bar.

The conversation turned into a more general direction. Mr. Dawson shared a recent frustration. He told the vice president that the country was failing to maintain its roads. National Highway One had many potholes that went the length of the plantation. Even though it was the country's job to maintain them, Mr. Dawson had tired of driving over them.

At the plantation's expense, he had every pothole filled with gravel. That lasted for one day. The next day, the potholes were all back, and vendors were beside the road selling gravel!

Mr. Washington roared at this. He felt it showed his countrymen were an enterprising lot and how foolish of Mr. Dawson was to waste his money on such a project. This made me wonder about the future of Liberia.

After settling down, the vice president brought up, "Speaking of gravel, have you heard of the diamond robbery in Sierra Leone?"

"No," replied Mr. Dawson.

"A Kimberley pipe yielded an unprecedented find. There are twenty-five pounds of raw diamonds of large size. The estimated value is over fifty million dollars. The thieves raided the diamond offices and killed most of the office workers. They left one wounded behind who is being questioned severely. Every police force in Africa is on the lookout."

Mr. Dawson said, "That much money could destabilize the entire region. There is a delicate balance in West Africa. If any one country had that much new wealth, it could lead to war."

"This is true, my friend. That is why if I found such a treasure, I would not share it with my government," stated the vice president.

For some reason, no one commented on this. Shortly thereafter, we all retired to our rooms to prepare for the evening.

After cleaning up and after dinner, the skipper and I donned our Red Sea Rig, coats, and all. While at the country club, we noticed it was air-conditioned, so we could go the full route. It was fortunate we did because all the other men wore the same.

At the club, I quickly discovered I was the youngest, including the wait staff. It was a mixture of European nationals and Liberian blacks. I found it strange that almost all the Liberians had American names until I was reminded of how the country was founded.

This was explained to me by a twenty-some-year-old lady by the name of Ellen Johnson Sirleaf. She referred to herself as an Americo-Liberian. This was how the returned freemen differentiated themselves from the native-born. There was a caste system in place. She was a member of the True Whig Party, while the natives formed the Republican Party.

I was even introduced to the President of Liberia, Mr. Tubman. I asked if he was any relation to Harriet Tubman of anti-slavery fame. Mr. Tubman proudly told me he was. I left it at that, wondering about the president's ancestors being against slavery in America, but as soon as they returned to Africa, they promptly created a caste system that effectively enslaved the natives.

The effects of that were still present today in 1959. I didn't feel this could have a good ending, but I kept my mouth shut wisely. In Hollywood, I learned that holding my tongue was the safest thing I could do in a social situation with strangers.

The lead topic of conversation was the stolen diamonds. The consensus was that if found, it was one's civic duty to keep them.

When the skipper and I retired for the evening, I wondered if Liberian society could continue to exist in its present form. The skipper felt that with American leadership, things would work out. I wasn't so certain.

Chapter 46

The next morning after breakfast, I was packed to leave. The skipper was staying for two more days to visit with his friend Mr. Dawson. My driver was instructed to stop at a shop on the road to Monrovia. It sold wooden carvings that made for excellent souvenirs of Africa.

I learned several things at that shop. The most important was that I had no idea how to haggle. My driver told me this was the way it was done and to be prepared to pay one dollar each for the carvings.

I thought it would be an offer and counteroffer until a price was met in the middle. I found out quickly that if I didn't pay, the wood carver's wife and seven children would starve. Also, the extended family needed help, and ten dollars each would be a good price.

I didn't know what to say to that, so I just looked at the salesman and shook my head no. The salesman then accused me of trying to steal his humble work of the first quality of the finest woods available. Then he explained how I could make an enormous profit by reselling them in America or donating them to a museum.

While the carvings of monkeys and elephants looked good, they didn't look that good.

The carver kept up a barrage of why I should pay ten dollars each. I finally came back with, "I will pay fifty cents each."

I thought the man was having a heart attack. I had to help him sit in a chair, and a young boy brought him water. Another child, a small girl, ran out and cried, "Don't die, Daddy!"

By this time, I was so confused that I turned to leave, not knowing what else to do.

This miraculously returned the carver to robust health.

"For you, I could see five dollars each, and only this small girl child will have to starve."

At that, the girl burst into tears and ran away. It would have been more convincing if I hadn't caught the impish grin she gave her father.

In exasperation, I finally said, "And your mother wears combat boots."

"How did you know? Have you been spying on my family?"

Now I was shaken up. I upped my offer to seventy-five cents each while waving a wooden elephant. As I did that, I realized something else. They didn't have elephants in Liberia!

I taxed the carver on this, who quickly informed me they had a zoo in Monrovia and that he had studied them there, which was why they were worth four dollars each, as he had to spend time in his studies.

All of a sudden, the scene struck me as hilarious.

I told the salesman between my gales of laughter, "You win. Four dollars each it is."

The driver, who had been watching and listening to all of this, shook his head in disgust at my poor performance. I also caught the wink the driver gave the shopkeeper. Was there a payoff involved with my shopping here?

I had given up and waited while the ten elephants I had purchased for family and friends were put into a large cloth bag.

As I started the door, the driver indicated he would be a few minutes. I thought to myself, he is negotiating his share of the loot.

As I stood by the automobile waiting for my driver, a car was speeding from the direction of Monrovia. As it came abreast of me, a bag was thrown out of the speeding vehicle.

It landed at my feet with a thud. I picked it up to see what had been thrown at me. It was hefty and felt like it weighed twenty pounds or so.

As I started to open the bag, another car came speeding by. This one had men with guns leaning out the window.

I put the bag I had picked up into the bag with my recent purchases.

The driver came out with a smile on his face. His negotiations went better than mine. As we were getting into our vehicle, two police cars came screaming in pursuit of the others.

I got into the backseat of the car as I had been told was proper when being driven by the plantation security force.

As we drove towards Monrovia to return me to my ship, I took a look at the contents of the bag thrown at me. The first look reminded me of Mr. Dawson's story of the gravel taken from the potholes and being sold. A second look brought to mind the huge diamond heist.

I sat in thought during the drive. While I was thinking about what to do, the driver asked if I minded if he listened to the radio. I didn't care.

When the radio was turned on, it confirmed that the stolen diamonds had surfaced in Monrovia and that the police were hot on the trail. The port was being sealed, and everything and everyone was being searched. Since there were no commercial flights out of the country today, the thieves couldn't use an airplane.

The driver laughed at that and said, "Unless they have access to a private plane, then they could escape to Nigeria."

"What about the Liberian Air Force?"

"What air force?"

"Oh."

As we approached Monrovia, I asked the driver if we could make a short stop at the British Embassy. I had some business there, and it would save me a trip later. Having the driver's mercenary nature in mind, I offered five dollars for the stop.

When we pulled into the embassy compound, I exited with my bag of elephants and other contents in hand. The driver asked what I was doing with the carvings.

"I'm sending a present to my godmother."

The driver, who didn't care, just nodded.

At the front desk of the embassy, I presented my British passport and asked to speak to an official. I had to wait fifteen minutes for a minor functionary. The young man looked like he was only a few years older than me.

Upon introducing myself, being certain to use the Honorable Richard Jackson as it appeared on my passport, I asked if the young man would let someone in the intelligence branch know that the "Mr. Jackson who has interesting things happen to him would like to speak to them."

The young man gave me a perplexed look and made a phone call. He gave the strange message to the person on the other end. He then handed the phone to me.

I had to go through my introduction again and was required to hand my passport to the young man, who disappeared for a few more minutes.

He returned with another man, who was in his early thirties. I felt that I was getting somewhere.

"What's all this about?"

Instead of answering, I opened the bag which was inside my bag of carvings.

"I would like to send my godmother a present."

The older man stopped cold. He turned to the younger man, "That will be all. Thank you for your help."

The now really confused young man left. After that, I was asked, "How in the bloody hell did you get these?"

I explained what had happened.

"What do you want to do with them?'

"Well, from the sounds of it, I couldn't smuggle them out of the country if I wanted to. They can't stay in the region, or they will destabilize it. So, I thought I would give them to Elizabeth."

"Elizabeth?"

"Yes, my godmother the queen."

That threw the cat amongst the pigeons. The man picked up the phone and made a call.

"Sir, I need you down here right away. We have a situation you need to be aware of."

An older gentleman joined us. The aide introduced him as Sir Guy Clarke, Ambassador Extraordinary, and Plenipotentiary from Her Majesty's Government to the Republic of Liberia.

After handshakes, I fully opened the bag containing over fifty million dollars in raw diamonds.

"I thought Queen Elizabeth could make good use of this."

"On behalf of Her Majesty's Government, I thank you."

"I'm not presenting these to the government. These are for the queen."

"My mistake. Are you certain that is the way you want this done?"

"Yes, I have no idea how this should be handled, but I'm certain Her Majesty will."

The ambassador was now over his initial shock. He sent his aide to find a scale, if nothing else, to grab a bathroom scale.

In short order, I was ready to leave with a handwritten witnessed receipt for twenty-seven point six pounds of raw diamonds to be presented to Her Britannic Majesty. They also agreed to mail my carvings to Jackson House in the US.

My actions were confirmed when arriving at the docks. Before I was allowed to board my ship, I was practically strip-searched. My clothes were all taken out of my duffel bag and gone through. While waiting, I heard the customs agents discuss the big shoot-out that had occurred near the Firestone Plantation. All the gangsters were dead and most of the police. The diamonds had disappeared.

After boarding, Popeye cornered me and had me chipping paint. I had to laugh at myself, from carrying millions in diamonds to chipping paint. Well, the intelligence people said interesting things happened around me. I was beginning to believe it.

Chapter 47

The next day we set sail for Spain for the final leg of my trip. We arrived in Barcelona on the last day of July 1959. I had received a certificate for sailing through the Straits of Gibraltar. As Popeye put it, I was becoming an old salt. If he had me for another six months, I would be an able-bodied seaman.

On that subject, I kept my thoughts to myself. Once was enough, and I never wanted to chip paint again. I talked with Popeye again about my plans for the container business. Popeye just shook his head and told me that was more than a simple seaman could handle.

Popeye added, "If you see your Aunt Sybil, tell her I said, hello."

"I will, and thank you for all your help and guidance."

'Well, I don't know how much guidance it takes to chip paint, but you did okay. Here are your pay packet and passport. You are welcome to sail with me anytime."

The skipper made a point of catching me at the gangway.

"I have received several interesting messages recently. Are you going to fire me now that you own the company?"

This was news to me!

"Not if you continue to share your golf balls."

The skipper chuckled, then went on, "I understand it is your company under your father's direction. I would say this anyway. You did a good job on this voyage, stepping up as a radioman when we needed it and working hard. You can sail with me anytime. Though, of course, I'm about to retire."

"What are your plans?"

"I am thinking about taking up charters. I have my eye on a handy motor vessel named *The Minnow*."

"Well, fair seas, Skipper, and don't get caught in any more storms."

"I'll try my best."

I was flying to Madrid from Barcelona to catch a flight to London. I was dressed in clean work clothes. All I had with me was my white tux dress clothes and work clothes. The clothes, while clean, showed the wear and tear of working on a ship. They were rust and paint streaked.

If I had looked in a mirror, I would have been surprised at what I saw. A fresh-faced young boy had left home. My face was now rough and weathered from being out in the sun and wind. My boyish beard had now come into a full black bristle that needed trimming every day and, in the evening, if I was going out. My arms and chest had filled out even more. I was pretty impressive at six foot five inches and two hundred and twenty pounds. All in all, I looked like a pretty rough character.

As I left the ship, a gentleman was waiting for me at the bottom of the gangway. He introduced himself and showed his identification from the British Consulate. He had been detailed to ensure I made my flight with no problems.

At the airport, I checked my duffle bag at the ticket counter. My escort talked to a supervisor, and the next thing I knew, I was walked to the airplane through a backdoor and shown my first-class seat. This was before other passengers were on the plane. I had an aisle seat.

The stewardess served me a cup of coffee after seeing if I wanted any alcohol. I was just getting comfortable in my seat when other passengers began boarding. One of the first aboard was a dark-haired Spanish beauty. She had the window seat next to mine. I thought this might be a pleasant flight.

It was not to be. A lady in her late fifties was accompanying the young lady. In no uncertain terms, she let it be known to the stewardess that the Countessa could not be seated next to the ruffian. This was in Spanish, so it was assumed that I couldn't understand what was being said, or if I could, the woman didn't care.

The lady escorting the Contessa was seated in the aisle across from me, so I stood and, in my most correct Spanish, asked the lady if she would switch seats with me, as I would be uncomfortable sitting next to such a beautiful young lady.

As the switch was made, the young lady in question glanced demurely at me. I gulped and wondered what had hit me.

The flight was uneventful, and I was ignored by the lady, who had never thanked me for changing seats. The stewardesses on the flight fell all over themselves to take care of me.

After exiting the plane in Madrid, I had a similar experience as in Barcelona. A young man from the embassy was waiting to escort me to my next flight. As before, I was boarded in private.

As I was settling in, I took my aisle seat and was surprised to see the Spanish beauty coming on board. As before, her seat was next to mine. I didn't even argue with the harridan following her. I stood up, bowed, and then sat in the other seat across the aisle.

The old lady talked urgently to the stewardess, who in turn talked to the flight captain. The captain left the plane and returned with two policemen who asked me to come with them. They wanted to know why I was stalking the Contessa.

I had to show my identification, and the British Embassy was called. By the time everything was straightened out, I had missed my flight.

I had to sit in the first-class lounge for four hours, waiting for the next flight to London.

Finally, I was on my flight and going to see my family. So much for pretty young countesses!

When arriving in London late in the evening, I was met by another polite young man who whisked me through customs with no problems. My family was waiting at the arrival gate. It seemed like forever since I had seen them.

It was a group hug, then individual greetings. When I shook hands with Dad, I noticed that Dad seemed to have shrunk, and then I realized no, I had grown. Mum gave me a fierce hug and told me, you have done it now. I didn't have a chance to question her because Denny and Eddie both wanted to shake my hand. They had grown also.

The only one who didn't seem different was Mary. I picked her up and hugged her. She told me that my beard was itchy and no girl would want to kiss me if I didn't shave.

While the family reunion was ongoing, the young man retrieved my duffel bag. We all boarded a large limousine and went directly to the Plaza Hotel on The Strand. By this time, the rest of the family and I were exhausted from a long day, so we retired immediately.

The next morning, we had breakfast as a family in our suite. The conversation was varied as my family filled me in on what they had seen in the last two weeks. Mum and Dad let the boys and Mary rattle on. In a short break, Dad indicated we needed several hours to discuss business. Mum let me know there were some items she had to cover.

I once more had clean work clothes as I had nothing else to wear. Mum let me know that this wouldn't do and that I needed a whole new wardrobe. She knew this would be the case and had planned for me to visit a tailor on Saville Row.

Before I was allowed to leave, a barber was summoned to give me a haircut. I hadn't had one since I left home. It was now hanging over my ears and touching my collar in the back. Denny and Eddie teased me about looking like a girl, but Mary told me she liked my long hair. This gave me an excuse to stick my tongue out at my brothers.

As I was getting ready to leave the suite, I was joined by one of the ever-present escorts. This one had been assigned directly from the palace and was to ensure I had the best smoothest service possible.

I made a mental note, give someone fifty million in diamonds, and you had a friend.

My escort took me to Gieves & Hawkes at Number One Saville Row. The door was locked, and we had to ring for an entrance. I doubted that I would have been allowed in without my escort.

In short order, I was measured up and was selecting cloth for my bespoke suits. Mum's instructions to them were four complete suits, each suit to have two pairs of pants and a waistcoat. There were also sports coats with appropriate slacks, plus all the proper shirts.

There was outerwear and, of course, a selection of ties. English-style cuff links had been ordered.

I was shown what a finished suit would look like. The buttons on the cuffs would be button-ups, my name would be embroidered inside the coat, the pants would be silk-lined above the knees, and there would be a hidden pocket inside the waistband. There were pockets on both sides of the inside of the jacket, plus a small pocket for my business card case.

I mentioned I would have to obtain a case and also cards. It turned out they had been ordered. The cards were for this trip only as they would merely state, "The Honorable Richard Jackson – The Plaza on The Strand."

After the fitting, I was taken to James Taylor & Son to have a last made for custom footwear.

I didn't want to think about what this was costing. My pay for the summer certainly wouldn't cover it. I knew the family had the money now, but it wasn't that long ago we were the working poor. However, I understood that proper clothing was a requirement in the circles we were now traveling.

With the help of my escort, I purchased several hats. I missed my Resistol cowboy hat. When I told my escort, James Barclay, James thought I should have brought it. It would have excited the girls in court; they would think I was an American millionaire rancher hunting for a wife.

That confirmed Equerry Barclay's thoughts on how rich these Americans were.

I don't know if he believed me when I said, "I'm not a rancher or wife hunting."

We had lunch at a restaurant near Harrods. James wanted to know if I had been to Harrods yet.

"Not here, just the one in Buenos Aires."

"When was that?"

"Last month. My ship had to unload its cargo."

"What were you doing on a cargo ship?"

"I was working as a deckhand."

All of a sudden, Mr. Barclay wasn't as certain about these Americans as he had been.

After lunch, we proceeded to Harrods, where I purchased casual clothes. Arrangements were made to have them delivered to the Plaza Hotel. I thought I got off cheap. I had only spent several hundred dollars at Harrods. I wanted to get back to running but needed a new pair of shoes. When I asked James where I could buy running shoes, James got a blank look for a moment and then realized that I was talking about trainers. Harrods had a small department that handled these, so we only had another stop.

When I went to pay for all my purchases, James Barclay told me my mum had set up a family account there and that I was to use it. Once more, I thought about how times have changed.

We caught a black cab back to the hotel.

Dad was waiting for me with a thick packet.

"It is time to go over the business, Rick."

Chapter 48

Dad updated me on the status of the container and modified tractor-trailer patents. They had been submitted and probably would be approved in short order as no one else was looking at this possibility.

We had purchased Narrow Freight Truck lines for our US hauling. We had made a large investment in the shipping line and entered into a partnership with Howell Trucking in Argentina.

Dad told me they were in negotiations to purchase a company that would manufacture the containers and another to do the trailer bodies to haul the containers.

"How much is this costing?"

"A little over six million so far, Rick."

"I don't have that much money!"

"You have close to it after your movie money, Detroit Faucet dividends, royalty payments from other faucet manufacturers, and the hairdryer licensing fees. However, Mum and I didn't want to deplete your investment, so we loaned you the money."

"Loaned me? How much and where did you get it? I know you have done well in real estate but not that well."

"Remember the find in the sub-basement at Jackson House? I went to Switzerland and opened that safety deposit box. It had over twenty million dollars in stocks and bonds sitting there since around 1920. The interest and dividends have been reinvested for the last forty years. We are now one of the wealthiest families in the world. If Forbes knew, they would have us in the top twenty-five in America."

"Wow! What about taxes?"

"If you remember, we were bringing everything into our name through the Bank of England. We were going to owe a bundle to the Crown until last week. It seems your donation of gravel to the queen took care of that issue. So, we are free and clear. Right now, it comes to almost two hundred million dollars."

"That is a lot of money. What are your plans?"

"It is not in the J. Paul Getty class, but it is getting up there. Mum and I are going to invest in the United Kingdom and the United States. We want a large cross-section of investments so we are not at risk from any one sector. We are also looking into Australia and New Zealand. We thought about Africa and South America, but other than the container business, we don't trust the politicians.

"Singapore, Japan, South Korea, and Hong Kong are good possibilities. I will be making a trip to the Pacific later this year to see what opportunities are there. I have a lot of learning to catch up on. This world is different from switching cars on the railroad. If it weren't for the contacts provided by Elizabeth, our banks, and the White House, I don't know what we would do."

"I didn't realize that the White House was involved."

"Mum and I back-channeled our good fortune to Ike. One of his people contacted us, and they feel if they help us make good business contacts, it will help America in the future. They are quite keen on Pacific nations."

"They feel that they will emerge as a manufacturing powerhouse. I have to say they are probably right. The war made them create a whole new infrastructure. We have profited in building it for them, but I wonder what it will lead to in the future."

"Wow, Dad, you have had to learn a lot in short order."

"I have, but at the same time, I have learned to find good advisors and listen to them. The trick is getting the right advisors; after that, it is easy."

"Somehow, I don't think it is all that simple."

"Rick, do you know we employ twenty people, most of them full-time between lawyers and accountants?"

"No, I didn't."

"If you count people like publicity and agents between us, we have another twenty people. This is a business, son, a real business. That reminds me, you should find a tidbit or two to give to your favorite news people."

"Since my voyage is over, I could let Susan Wallace fill them in on my summer vacation."

"Give her a call this evening as it is the middle of the night in LA right now."

"I will, Dad."

At dinner later that evening, we talked about our plans for the next month. Today was Monday, August the third. The family and I had a private audience with the queen and Prince Phillip on Thursday, the sixth. There would be a public audience that we would attend on August 26.

We will be attending a horserace on August 23. I wanted to know why we were going to a horse race. Mary had the answer to that.

"So, Mum and I can wear fancy hats, silly."

I realized immediately that was a conversation I didn't want to dig into, so I left it. It sounded like fun. I would have made a fuss if I knew that I had to wear a grey morning suit and a top hat. It was far too late when I learned these details later.

Then Aunt Sybil would be coming to London from the wilds of Essex for a visit. I wondered if I should mention Popeye. I would talk to Mum about that when I had a chance.

There was also a dance at the American Embassy to which my parents and I were invited. Mum liked the idea of another chance to dress up. Dad and I held our tongues. Who was going to tell their wife and mother that they found it boring, especially since I now knew she was a top MI6 agent? Telling Ms. Bond that she couldn't dress fancy could be hazardous to her health, or at least to her happy home life.

Denny and Eddie were excited about seeing the Tower of London, where they chopped heads off, and the other tourist spots around town. And oh, did I know they chopped off heads at the Tower of London?

I had the impression they thought it was still done, and they were hoping for a live performance, at least for the head chopper. If they wanted to see that, they would have to go to France, where they still used the guillotine. I wasn't sure if it was public or not.

After dinner, I called Susan Wallace and updated her on my travels for the last two months. She was disappointed that I hadn't any pictures from my trip. I told her the British Embassy in Buenos Aires or the Firestone Plantation in Liberia might have some as there were photographers at the events I attended there.

I left her with the problem of passing my story on to the news people who I tried to keep on my side by giving them innocent inside stories. She also had a problem obtaining the pictures. I began to appreciate my dad's comment about hiring good people and letting them do their job.

The next couple of days were busy. I started each day with a run on Rotten Row in Hyde Park. I would start at the speakers' boxes on Hyde Park Corner, which were occupied even at first light. I had to make four round trips, end to end, to work in five miles while James Barclay listened to the speakers to while away his time. The dapper James was not going to get all hot and sweaty, thank you very much!

After returning to the hotel to clean up and have breakfast with my family, we boys were given a tour of London by James. This was repeated almost every day for several weeks of our visit. On Wednesday afternoon James and I returned to the tailor shop on Saville Row for the final fitting of the suit I would be wearing to meet the queen on Thursday. They hoped to have everything else finished before I left England.

Oh, and I wasn't to worry. My morning suit would be ready in time for the Ascot Race we were attending. This was the first I learned of my wearing a fancy suit in public. My initial thought was no way, and then I realized that I would be fighting Mum and Mary, and I couldn't possibly win that battle. I would just pretend I had a part in a movie.

I mentioned that to James Barclay, who hadn't heard anything about me being in movies. During lunch, I told James about the two movies, one about a cowboy and the other about young Robin Hood. The Robin Hood movie intrigued James the most. He had many questions, especially about the fact that I had some ability with a longbow and had training in the use of a quarterstaff.

When I described my run-in with bank robbers in Los Angeles and how I had forced them out of hiding by firing arrows into the open-roofed building they were hiding in, James seemed to reach some decision and changed the subject.

Chapter 49

Thursday morning was spent getting ready for our afternoon appointment with the queen. Gieves and Hawks delivered my suit to the hotel, and James Taylor & Sons had the correct shoes ready and sent them to the Plaza. I was surprised when there were also suits for my brothers and father. I made the mistake of saying something where Mum could hear it.

"Men," was her comment. Mary echoed her, even though she had no idea what Mum was talking about.

It took me more time than usual to get ready. With my brothers fighting for the bathroom, it took us all longer. We were still waiting for Mum and Mary. Lady Caroline, a Lady in Waiting for the queen, was assisting them, but it still took forever, at least in my estimation.

Mary was a picture in her dress and hat. I hugged her, and as I did, I noticed something.

"Is that perfume you are wearing?"

Mary answered me seriously, "Yes, all young ladies need their special scent. Mum and Lady Caroline helped me pick this out at Floris; it was made just for me."

"It smells nice, just like a young lady should."

"Of course, silly, I won't be wearing perfume to drive the boys mad for a long time yet. I will be quite old by then, most likely thirteen or fourteen."

"Yes," I replied. "You will be in an old sad state by then and will need all the help you can get."

"Mum! Rick is teasing me."

"As well he should, dear. Now it's time to leave."

As a family, we trooped to a waiting limousine. As we went through the hotel lobby, Rick could hear staff telling other guests we were off to see the queen.

As we were driven through the gate at Buckingham Palace, it sunk in to the entire family. We were about to have an audience with the Queen of England! Even Mum seemed a little nervous. This, more than anything, gave me pause. I saw how she faced Russian agents without flinching. Now she was nervous.

The tension in the family rose as we were escorted into the depths of the palace.

It all dissolved when the two old friends and comrades in arms met formally. There had been a quick reunion earlier, but this was official. The formal entrance turned into a hug by the two ladies.

Mum introduced each member of our family to the queen. When it was my turn, I gave a bow worthy of Hollywood with flourishes that I had practiced in private.

The queen commented dryly, "We will have to keep an eye on this one. I may have to have him beheaded if he causes too many scandals."

Startled, I looked up to see everyone laughing at me. Maybe my little joke wasn't such a good idea!

The queen turned serious and told me, "You have Our Thanks for the diamonds. If they had been captured in West Africa, they would have caused untold problems. We are having them sold. The monies will be returned to each of the countries in the form of foreign aid. Some will be kept for Peg's department, so she is in very good odor with them at the moment. They wanted to recruit you."

My mind almost froze up. They wanted me to be a spy, like that James Bond guy, how cool. My name is Jackson, Rick Jackson!

"However, your Mum asked what they would do when their highest officers all disappeared from the face of the earth, so they decided that wasn't a good idea. She has allowed you to be designated a Queen's Messenger."

Queen Elizabeth handed me a small pin for my suit lapel. It was a silver greyhound.

"I would like to talk to your parents in private, so Mary, Denny, and Eddie will start on a tour of the palace. Rick, you will meet with the head messenger for a few minutes."

Lady Caroline escorted the children out. Before leaving, Mary performed a little curtsy. She had practiced with Lady Caroline. The queen proved why she was the queen and that she was also a mother.

"We may have to behead this one also."

With a large grin, Mary backed out of the room like she had been taught.

Lady Caroline led the children off on their tour. I was taken to meet Mr. John Norman.

Mr. Norman was a very grave man who looked like he had seen it all for a long time. I immediately sensed no teenage nonsense here.

After a very brief introduction, James Barclay left us alone.

Mr. Norman was all business, handing me a package.

"I understand you have performed exceptional service for the Crown. Because of the type of service and the fact that you may perform other services in the future, it was determined that some protection should be given to you for those times."

"A Queen's Messenger hand carries highly confidential information, with diplomatic protection. To that order, there is a new diplomatic passport in the package. There are several ties with the greyhound pattern to discreetly inform those in the know that you are a messenger.

"That is the norm for all messengers. Next are several highly unusual items. When traveling, the bag containing the message is sacrosanct, not the messenger. To that end, the bag is sealed with a numbered seal and is accompanied by its passport containing the number of the seal.

"You have an open numbered seal and its accompanying passport. The queen has entrusted this to you, and you are only to use it at need. You will have to account for its use later, and we are notified when a bag passes an international checkpoint so that we will know. Do you understand?"

"Yes, sir, I do."

"Now I have a personal question, did you sing "Brothers" with Mr. Sinatra?"

"Yes, sir."

"May I have your autograph? I love that song."

At that, Mr. Norman handed me the sleeve which held the forty-five record for me to sign. I signed, thinking you never know.

After that, Mr. Norman broached another subject.

"I understand that you work with the longbow and quarterstaff?"

"Yes, sir."

"Would you like the opportunity to practice while you are here?"

"I would love it!"

"Fine. Mr. Barclay will take you to the Tower where the Yeomen of the Guard work. They have several people who are quite skilled and will be delighted to work with you if you are as good as the reports."

No pressure there, I thought.

At that, my interview was ended. Mr. Norman shook my hand as he opened the door.

"I have served the Crown for a long time. You are the most unique messenger I have seen. Please don't fail the queen."

That simple statement sent cascading thoughts through my mind. The public embarrassment of not performing well with the bow or quarterstaff became nothing. At the same time, I heard bullets rattling off the front of a landing craft and the sound and fury of a hurricane.

"I will try my best, sir."

I was then taken on my tour of the palace. It didn't include the royal family's private apartments, but I appreciated the history I saw.

One display had medals presented to Indians during the 1700s. I commented to James that I had seen one from King George III to Chief Blackhoof. James had no idea who that was and showed little interest.

Everyone met back at a small dining room where we had lunch with the queen, Prince Philip, eleven-year-old Prince Charles, and nine-year-old Princess Anne. Charles and Eddie hit it off and talked about things that interested eleven-year-olds, namely locking people in the Tower, throwing them from battlements, etc.

Princess Anne found her doll baby in Mary, who had just turned five. They discussed the important things in life, like what to do if you spill the tea on your dress at a tea party. Anne also was heard to confide to Mary that Denny was quite handsome.

Denny was embarrassed by being admired by a little girl. He was fourteen and didn't need this nonsense. Instead, he turned his attention to the adults. I did the same.

The adults in the party were acting like younger versions of themselves, remembering antics from wartime London. Nothing serious was discussed, just old friends getting together after a long absence. I did find myself the center of attention as my summer vacation from the previous year was described and how it had changed the family's fortunes. After a long relaxing lunch, the queen was notified that her next appointment was here.

Elizabeth sighed that some days it never stopped. The Prime Minister had a bee in his bonnet about something new. He always seemed to have a bee in his bonnet.

Chapter 50

We returned to the hotel together. A note was waiting for me that the American Embassy would like to have a word with me. I showed it to Mum. She told me this was expected. Some chaps there wanted to talk to me about Cuba and what I had seen. The note told me to call when I was available. I took this as a good sign as they were being polite.

When I called, I was put right through to my contact, Mr. Gerry Droller. Mr. Droller was in London expressly to talk to me. Droller asked me if I was immediately available. This resulted in me taking a black cab to the embassy.

After identifying myself at the front desk, I was escorted to a room where Mr. Droller was waiting for me. After a very perfunctory introduction, Droller started questioning me. I didn't feel like it was a hostile interrogation, but it certainly was intense.

It was explained that the same questions would be asked in different ways to elicit memories. I also remembered from hearing Mum talk at various times that it was a check on the facts of my story.

There were general questions about what I had done on the voyage, identifying the various crew members, and if they would have any information. The questions homed in on my trip to the cantina, where I saw the Russian soldiers and the unit badges exchanged. Droller was trying to establish where this cantina was, what transpired, and other clues of what was happening. The only new information I was able to provide was R12 and a name, Statsenko. I had no idea what an R12 was or who Statsenko might be, other than apparently the commander.

Droller thanked me and gave me a card with a U.S. telephone number to call anytime if I remembered anything else.

As I was parting, Droller did ask me if I had met anyone named Frade in Buenos Ares.

I replied that I had danced with a girl with that last name at the American Embassy, but that was it.

Droller smiled and let it drop.

The next day I was driven to the Tower of London.

The Tower of London was nothing like I had pictured it. I had the tower right, though it appeared shorter and squatter than I thought it would be. I hadn't expected all the other buildings inside the curtain wall. It was like a small town inside the tower. I hadn't realized that the Tower was a full-fledged castle in its own right.

I was introduced to several Yeomen of the Guard. Instead of their fancy beefeater's uniforms, they were in regular British Army work uniforms. Cyril Smyth was to practice the quarterstaff with me. We both warmed up. I wondered why they had selected Cyril; he was barely five foot seven inches tall. He must have weighed one hundred and forty-five pounds. I felt like I towered over him, pun intended.

It didn't take a full minute for me to learn I was overmatched. I had never seen anyone with the speed this man had. Plus, though he was small, the power of his blows was devastating. After a sharp exchange of blows, Cyril backed off and told me that I was trainable.

Humbled, I was encouraged to hear this. A series of lessons were started, the first showing me how to brace a leg and bring my whole body into a blow. The lessons only lasted fifteen minutes, but I felt I had advanced to another whole level. Now all I had to do was practice forming the muscle memory required.

During the training, I also learned that Cyril was trying to revive the art of quarterstaff fighting as a sport. He dreamed of reforming the Company of Maisters, the original quarterstaff group of medieval England.

Next, I had sword practice with several different gentlemen. They weren't as good with the sword as Cyril was with the quarterstaff, but I still had a good workout. I felt I was equal to or better than they were. Since I knew the history of my instructors in Hollywood, this wasn't a surprise.

When I thought about it, even Cyril wasn't a surprise. I had been taught real sword fighting in the US, but only Hollywood quarterstaff showmanship. The quarterstaff was now a historical oddity. Of course, it was an oddity that could kill you in a heartbeat.

Then I was taken to another area that looked like a long narrow alley between buildings. At the other end were two archery butts. They must have been one hundred and fifty yards away, not a clap shot, but not a difficult one either. After examining the equipment presented, I easily bent the fifty-pound pull bow that I had been given to use.

Five releases and five bullseyes convinced my instructor I knew what I was doing. They weren't Robin Hood shots where he split the arrow, but the pattern could be covered with the palm of my hand.

After a discussion about my personal bow's characteristics, I was told I was free to practice anytime I wanted, and they had nothing to teach me. My form was correct, and I obviously could aim. They didn't have a longer range for me to work on within the City. If I could leave town, there were several places I could go.

I joked that Sherwood Forest would be great. I quickly regretted that poor attempt at humor as I was informed that there was an annual archery contest at the Forest on August 25, and they would be glad to enter me. I tried to back down but found it to be a losing battle. From the side conversations, I began to understand why.

They thought I was good enough that if they entered a Yank, they could make some early money in the betting. Of course, I wouldn't go all the way, but most of the bettors would write me off immediately when they saw I was an American.

James Barclay wasn't helpful at all. He offered the use of a Queen's Park outside of London to practice at longer ranges. This put in motion my morning ritual for the next two weeks. James and I would go to the park at first light, where James would watch my warm-up and run. Afterward, I would work out with a sword, quarterstaff, and then the longbow. The Yeomen of the Guard joined us; it was a good time.

I was also smart enough to call my publicity agent Susan Wallace in the US. She told me she would arrange for my bow to be shipped over. Later I was to regret that call when Susan showed up with not only my bow but with a costume from the movie. The studio even arranged for a camera team from Pinehurst Studios to film the event.

That was several weeks in the future. In the meantime, I had finished my workout at the park and needed a shower desperately.

James dropped me off in front of the Plaza. As I stepped out of the cab, I walked right into a young lady. I grabbed her to steady her as I had knocked her off balance. A loud sound of disapproval made me turn to see an angry-looking Spanish lady standing there. It was my nemesis from my flight from Spain! The young lady was the Contessa.

I let go of the young lady, who gave me a careful look and a small smile. The Duenna immediately took her charge by the arm and hauled her away. She told her charge loudly in Spanish, "That man is following us. I have a good mind to report him to the police."

I thought about saying something but shrugged and moved on. The girl was cute, but she looked like a lot of trouble, or at least her escort did.

After lunch with the family, I accompanied my two brothers to Covent Garden Market. There were supposed to be many shops dealing in all sorts of oddities and a general circus atmosphere, so we were all anxious to take a look.

One of the first shops we found was an antique store. It held many treasures that fascinated me, but not so much as my brothers. As my browsing slowed down, they became impatient, so we finally agreed that we would separate. After checking that our watches showed at the same time, we agreed to meet in front of this shop in one hour.

The boys took off. I remained in deep thought, wondering how I could convince Mum that I needed the matched set of early nineteenth-century dueling pistols. A clerk was helping me by explaining that they could prove these had been used in a duel where one of the participants had died. This point was most telling to me, and I was almost ready to buy them and take my chances with Mum when I was interrupted.

"Christina, it is him!"

I turned to see Lady Pamela and her niece, whom I had saved in New York. I had never learned the niece's name.

Christina wasn't impressed as she replied, "So what? He is just a commoner."

Lady Pamela turned upon her niece and scolded her, "Young lady, this is exactly why your parents sent you here from Sweden. To learn some manners and spend time with real people instead of that snobbish crowd of young nobles you run with."

I stood there and didn't take in the exchange. All I saw was the beautiful Scandinavian blonde girl with a figure that a movie star would die for. She was so blonde her eyebrows were almost invisible. I wanted to know this girl better!

I didn't have a chance to say anything because there was a commotion in front of the store.

Two bobbies in their tall hats were escorting my brothers to me.

One of the policemen asked me, "Sir, are these your brothers?"

As I was trying to decide if I should try to disown my brothers as a joke, the two ladies turned and moved away. I did hear Christina say, "I told you he was common trash!"

I decided this wasn't the time for humor and answered with a simple, "Yes, sir."

"We are going to have to take them to the station for questioning, but they stopped several shoplifters who assaulted the store clerk after she caught them in the act. We need to document their testimony, but it looks like we have a couple of heroes here. They asked that you accompany them for their statements."

I had become wise enough in legal issues to ask, "None of us are of age. Should one of our parents be present?"

"Oh, sorry, sir. I thought you were over eighteen."

"No, I'm only fifteen."

"They do grow you Yanks big! We do need an adult present. Where may we contact your parents?"

I was a little uncomfortable with this question because I could see what was coming, but I had no way out. "They are at Buckingham Palace visiting Queen Elizabeth."

"Come now, young sir. This is a serious question!"

In reply, I handed the bobbie James Barclay's card. It had his name, title, Equerry to the queen, and phone number at the palace.

"Oh, excuse me, sir. This is most surprising and unusual."

"No problem, officer. I find it hard to believe myself."

While this brief exchange was occurring, Denny and Eddie were all smiles. I looked at them and asked, "Less than ten minutes alone, and you manage to find trouble?"

A very non-contrite Denny replied, "I know. It usually takes you longer."

In the meantime, one of the bobbies had borrowed the shop phone. Fortunately, James was at his desk and told the police he would arrange for one or both of the parents to be at the station for the statement.

At the station, both Mum and Dad came in accompanied by Lady Caroline and James Barclay.

Our wait hadn't been long, but we were well treated. As I sipped on a cup of the strongest tea I ever had, I watched the comings and goings at the stationhouse. During the hour wait for my parents, I had concluded that having parents who visited the queen was good, even if you weren't the criminal.

When Mum identified herself as Viscountess Jackson and showed her passport, the police fell all over themselves in finding chairs, tea, and even inquiring if she would like crumpets. I hoped she would want them because I was hungry, and besides, I had never seen a crumpet.

From my brothers, I expected to hear a tale of how they used their martial arts to overcome the criminals. What happened was that the shopkeeper was being distracted by one of the two thugs, who were in their twenties. When the shopkeeper noticed the other man stealing, she yelled and started after him. The one talking to her grabbed her.

At this point, enter Denny and Eddie. They were going by the open front shop and saw the man grab and throw down the shopkeeper. Eddie charged in front of one as the two thieves headed for the front door and went down on his hands and knees. One of the men tripped over him and had a hard bad landing, knocking him unconscious.

The other had run past the boys when Denny nailed him with an all-American flying tackle. The man had the wind knocked out of him, so Denny just sat on him until the police arrived.

The police recorder took this statement. During the proceedings, more men came into the room, one by one. It was obvious that word was being spread throughout police headquarters and that higher-level officials were getting in on the act.

At the end of the boys' questioning, which was more of a praising session for their quick action, one of the better-dressed gentlemen spoke up.

"Your timing was impeccable. The government is starting a campaign to strengthen our commercial ties with America. A magazine photography crew present to show the Covent Garden Market in its best light caught pictures of you after you subdued those thugs. I mean it when I say thugs. They both have been remanded for assault and theft previously."

Chapter 51

After that, our entire Jackson party retired to the hotel to discuss events. Mary was impressed with her two brothers. Now all her brothers were heroes! Mum and Dad were a little more cautious in their praise, but it was obvious that they were proud of the boys. I was also proud, but it seemed a little weird that I wasn't the center of attention. Not that I begrudged my brothers the attention. It was just different.

Lady Caroline and James Barclay had stayed behind when we left and were trying to extract more information from the police and the other high-ranking personnel there. It turned out the man who had talked last was from the Lord Mayor of London's office.

Lady Caroline explained the mayor's office was going to seek permission to use the pictures of the boys with their captives as part of an advertising campaign. They may not appear for some time, as this was a long-term campaign. The advert people are calling it *The British Invasion*. It will include the arts, fashion, and music. Denny and Eddie were considered to be photogenic, and they were already talking to some fashion designers in the West End SoHo district about using the boys for models.

Dad asked, "What does the palace say about this?"

"The queen does not mind it being mentioned that they visited her, but beyond that, there will be no royal involvement. "

"Fair enough, it's about time these two scoundrels started earning some money to help support the family."

Since Dad had a wide grin when he said it, the boys weren't worried.

Mum was more at ease with the situation. "Whatever will be, will be, just like the song."

After exercising, the next day I spent sightseeing. Besides Parliament, St. Paul's, and Westminster Abbey, I visited several offbeat places, such as the fictionalized 21 Baker Street. One church I saw was interesting. It was the model for the church used on wedding cakes.

Thursday started with my morning exercise and a trip to the archery range at the Queen's Park for practice. When I returned to the Plaza on the Strand, Mum was waiting for me. She had some information she needed to share.

"Rick, there has been a leak in MI6. Part of the information leaked was your involvement in identifying the Russians in Cuba."

"How did they find out that there was a leak?"

"We have our spies inside Russia. They report back what new information they have received. Your name and identity were amongst the information compromised."

"What does it mean?"

"Right now, not a lot. The Russians have expanded their file on you."

"Expanded my file? That means they already have a file!"

"What did you expect? They know who tossed those bowling ball bags over their embassy fence."

"Oh yeah, I had forgotten about that."

"You can bet they haven't nor ever will. That made an impression on them and reminded them to keep family out of things."

"Won't that keep me safe? I'm part of your family."

"I'm not certain, Rick. You may now be considered an agent in your own right and as such, fair game."

"What do I do? I don't know anything about spy stuff. Sure, I have read books, but I don't know what you call tradecraft."

"I had a conversation with my contact. Once we return home, you will be given some training. Not how to be a spy, but how to recognize if you are being followed or if your room has been searched."

"MI6 is willing to do that?"

"I was insistent."

Rick paused a moment, thinking how insistent Mum could be. He was glad he wasn't present for that conversation.

"Now, let me tell you something humorous."

"What could be funny about this, Mum?"

"Our spy is inside their file room. When they expanded your file, it made the rounds of the room. Over half the employees volunteered to seduce you if needed."

"Half the employees are young girls?"

"Most are neither young nor girls."

"Oh...Oh!"

Mum burst out laughing at her freaked-out son. She didn't want to leave me scared. Now I had more to think about.

On Friday, Denny and Eddie went to the West End for their fashion photography session or photoshoot, as the now veteran model Eddie reported upon return. They even had copies of several of the pictures from Carnaby Street.

Dad and I kept straight faces as we viewed the pictures. After the boys left the room, we exchanged a look and burst out laughing.

I said, "Did you see how long the points were on those shirt collars!"

"I was looking at those bell bottoms on the jeans."

"Those styles will never be popular!"

Dad returned, "Those short dresses those two birds were wearing might make it."

"Yes, I noticed those, very nice."

Mum broke in, "You two are typical male pigs. I thought the boys looked nice, but Mary will never be allowed to wear one of those mini-dresses."

That stopped Dad and me in our tracks. We didn't want to think of Mary as a young lady. We would have to kill too many teenage boys.

The next few days I settled into a routine of exercise, target practice, and sightseeing. Sunday night, things began to change. My British aunts, uncles, and cousins were gathering in London for a visit. My parents had arranged rooms for the whole family at our hotel. Saturday evening was the first get-together.

The extended family had dinner in a private dining room. After dinner, I spent time with my cousins Irene, Sandra, David, Edward, Paul, and John. All of us were born within six months of each other. The war was a busy time.

Our conversation was stilted at first. While David, Edward, Irene, and Paul lived near each other, Sandra, John, and I didn't know the others. By late in the evening, the talk became easier. I caught the most questions as I was the oddity of the family, an American movie star, and a singer. They wanted to know what my life was like.

They loved the glamor part but agreed that I had to work hard to make it happen.

I made certain to ask about them. John was planning on joining the British Merchant Marine. He wanted to start as an apprentice engineer and work his way up, and he had many questions about my summer job. He thought the equator crossing was cool and couldn't wait for his turn. I warned him to have mints with him to help the taste that would be left in his mouth.

David was looking at becoming a pharmacist through an apprenticeship program. This was different from the American education system. Paul talked about owning a black cab in London. He had several rides and thought it neat how the drivers knew every street in London.

Edward wasn't sure what he wanted to do, and his parents considered emigrating to New Zealand. Both the girls planned to obtain what they called their MRS Degree as soon as possible and start a family.

I had seen enough of London that I was able to be the guide for my cousins the next day. We used the tube for our excursion. We had fish and chips wrapped in newspaper for lunch. Our cousins quickly became acquainted, laughing and teasing each other the whole day. It was the best time I had in a long while. I had not spent time with kids my age for some time. If you only counted family or close friends, it had been almost a year. As we called ourselves, The Cousins roamed London and had a ball. We even shopped on Carnaby Street. We boys refused the funny-looking trousers and couldn't talk the girls into the mini dresses.

When we went to the Tower of London, I was able to give my cousins a behind-the-scenes tour. To the girls' disappointment, even I didn't have the influence to let them try on the Crown Jewels. Edward had a camera and took many pictures of our group. The Yeomen took pictures of our entire group, so Edward wasn't left out.

I had a thought about the pictures and let Edward know he could make a few quid by selling them to the tabloids. The London scandal sheets loved anything with an American being silly. It was no problem for the group to be silly with me. Nothing that was embarrassing, just silly. Everyone got into it, and they agreed everyone but me would share in any profits. I started to regret my thought when they took me back to Carnaby Street and dressed me up.

It wasn't a total loss, though, as Irene and Sandra posed with me in miniskirts. I figured no one would notice my silly pants. It was over the top when they put a wig on me, where my hair went down to my shoulders, and a fake mustache. I knew this stuff would never catch on, which was a shame as it would do wonders for my hairdryer sales.

All too soon, the cousins had to leave, and after all the fun, I was disappointed to part. It reminded me that I had become a grind about work and life and that I did need some time to be a teenager. It was very satisfying to make money, and I enjoyed what I was doing. Going through school fast was still a goal, but I had to, as Sandra put it, "Lighten up."

Chapter 52

After the cousins left, I was informed that I had to learn to dance. Mum told me about the dance next week at the American Embassy. Even though the Americans sponsored it, a good deal of British society would be there.

As she told me, "You have never learned to jitterbug, much less any of the formal dances. I have arranged for a dance instructor for all of you here at the hotel."

I tried to get out of it, but Mum wouldn't have it.

"Rick, you don't want to be embarrassed, and besides, you will probably need it in your acting career at some point."

I couldn't refute that, so I gave in as gracefully as any teenager, which meant I didn't slam the door on the way out.

After my usual morning workout and practice sessions, I adjourned with my brothers and sister to the hotel ballroom, which had been reserved for the instruction. We were introduced to our dance instructor, Mrs. Colleen Burke, and several other children whom Mrs. Burke had selected for their dancing ability to be our partners.

My partner was a young lady by the name of Alice Burke, the younger sister of Colleen. It turned out that she was twenty-five years old, and her only interest was in the money she would make. She wouldn't even make small talk with me as I was only a kid.

It didn't hurt my feelings at all. I was having too much fun observing Mary. Her partner, a boy of about seven, was just the right height for her and was treating her like a precious object. Mary was in princess heaven!

We went through them all, from the waltz to the foxtrot to the mambo. When they were about to start the tango, Lady Caroline cut in. She had been sitting with Mum, and they had been whispering back and forth.

It turned out Lady Caroline could tango. Between us, we did a number.

Colleen wanted to know how I had suddenly gotten so good at the tango when I was barely competent at the others.

I blushed as he told her I had learned from some sailors in Argentina. This caused Colleen to laugh in huge whoops as she knew this story. The more I tried to explain I had not been in a house of ill repute, the greater the laughter became. Mum, the traitor that she was, joined in with Colleen and Lady Caroline. The rest of the kids joined in even though they didn't know the joke.

Later Denny and Eddie cornered me for the inside story. When I explained it, I also had to educate Eddie on what went on in those places. Denny took it all in stride, Eddie not so much as he went, "Yuck!"

This set the pace for the next several days. Work out, dance, and sightsee. I felt I could be a tour guide. I loved riding the tube on the Elephant and Castle line, just because of its name. On a Wednesday the following week, I had the duty of being an escort to Mum and Mary when they went hat shopping for the horse race we would attend on Sunday.

It turned out to be a fun event. It was a posh shop, and they were used to bored men, so they had chairs set up and tea available. I was learning to drink tea, but it would never be a favorite. Sitting and sipping my cuppa was still fun while Mum and Mary paraded their hats.

The young shop girls flirted with me, but I decided that I had better stay out of trouble, at least for today.

The next day we visited the palace again. It was a dreary rainy day, so we had to stay inside. Dad was involved in business meetings while Mum and Elizabeth chatted about old times. The other kids and I sat listening to the queen and their Mum, but it was boring.

Who wanted to hear about the old days? All they had were air raids, blackouts, and a bomb or two....

Prince Charles finally asked, "Mum, could we play hide and seek."

"That is a good idea, Charles. Explain the rules and get the gear for your guests."

Charles led the group to his room, where there was a box. There was a stack of straw hats with a dark blue band that Denny called a boater. This received a quick correction from Charles. These were Harrow Hats.

"The rules are simple; one person is it. I suggest Rick as he is the eldest. We all wear hats, so the staff knows what is going on."

I wasn't going to dispute this with the future King of England, even though he was only a kid. Who knew? His Mum was as old as mine. She might die tomorrow.

"Okay, I will be it. What else?

"You can hide in any room that doesn't have a yellow ribbon tied around the doorknob. Those are off-limits. Oh, and the person who is it gets to carry a torch."

I was disappointed when I was handed a flashlight. I had images of running through the castle with flames trailing behind me.

After the obligatory count to one hundred, I started my hunt. I went counterclockwise out of the great hall as I liked the word widdershins. Quickly it was apparent that most of the castle was off-limits. It was a good thing. Looking in seven hundred and fifty rooms would have taken several days at least.

I heard people talking in one room. Since the door was wide open, I looked in. It was a group of dowager ladies. All sixty or older, they were dressed in what I thought of as Sunday best on Easter. Unfortunately, I was too close to the entryway and was noticed.

"Young man, this meeting is for ladies only," stated the woman at the head of the table. I realized that I was facing the Queen Mum.

"Sorry for the interruption, ma'am."

As I turned to leave, I heard a titter. It was a young lady's titter, Mary's!

I continued down the hall as though I had heard nothing. Hiding in a small alcove, I waited.

As I was waiting, I heard a sound in the distance as though someone had tipped over a load of empty trash cans.

Less than a minute later, my sister backed out of the room, giving a perfect little curtsy as she left. She skipped away in the other direction, so I trailed behind. As I passed the open door, I heard a soft "Tally Ho." This was followed by general laughter.

I kept behind Mary as she looked for another hiding place. Soon she peeked into a fireplace. This was not your home-sized fireplace. It was your roast an ox in the palace size.

Mary walked into it and disappeared out of sight as she went over an edge. I peeked into it, and Mary was not in sight. About that time, I heard a thud and an "Ow!"

The game is forgotten. I stooped a little to walk into the fireplace. At first, it was as though Mary had disappeared. Shining my torch, I realized that the depth was different to one side. You could not see from looking in from the front that one side had a recess about three feet deep. Furthermore, there was an opening in the wall. Even this opening was difficult to see because the wall behind the opening was identical to the front wall.

From this opening, I could hear Mary crying quietly.

I went to my hands and knees and stuck my head into the opening. The space between the two walls turned to the right. Just immediately past the opening, the floor dropped away. Since the space between the walls was only several feet wide, I had to twist around but was able to shine my torch into the hole. Mary was sitting at the bottom of the hole. She had fallen about four feet.

I asked her if she was okay.

"I skinned my knee, and it is bleeding."

"Can you stand up?"

Mary did but found out quickly she had sprained an ankle when she fell.

I decided I had to go in and lift her out. It was tight quarters, but I managed. As I was going in, I was stopped by a voice. "Sir, may I help you?"

I backed out and found a palace footman standing there.

I explained that we had been playing hide and seek, and my sister had fallen into a pit of some sort.

"Oh, that is part of the old ash removal system. It is a regular warren down there. Tell her not to go any further."

I promptly relayed this to Mary as I went down into the small pit. I lifted her to the footman. I realized that most of the damage had been to Mary's pride.

As I was climbing out of the pit, my flashlight, which I decided was much better than a flaming torch, was shining on a name. "Edward Jones 1839" was written in chalk. I thought that was cool and wondered where I could find some chalk for myself. After a moment of thought, I realized the queen might not be amused. From there, I remembered the chopping block I had seen at the Tower of London and decided that I wouldn't mess the place up.

I did mention it to the footman, who, for some reason, got excited. As the footman informed me as I carried Mary on our way to the palace infirmary, Edward Jones was famous. He was called Boy Jones and intruded on Queen Victoria numerous times from 1838-1841.

He was a young lad, and the only way they finally stopped him was by forcing his enlistment in the Royal Navy. One thing that never had been settled was how he moved around the palace so easily. Now the mystery may be solved!

At the infirmary, it was quickly established that Mary's damage was slight, a skinned knee that was bandaged and an admonition to remain off her feet for the next day or so. No running!

Another footman had been dispatched, and Mum was summoned. She arrived in short order, accompanied by Queen Elizabeth. After the proper fussing, Mum let me know I was the only child not in trouble today. Denny and Prince Charles had knocked over a suit of armor. The queen didn't care about the armor, but she was afraid the Palace Historian was going to have a heart attack.

In the meantime, Princess Ann and Eddie had found a large bowl of trifle pudding in the kitchen and had eaten so much that they both had belly aches.

While not in trouble, Mary was to stay with Mum.

Elizabeth told Peg, "Why doesn't Rick join Christina? She is waiting on Lady Pamela, who is meeting with Queen Mary."

I was led to a parlor-type room where Christina was looking bored to tears. Her face lit up when I joined her. She had a book but wasn't interested. I saw it was by the founder of the Bow Street Runners and was a rollicking good tale, but my attempt to talk about it was quickly deflected.

She wanted to know about Hollywood, who I had met there, and how much money could be made in movies. Was I going to pursue a singing career, and what sort of royalties would I receive for "Brothers"? I absently answered her questions as I admired her features, especially the two prominent ones. I wondered if I could find some way to spend time alone with her.

Christina went on to ask about Mum's title. She appeared disappointed when she found it wasn't hereditary but quickly turned the conversation to where I lived. I told her all about Jackson House except for the sub-basement. I may have inflated it a bit.

I finally was able to change the conversation to plans. After discussing our calendars, we found we both would be going to

Epsom Downs for the Classic and the dance at the American Embassy. We agreed we would spend time together and that she would be my dance partner. As we parted, I had thoughts of holding her close, remarkably close.

Chapter 53

The rest of the week flew by. My regular exercises and practices, archery, quarterstaff, and dancing, took up most of my time. One evening our family did find time to attend a play. Though the play twisted and turned like three blind mice, I didn't like Sergeant Trotter from the beginning, so I wasn't really surprised at the ending.

Early on Sunday, we, along with many others, boarded the royal train to go to Epsom Downs. The cars were all in the royal households' claret color. The engine was a steam engine named King Edward I. Denny, and Eddie thought this train was so cool, unlike the U.S. working stock. Dad and I exchanged glances. We both remembered the last train we had been on.

We boarded a regular passenger car while the royal family entered their private carriage.

For the day, all the men wore what were called morning clothes. Ours were a dove grey coat with striped trousers. Each had a matching top hat.

Mum wore a white linen two-piece sheath dress, with three-quarter length sleeves on the jacket, which had wide lapels.

The ladies all wore large, wide-brim hats with a teal blue satin ribbon, matching gloves, handbag, and shoes. These were a race day staple, at least in certain circles. Mary was the cutest of all in a daytime princess dress. It had a full cotton skirt with crinolines. The neck was round, and the sleeves were capped. She had a light blue silk ribbon around her waist. Her hat ribbon and accessories matched the ribbon. Instead of a large handbag that could carry a cannon, she had a small purse. I asked Mary why she was wearing a fancy hat.

Her reply was, "It is fun, silly."

I knew when to quit when behind.

On the train ride, I found myself wedged against a window by Christina. I had no complaints about this, as one of her large breasts was rubbing up on my arm. I found it to be quite pleasant and was in no hurry to arrive at Tattenham Corner railway station. I had a pleasant conversation on the way.

She was most interested in my lifestyle and future intentions. She extolled the virtues of a continental lifestyle of skiing in the winter, the French Riviera, gambling at Monaco, and various worldwide excursions. She also had further inquiries about my family finances, as she had heard we had serious money.

The lifestyle didn't seem very worthwhile to me, and I avoided the family finance questions, but I didn't argue. I was smart enough to know that I might lose that wonderful closeness I was feeling.

Unbeknownst to me, Mum sitting behind us heard it all.

Mary was bored, so she tried to join in with us but was shoved not so gently out of the seat by Christina, who told her that she and I wanted to be alone. Mary accepted this, but Mum was frowning. I was looking out the window at the time, so I didn't notice this treatment of Mary.

The race day was fun. We were in the royal enclosure and were treated like we were members of the royal party. Since we were, this made perfect sense. I felt like a real toff with my top hat and walking stick, what I would call a cane without a curved handle. My only regret was that I hadn't thought to look for a walking stick with a hidden sword.

The big race of the day was the Epsom Classic. The winner was Parthia, ridden by Henry Carr around the mile-and-a-half course. Dad won a bundle, but Mum dropped a bundle, so it was a wash. A tired but happy crew, we worked our way back to the train.

At the station, a large crowd was waiting to see the queen and Prince Philip.

The police had formed a human barricade by linking hands so the queen and her family could pass through. I at first thought this was funny, all the police holding hands. Then my eye caught sight of a man close by, pulling a revolver out of his coat pocket. It was the largest pistol I had ever seen.

One large step and I brought my cane crashing down on the man's arm. I had been practicing with a quarterstaff and had learned to bring my entire body into a blow. The man dropped the pistol and fell to his knees with the agony of a broken arm. I took him down to the ground and held him there. There was no fight in the man as his shattered arm was nothing but pain as he went into shock. My cane had splintered with the blow.

The crowd was a scrum, some trying to move back, others moving in to see the commotion. The police whisked the royal family aboard the train. They quickly pushed the crowd away from me and the man I was holding down. Two bystanders very quickly told the police about the man pulling a gun and my action.

One of the bobbies recognized the man as a known IRA terrorist.

As I started to rise, I was told, "Stay on your knees."

I looked up and saw a wickedly grinning Queen of England standing there holding a cheap cricket bat. She had picked it up from a souvenir stand at the station. It had Epsom Race Day printed on it.

She then proceeded to tap me on each shoulder and said, "Arise, Sir Richard Jackson, Knight of the Garter."

I could do nothing but gape. While I stood up, flashbulbs were going off everywhere.

Elizabeth started to hand me the cricket bat but changed her mind.

"This will be my addition to the weapon collection at the Tower!"

In a moment of clarity, I presented my broken cane to the queen.

"This is the real weapon of the day; will you take it as a remembrance?"

"Gladly, Sir Richard."

At this point, our party boarded the train as the crowd was now augmented by reporters shouting questions.

Once on the train, Mum took a distraught Mary into her arms.

I heard her tell my sister, "It's all right, dear. It's the men's job to take care of the ladies."

When we were halfway back to London, Prince Phillip came forward to talk to my Dad.

"Jack, Elizabeth, and I have talked it over. It will be a press nightmare you have never seen when we get off the train. We would like to move you to Buck House for the remainder of your stay. The press will make your life a living hell if you go back to the Strand."

My parents glanced at each other, and Mum nodded yes.

"We will gladly take you up on your offer. We will have to retrieve our personal belongings, though."

"That will be taken care of. Everything will be delivered to your rooms at the palace."

"Thank you."

"No. Thank you. Your son probably saved our lives."

"He did. I'm proud of him."

"One can only hope one's son will grow up like Rick."

Upon returning to London, the cars of the queen's train were unloaded in a private section, and we were carried away in limousines to the palace. Our family was shown to a suite of rooms. All of our gear had already been delivered and put away. This was royal service!

Dad told me I should try to contact Susan Wallace, my publicist. She deserved a warning of what was about to break.

She picked up the phone on the first ring.

"Rick, what have you been up to? The wire services are going mad about you saving the Queen of England from an IRA gunman."

I told her the story, including my being knighted with a cricket bat. Of course, Susan wanted to know if there were pictures. I knew photographers were there but didn't know if they had any pictures. Susan told me she would find out.

"Rick, the studio wants you in costume for the archery contest you are entered in. They think it will be wonderful publicity for *Bandits of Sherwood*.

"I will bring it over to you and your regular equipment."

"Thanks. That will help. When will you be here?"

"I can be there tomorrow. Is that okay? I will arrive at Heathrow at 7 a.m. from LA."

"Yes, I will see about a room for you."

"I tried your hotel, but it is booked."

"I'm sure there is room for you with us. I will have a car pick you up at the airport. What airline?"

"TWA."

"Okay, see you tomorrow morning."

After hanging up, I talked to Mum, who in turn arranged a room for Susan near our suite in the palace. I couldn't wait for her surprise when she arrived.

It worked as well as I could hope. The next morning, I was waiting at one of the side entrances where Susan would be delivered. She looked as good as anyone could after flying from Los Angeles to London all night. In other words, she was tired and worn out.

Her words to me were, "I will get you for this. I suppose you have an audience with the queen lined up?"

Sometimes life is cruel. By bad luck for Susan, she had no longer spoken those words when Peg and Elizabeth came out the side door. Fortunately, my Mum took in the situation instantly.

She turned to Elizabeth and said, "I must get this poor child to where she can clean up and rest. I will formally introduce her later."

I just about said, "This isn't the queen's first rodeo." Luckily, I kept my mouth shut.

Chapter 54

Later that day, Susan and I talked. At her suggestion, representatives from the queen's staff were brought in. There would have to be a press conference about my actions at the track, but we should all be on the same page. After an hour's discussion, I agreed to say as little as possible.

The press conference was set up for the next morning. It went well till almost the very end. I was proud of being able to answer modestly without really saying anything. It wasn't quite "Ah shucks, ma'am," but it was close to it.

One of the last questions was from a reporter who looked like he was a stuffed sausage.

"Why do you dislike the IRA?"

"I know enough of the English, Irish situation to know that I know nothing."

"Then why did you hurt that man?"

"I didn't care what group he belonged to. It could have been the Flat Earth Society trying to harm the queen. What if it had been your Mum? Would you have wanted me to stop him?"

"I say, you are not being fair, and speaking of fairness, why did you have to break that poor man's arm?"

"You're correct. I wasn't fair. Fairness would have me doing the same to him as he was trying to do to others."

"You mean kill him!"

"Yes, that would have been the fair thing to do. Now that I think of it, it isn't too late to take him to the Tower and put him to the chop."

At that, I made a gesture to all the other reporters. "Please note that this gentleman thinks it fair that we execute the man immediately."

This brought out a round of laughter as my fat questioner was a well-known IRA sympathizer. Most of the newspapers took great glee in reporting my twisting of the reporter's remarks.

A typical headline was, "Give him the Chop says IRA Reporter."

Afterward, Susan just shook her head. The queen's staff loved it. I had said what they couldn't say. They could blame it all on the barbaric Yankee.

After the news conference, Susan and I called our friendly reporters in the States and gave them some special quotes on the incidents. I was beginning to appreciate how a friendly press connection was good.

The next few days went quickly for me. It was exercise and practice with my bow. I was taken out to a private area of Windsor Castle, where I was safe from reporters and the general public. The attempt on the queen's life had made world news, and there were pictures of me taking down the gunman.

I received letters of congratulations and thanks from many world leaders. I gave them to Susan, who had organized a team to handle all the mail on the incident. While they wrote out thank you cards, I had to sign them. Autographs to fans were one thing, responses to heads of state another.

The British Boy Scouts and the Boy Scouts of America both notified me that I would be given an award for my heroism. I was able to go to Gilwell Park the next day and was told by BSA that their presentation would be next month at the White House. At Gilwell, I was glad I didn't have my BSA uniform with me as some of the lads there commented that American Scouts looked like Christmas trees with all their badges.

The day after that, our family, Susan, and I were all escorted from the palace and trekked to Nottingham for the Sherwood Forest archery contest. I learned what really good archers were. I came in a respectable third, but it was a distant third. The winner had split an arrow in the bullseye, ala Robin Hood. I wore my movie costume and was the only one there in period costume, at least a Hollywood definition of the style worn. I didn't mind not winning, but Cleese, a young college kid, kept making remarks about "Men in tights."

Christina was there and flirted with me the whole day. She made certain that she held my arm with her large breast rubbing against me. During our conversations, she let me know that she would be glad to attend any red carpet events with me once I was home. All I had to do was send her an airline ticket, first class, of course.

When it was time for me to receive the small trophy, I turned to pick up Mary to take her with me, but Christina grabbed my arm and dragged me to the stage with her. If eyes were daggers, Mum and Mary would have done her harm.

Each day when possible, I continued my dance lessons. I was passable in most of them, nothing great. The one dance that I seemed to do well was the tango. Lady Caroline was my partner for these dances. We had developed a routine for "La Cumparsita".

When we danced, did it become a parade of misery? Our instructor told us we could win dance contests with it, but unfortunately, it would be our only dance as I seemed to move like a cow for the others. I had the impression she didn't think cows were graceful.

The night of the dance finally arrived. The whole family had been looking forward to it. Not for the dance so much, as it was the last event of our summer vacation. We were all ready to go home. And what home we would be going to! The builders had been keeping Mum posted on their progress, and all major items in the renovation of Jackson House were completed.

Peg and Elizabeth had talked it over with palace security, and if the queen ever visited Los Angeles, her party would be staying at Jackson House. It met all the security requirements and was certainly spacious enough.

Dad was more than ready to go home; he had been conducting business all along. His had truly been a working vacation. He took me aside the morning of the dance and updated me on the new container business and its allied projects.

"Rick, this has taken off like a rocket. The first customers have loaded containers. Their cost is a quarter of what they would normally pay for shipping, and the loading and unloading time has been cut in half. The cargo ships have had days cut off their port stays so far. As more ports gain the capability, it will be even more effective.

"You will make a fortune off the container manufacturing. I don't even know how to describe what the truck and ocean lines will make. Within five years, you will be worth more than John Paul Getty! Money will never be a concern again. What are you going to do with the rest of your life?"

"Dad, I haven't thought that far ahead. I knew there would be serious money involved, but this is insane. I have to think about this. I have wanted to help get mankind into space, but how is the question."

"Well, no hurry, you aren't even sixteen yet."

"Dad, what are your plans?"

"Good question. Everything I have going is getting beyond me. I have plenty of staff with checks and balances on the finances. I think Mum and I will be looking for some causes to support, like curing cancer."

"Yeah, you missed out on polio; I guess cancer is the next big thing. It might take ten or more years to find a cure."

"From what I know, Rick, it may be much longer than that."

"Oh."

"Anyway, have fun tonight. They invited children for the first two hours."

"You mean I can only be there for two hours?

"No, silly, that is for Mary and the boys. Here, they consider you an adult. Why I don't know, but they do."

I thought a couple of dark teenage thoughts, then let it go.

The night of the dance, all dressed in our finest, we gathered in our parents' suite at the palace. The men were in black jackets with tails and white ties. The ladies wore formals. Mary was even wearing a tiara. It looked almost real. I asked her where she got it.

"Anne loaned it to me."

I gulped. This was the real thing. No wonder it looked so good.

"Be careful, shortcake. We might have to sell the house if you lose it."

"Anne thinks you're cute. If I lose it, she wants you to make up for it."

"Oh."

At that point, I found something else to do. I remembered that chopping block in the Tower.

When we arrived at the dance, the first person to greet me was Christina. She had her dance card out for me to sign. She wanted all the slow dances with me. I was glad to sign. I loved holding her close and tight. I wondered if there were any dark corners we could find.

All went well for the first two dances. As we sat down, Mary came up to us, holding a cup of chocolate. You could tell it was chocolate by the ring around Mary's mouth. As I wondered where she got it, Mary stumbled.

Mary stumbled right into Christina and spilled the chocolate down the front of her dress. Christina grabbed Mary and started to shake her.

"Horrid brat! You've ruined my dress!"

I grasped Christina's arm in a grip of iron. I peeled her hand off Mary.

"We are done."

"Fine, you lout! You can't dance. I don't know why I'm wasting my time with you and your jumped-up family!"

"Well, you don't have to bother anymore."

As I turned to walk away, I noticed Mary had run to Mum and was sitting on her lap. Poor tyke, I thought.

I may not have thought that if I had heard the exchange between Mum and Mary.

"Mummy, it worked!"

"I saw and heard, dear. Good work! As I told you, it's the lady's job to take care of the men."

I went out to the hallway to cool off. I saw the Spanish girl I had been running into all summer. I was about to go and finally introduce myself when her duenna caught my eye. If looks could kill! I decided I had enough woman trouble tonight and returned to the dance.

I saw Christina sitting alone at a table in her chocolate-stained dress. She glared daggers at me when I went by. I hoped I would make it out alive. All of a sudden, I started laughing. I had fought gunmen! Why was I afraid of a few young ladies and their guardians? I might make an exception for the girl in Argentina; now, her guardian was plain scary. Her dad had sent me a bullet. Now that was something to take seriously.

I went over to the bandleader and slipped him a tip. I then approached Lady Caroline.

"Rick, I saw and you Christina had a tiff. I hope it was permanent as I intensely dislike that piece of Eurotrash."

Ignoring that comment, I held out my hand and asked her to dance. The opening notes of a tango were playing.

We proceeded to the floor and danced. It was the most intense dance I have ever done. The emotions that were flowing through me added to the controlled violence of the dance. The floor cleared as other couples stopped to stare. This was special.

When the dance ended, the room broke into applause. We bowed to our audience.

Lady Caroline heard me mutter, "Can't dance, can't I?"

I spent the rest of the evening dancing to almost every dance. All the young ladies there wanted a turn with the American hero and world-class dancer. Well, granted, my dancing with them was mediocre, but they had seen the tango.

That was how it would be referred to in the next day's gossip papers. They also reported the end of the budding romance between Sir Richard and Christina. From the way it was reported, there was no love lost between Christina and the press. Such terms evinced this as "dodged a bullet."

The next several days were a blur to the family. We were all on a plane bound for Los Angeles. Summer vacation was over. We were going to our new home to start a new life. All were affected by events. Mum and Dad had pretty well decided that they would be, for a better word, socialites, supporting charities and worthy causes. Teams of auditors, lawyers, and accountants would keep track of the professionals hired to run the businesses.

I agreed to operate my businesses the same way. My business and the family would not be intertwined but run in the same manner. I knew enough to know that I didn't know how to run a business on any level, much less this high of a level. If I had pocket money for gas, I would be happy.

Well, maybe a new car each year, and maybe an airplane, as I wanted to learn how to fly. Oh yes, and a beach house. Maybe something up in the mountains would be nice. But my wants were modest! Maybe a warm fire and some chocolates to eat would be "loverly."

I thought of this as we flew over the pole. I also reviewed my summer. The time on board the ship was worth doing, but I wouldn't want to do it all the time. I wasn't cut out to be a sailor. That stuff they made you drink when crossing the equator confirmed those thoughts.

I also thought about the girls I had met. I would always remember that night in Argentina and the wonderful sight I had beheld. I hoped to behold many more of those! The well-protected shy Spanish girl would always be a "wonder what if" memory, but I would never know. Then there was that wretched Christina. How could she have fooled me? Of course, I knew exactly how she had fooled me. I would have to remember in the future that a large boob rubbed against me was probably a danger signal. The danger was that all logical thought was about to depart.

I also wondered what being Sir Richard and a Queen's Messenger would mean in the future. There were also the promised spycraft lessons coming up. I looked forward to learning how to recognize a tail and evade them. I could see it now. I would introduce myself as "Jackson, Richard Jackson."

Then I had to make decisions on what to do next. I didn't have a movie offer in hand, so I was at a few loose ends. Of course, I had to have schooling, but no way was I going to a high school. Then there was a pilot license. I was going to get one.

The sub-basement of Jackson House might still have some mysteries to yield. Who knew where life would take me?

As I played with these thoughts, I fell asleep as the great jet flew through the sky.

The end for now

Back Matter

To be continued in Book 6: Surfing Dude The Richard Jackson Saga[1]

https://www.enelsonauthor.com/[2]

If you want to be on the mailing list for new releases, go to my website and contact me with Mailing List as the subject.

For information on hiring Janet E. Rupert to edit your fiction project, email:

janeteditorrupert@gmail.com

---

1. https://www.amazon.com/gp/product/B07XLVFDZS

2. https://www.enelsonauthor.com/

Other books by Ed Nelson

The Richard Jackson Saga

In the Richard Jackson World

Stand-Alone Story

Cast in Time Series

Did you love *Star to Deckhand*? Then you should read *Surfing Dude* by Ed Nelson!

Surfing Dude has Rick working and living in California while preparing for a surfing movie to be filmed in Hawaii. Continuing his heroic ways, he finds that like the rest of the world, films do not always go as planned. From chipmunks to tigers the animal kingdom has its dangers. Throw in a group of crooked town officials, follow up with a flight crew down with food poisoning, and our young man has his hands full. While money keeps pouring in, he doesn't seem to have much luck with pretty girls, at least the luck a fifteen-year old boy wants. For the young, this is a coming of age adventure; for those who lived it, a trip down memory lane, and for those with a search engine Easters Eggs galore. This tongue in cheek saga is all true, give or take a lie or two.

www.ingramcontent.com/pod-product-compliance
Lightning Source LLC
Chambersburg PA
CBHW070304260626
47160CB00003B/705